# Praise for *Christmas Ever After*

"A wonderfully festive setting… The cast is charming and the
atmosphere's enchanting."
—*Publishers Weekly*

# Praise for *Christmas Camp*

"VERDICT a charming movie-to-book crossover that would
be right at home on the Hallmark Channel and a winner for fans
looking for a touching holiday read."
—*Library Journal*

# Praise for *Finding Christmas*

"Schaler's smart, appealing protagonists will keep readers turning
the pages, and the plotting is pitch-perfect, leading to an
inevitable but charming happily-ever-after.
Sweet as a Hallmark Channel movie, but never saccharine, this
innocent tale will satisfy fans of both romance and Christmas."
—*Publishers Weekly*

# Praise for *Once Upon a Christmas Carol*
## Top 10 Audible Bestseller

"This book is a must listen! I love how there were different
narrators and how the music weaves in and out. I swear I felt like
I was in the front row of the Christmas Eve performance when
Anna and Rachel were singing. I literally had tears in my eyes."
—**Kimberly, Audible Review**

## Praise for *Every Day Is Christmas*

"This is a beautiful story about love, forgiveness, second chances,
and the true meaning of Christmas… I highly recommend
*Every Day Is Christmas* along with all Karen's other books!"
**—Karen Cowee, Librarian**

"*Every Day Is Christmas* is an uplifting must-read
for the holiday season!"
**—Caroline D, NetGalley**

"*Every Day Is Christmas* celebrates the magic of the holiday season
and the power of love to change lives. It is a perfect choice for fans
of a feel-good story filled with hope, love, and the
joy of Christmas miracles."
**—Markie B, NetGalley**

## Praise for *Love Always, Christmas*

"This book was everything for my Christmas loving heart…
It's a journey I'll return to every year."
**—Eric, NetGalley**

"*Love Always, Christmas* was so much fun! Karen Schaler's
books always hit the mark! Enjoyed this one! 5/5 stars."
**—Kat, LibraryThing**

"A beautiful story about life, love, and family…
I loved this book. Devoured in one day."
**—Peggy, Goodreads**

## Praise for *A Royal Christmas Fairy Tale*

"[A] sweet Christmas charmer… Royal family enthusiasts and
fans of wholesome romance will embrace this enjoyable love story."
**—*Publishers Weekly***

# A Ruff Royal Christmas

KAREN SCHALER

HAWKTALE PUBLISHING

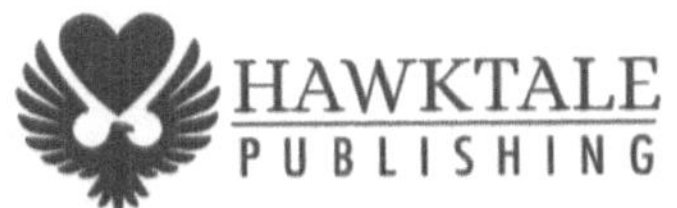

Cover design by Kristen Ingebretson
Edited by Elizabeth Mazer and Mira S. Park
Interior design by Ramesh Kumar Pitchai
Cover art illustration details Shutterstock
Author photograph Scott Foust

Library of Congress Cataloging-in-Publication Data has been applied for.

ISBNs 979-8-9885435-6-5 (trade), 979-8-9885435-7-2 (hardcover), 979-8-9885435-8-9 (ebook)

PUBLISHER'S NOTE

The recipes in this book are meant to be followed exactly as written. The publisher and author are not responsible for any of your adverse reactions to the recipes found in this book, or for your individual allergies or health issues that may require medical assistance.

# A Ruff Royal Christmas

Dearest Readers,

What a journey this has been to write this story for you. I'm incredibly grateful for your support in reading my Christmas novels, listening to my audiobooks, and watching my holiday movies. Your kind words of encouragement have kept me going through some very difficult times.

After my debut novel *Christmas Camp* came out in 2018, I planned to have a new holiday story for you every year—a tradition I cherish. Even during the pandemic in 2020, when I had to start my own publishing company to release *Christmas Ever After*, I was determined to keep bringing you new stories.

Despite a heart-wrenching battle with my dad's health, I continued writing, hoping to bring joy and positivity into your lives. While I faced those challenges, little did I know another test awaited me on Christmas Eve in 2023, when I broke my hand hanging Christmas stockings for my dad, which brought my writing to an abrupt halt. Sitting alone in the ER, all I could think about was when I'd be able to start writing again.

Though surgery wasn't needed, my recovery would take more than a year due to complications. I'm still in physical therapy today. This meant 2024 was the first year in years I couldn't share a new Christmas story with you, and it broke my heart. But thanks to my amazing physical therapists, Charlotte and Brian, I'm thrilled to finally share *A Ruff Royal Christmas*.

People often ask how, after writing seven bestselling Christmas romance novels, four Christmas movies, and a Top 10 Audible Original, I continue to come up with original Christmas ideas.

My answer is simple: be observant. What's happening around you? What's going on in your own life? Who inspires you? Who and what would you want to read about?

This is how *A Ruff Royal Christmas* came to be. During countless hours in physical therapy, Brian, my PT, had a TV show called *Lucky Dog* on in the background, featuring shelter dogs that are rescued and adopted into new "furever" homes. Combine that with meeting two incredible new friends, Alicia and Terri, who have rescued six dogs, and my answering the call from fans of *A Christmas Prince* for another royal romance, and I knew this story was meant to be.

A true labor of love, I hope this story helps you embrace the true meaning and magic of Christmas. Please share it with fellow animal lovers so we can empower as many people as possible to support shelters and rescue groups.

Merry Christmas!

XOXO,
Karen

**For Alicia and Terri,**
whose hearts and home
overflow with love for their six rescue dogs.

**And to every animal adoption shelter,**
rescue organization, devoted staff member,
trainer, veterinarian, and compassionate "furever"
parent who gives animals in need the
love, care, and second chances they deserve.

# Chapter 1

Princess Ava loved that she had a secret no one knew about. Impeccable in her classic winter-white pantsuit and designer heels, she held her breath as she stared up at the spectacular twenty-foot Douglas fir Christmas tree that dominated the Grand Hall of Vailgate Castle. The magnificent centuries-old castle was perched high on a snowy hilltop overlooking the small, enchanting Eastern European sovereign state of Skydovia.

Ava knew this was the moment of truth.

Never taking her eyes off the tree, she pushed a button on the sleek small silver remote she was holding.

Suddenly, like a scene out of an action movie, two men dressed in black dramatically dropped from the ceiling on cables, jerking to a stop in the middle of the Christmas tree.

Ava cringed as the men spun wildly, arms and legs flailing like drunk ballerinas.

Clearly, she still had work to do to perfect her Christmas tree decorating invention—one of her many creations she kept under wraps.

"Are you two okay?" she called out to the dangling decorators.

The men batted branches out of their faces as they desperately tried to grab onto to each other to steady themselves.

"Yes, Your Royal Highness," they called in unison, still spinning.

Ava frowned. She knew they were only saying that to make her feel better when in reality, they looked nervous and completely out of control.

Trying to figure out where she went wrong, she did some quick mental calculations as she studied the cable system the men were suspended from. She had envisioned it working like one of the cable and pulley systems you saw in theaters for musicals like *Peter Pan* and *Mary Poppins* that had people soaring gracefully through the air. But right now, there was nothing graceful about her two middle-aged decorators who were crashing into each other.

"Hold on, I'll bring you down," she called up to them.

"No. It's okay. We're fine," one of the men insisted, forcing a smile. "We just need to…get the hang of this."

The men chuckled at their own joke.

Ava did not. She didn't see the humor in any of this. What she saw was a problem that she didn't have time for.

There was a reason people called her "Princess Prim and Proper." At thirty years old, she proudly took after her father as someone who was disciplined and diligent. She took her role as the only child and sole heir in the royal family very seriously.

It was her father, Prince Fredrick, who had asked her to invent something to help decorate all the towering Christmas trees in the castle to replace the ladders and complicated scaffolding the royal decorators usually had to use.

While her father had a knack for dreaming up unique ideas to make life easier, she found ways to bring his ideas to life. It was something they always did together, their own secret hobby, because few people knew she was a highly skilled mechanical engineer who had graduated at the top of her class.

She smiled, remembering how they'd always made such a great team—until cancer took him away. Now, she was struggling to carry on alone.

As a flood of memories washed over her, Ava fought off tears as she twisted a men's eighteen-karat gold watch around her wrist. It was way too big for her but just tight enough that it wouldn't fall off.

She allowed herself only a fleeting moment of grief before shutting it down completely. Burying her feelings was second nature. If she let herself feel too much, the pain might consume her—and she didn't have time for that. She had a strict "no tears, no self-pity" rule. She had a job to do.

She'd promised her father she would pick up where he'd left off and continue to uphold her royal family's legacy with dignity and pride. Right now, top on that list was taking over her father's job of planning the annual Christmas party that was held on Christmas Eve and benefited local charities. She was determined to make sure this first holiday party without him was their most successful party ever in honor of his memory.

She also felt added pressure from knowing her mother, Queen Kathleen, was counting on her. While her exuberant, vivacious mother was always the life of the party, when it came to planning one, she knew her mother was royally unprepared.

Ava took a few steps back to admire their towering Douglas fir Christmas tree. It was a beauty. Her father had always said "the bigger the better," and this tree fit the bill, soaring toward the vaulted ceiling. Its fragrant emerald branches were adorned with a lavish mix of hand-carved wooden angels and nutcrackers, gold-dipped stars and snowflakes, and plush velvet hearts.

Rich crimson velvet ribbons with gold filigree were woven throughout the tree. But the real showstopper was the Christmas tree topper. It was a giant glittering gold star featuring the family's royal crest that was covered with rubies and emeralds. Adding to the magic were hundreds of white twinkle lights.

When Ava looked up and saw the decorators were almost steady, she felt a little more hopeful that her invention was actually going to work.

"If you're sure you're okay, I'm going to move you to the top of the tree so you can get started," Ava said.

"We're fine," both decorators called out in unison as they held on to the cables that kept them suspended in the air. "We won't let you down," one said with a confident smile.

Ava wished she felt his confidence. To pull this Christmas party off, she had to have every second perfectly planned and accounted for. She couldn't afford any delays. This Christmas tree needed to be finished today to stay on schedule.

"Okay, hold on. Here we go…" Ava said, biting her lower lip as she pressed the remote button, watching the decorators rise higher up the tree. This time, they barely spun at all—a huge relief. When they reached the top, she flashed them a satisfied smile.

"Very good," Ava said. "Now you can get started with the lights." She stepped back to get a better look at the tree.

The designers exchanged confused looks.

"But the lights are already on the tree," one of them pointed out.

"And they look beautiful," the other added eagerly.

Ava frowned, shaking her head. "No, the lights are all wrong—" she started, but before she could finish, five more designers entered the hall, each carrying giant Christmas wreaths.

She turned to them. "If you can all just wait over there, I'll be right with you to inspect the wreaths as soon as I'm done here."

The five designers lined up, ready to present their wreaths—except one guy who wasn't holding anything or wearing the all-black uniforms everyone else was. He was in jeans, a red fleece, and hiking boots, looking confident and laid-back, like the kind of guy who chopped down trees, not decorated them.

He glanced up to the dangling decorators. "Whoa. What's going on here?" he asked, stepping closer. "This is wild."

Ava, startled by his approach, took a quick step back and held up her hand. "Stop. Hold it right there. Don't move."

He froze, then chuckled. "Why? Is there a problem?" He flashed her a sexy, confident smile.

Ava's heart skipped a beat. For a moment, she forgot everything else. *Focus,* she told herself. *Ignore how good-looking he is.* She crossed her arms in front of her chest and locked eyes with him.

"Yes, you. You're the problem," she said firmly. "I told you to line up over there, and I'll be with you in a minute. To check you out."

His eyebrow arched.

Ava blushed and rushed on. "I mean, to check out your..."

"Go on," he grinned. "To check out my...what?"

"Your wreath," she finally said, annoyed with herself for feeling so flustered.

His piercing blue eyes lit up, amused. Ava pursed her lips and squared her shoulders. She refused to be distracted. "Please go over there and join the rest of the decorators."

"Oh, but I'm not—" he started, but Ava cut him off.

"I'll be with you in a minute." She turned back to the Christmas tree.

Then she heard it. Someone whistling "We Wish You a Merry Christmas." She spun around just in time to see the handsome stranger stroll right past the decorators and out the door.

"Where is he going?" Ava asked, exasperated.

"How exactly would you like the lights?" one of the dangling Christmas tree decorators asked, forcing her attention back to the tree.

She walked over to a strand of lights on the tree, picked them up, wrinkled her nose in distaste, and let them fall back onto the tree. "We need all these strands of lights to be five inches apart. Not six inches, not four inches—five inches, just like my father always did. He always believed the more lights the merrier, and that they need to be exactly five inches apart to get the full impact. It's our tradition. Do you have the measuring tape I gave you?"

One of the decorators scrambled to pull a measuring tape out of his pocket. He held it up like it was a winning lottery ticket. "Yes, Princess, it's right here."

Ava nodded, pleased. "Wonderful, then you shouldn't have any problems. Remember, five inches. We have more lights if you need them."

Both designers bobbed their heads up and down as they got started adjusting the lights.

Ava watched them, eagle-eyed.

When her private secretary, Edgar, entered the Grand Hall, Ava could barely see him because he was struggling to carry a massive display of pink roses.

"Princess, the florist sent these for your approval for the party," Edgar said, catching his breath.

Ava's eyes widened when she saw the flowers. "What? No, I specifically told them I wanted red roses. This is a Christmas party, not Barbie's birthday."

Edgar swiftly pivoted to leave. "I'll take care of it."

"Thank you, Edgar," Ava said, grateful. She could always count on Edgar. In his sixties, dignified and unflappable, he always exuded an air of confidence that felt very reassuring to her. He had loyally worked for her father for twenty years. When her father had passed away, she'd asked her mother to let him stay on and work for her, and she'd happily agreed. Edgar had taken on the role of not just her private secretary but her trusted friend and confidant. Her father had trusted him implicitly, and now so did she. She knew when Edgar said he'd take care of something, he always did.

"Oh no!" one of the decorators yelled.

Ava gasped when she looked over and saw that the giant Christmas tree was starting to sway back and forth.

"Oh my God, what happened?" Ava cried out. "Be careful!" She ducked as a crystal angel ornament fell off the tree and narrowly missed hitting her. It hit the marble floor and smashed into pieces.

Ava winced when she saw the broken angel wings. "Oh, this can't be a good sign—" She was cut off when more ornaments started to rain down on her. This time, she was hit by a snowflake that bounced off her before hitting the floor.

The designers held up their hands like they were being arrested.

"We didn't do it," one designer cried out in distress.

The other designer nodded his head in frantic agreement.

"I know," Ava called up at them. "It's not your fault. I'm more worried about you getting hurt—"

"We're fine," they said together.

"Please be careful. When you move the lights, try not to tug or pull on the branches, okay?"

Both designers nodded.

Ava sighed as she picked up what was left of a broken angel off the floor. "Some of these ornaments have been in my family for generations." She circled the tree, checking for any other ornament casualties. She was relieved to only find a few damaged snowflakes.

Trying to calm her jangled nerves, she shut her eyes and inhaled the signature scent of the Douglas fir. The fresh blend of evergreens, wood, and a hint of citrus stirred a rush of Christmas memories—of the times she would go with her mother and father to pick out the perfect Christmas trees for the castle.

She remembered how thrilled she'd been the first year her parents had let her go with them to their royal Christmas tree farm. She'd been only five years old, but she could still remember it like it was yesterday. It was one of her favorite Christmases ever.

As she stared up at the Christmas tree now, she hoped her father would approve. When she took a few steps back to take a picture of the tree, she almost tripped over a blur of black-and-white fur zooming by her.

"Whoa! What the—" Ava exclaimed, stunned, as she watched a border collie, with a giant strand of garland in his mouth, race around the Christmas tree like he was having the time of his life.

"Look at him go!" Queen Kathleen exclaimed, laughing with delight as she entered the Grand Hall. An effortless blend of glamour and charm, the fun-loving queen was the polar opposite of her more reserved, rule-following daughter.

Ava gave her mother an incredulous look. "Mother, what is a *dog* doing in here?!"

Her mother's joyful smile lit up the room. "That's Stormy. I got him from the shelter. Isn't he adorable?! He's a Christmas present."

"For whom?" Ava asked, still in shock. Her eyes grew even wider when she saw the sparkling, bejeweled, red Christmas collar around the dog's neck.

"For us!" her mother answered, bubbling over with enthusiasm.

Stunned and horrified, Ava could only stare at her mother. When she finally found her words, they came fast and furious. "What? No! We can't have a dog. We have too much going on. The party. My engagement—"

She was cut off when Stormy stopped zooming around and started barking at the dangling decorators. He was wagging his tail, wiggling around, excited, like he wanted to play.

Her mother laughed and happily waved at the decorators. "Hello, up there! Well, aren't you two brave letting my daughter fly you through the air like holiday superheroes. You're doing a wonderful job."

The decorators, delighted, beamed back at the queen. When they tried to bow to her, it was comical, but heartfelt. You could tell they adored her.

As Ava impatiently marched up to her mother, she could hear her father's voice telling her that after he was gone, it would be her responsibility to rein her mother in. Even though he'd warned her that trying to control the queen's exuberant behavior would be like trying to harness a tornado, he'd made her promise she would try, insisting the future of the monarchy depended on it.

*No pressure,* she thought, as she watched her mother run after Stormy, laughing like a child. Growing up, she'd never minded being an only child, but right now she wished she had a sibling to help handle her mother, because she felt helpless.

The problem was she'd never had a close relationship with her mother. Over the years, instead of getting to know each other better, they'd only grown further apart.

They were like fire and ice.

The queen was the fire. Ava knew her mother could quickly ignite, and things could get out of control really fast. At least, that's what her father had always told her. So, the princess grew up never getting too close to her mother, so she wouldn't be burned.

"Mother, are you listening to me?" Ava asked impatiently as her mother continued to chase Stormy around the Christmas tree. "What were you thinking? We can't have a dog."

Her mother ran up to her, excited. "Yes, we can, and now we do! With your father gone, I thought Stormy would be good company for both of us."

Ava watched Stormy sniff and then paw at a box of decorations. The box flipped over, scattering velvet heart ornaments everywhere.

"No! Don't touch that," Ava demanded.

Too late.

Stormy was already batting a heart around like it was a soccer ball. He stopped when he discovered another box and started sniffing it.

With a shaking finger, Ava pointed at him, exasperated. "No! Leave that alone. Don't you touch anything."

Stormy stopped eyeing the box and glanced over at Ava. He wagged his tail and barked. Clearly, he thought this was some kind of game, because he eagerly flipped over the box and gave Ava an adoring, innocent look as if to ask, *Is this what you wanted me to do?*

"No!" Ava gasped. "Stop that!"

When Ava headed for Stormy, her mother stopped her. "Ava, you stop. You're hurting his feelings. He's just having fun."

"*His* feelings?" Ava laughed, losing it. "What about *my* feelings?"

Stormy ran up and barked at Ava before he started running in circles around her. Her mother and the decorators laughed merrily.

"Mother, stop laughing. You are encouraging him. This is *not* funny."

Her mother laughed louder. "Oh, but it is. If you could see the horrified look on your face. You're looking at him like he's…the devil."

Ava didn't blink. *Devil dog, yes, that about sums it up*, she thought.

"Anyone can see how adorable Stormy is," her mother continued. "Just look how much he already loves you."

Ava, stunned, fought to find her words. "*This* is your idea of *love*? A dog that looks like he's going to attack me?"

"Attack? He's a border collie. That's just what border collies do. They were bred to herd sheep."

"Are you saying I'm the *sheep* in this scenario?" Ava sputtered, beside herself.

Her mother nodded, smiling. "Yes, my darling daughter, and a very fine sheep you are."

Ava's eyes narrowed. She could see her mother was having a wonderful time with this whole thing, while she, on the other hand, was fighting to not completely lose it. This was always their dynamic, and frankly, she was getting tired of it. She took a deep breath, determined to put a stop to this chaos. "Mother, can you please stop joking around for once? This is serious." Ava tried to think what her father would do in this situation, but her mother had never brought home a dog before. This was virgin territory, and she knew it was up to her to handle it before things really spiraled out of control.

"I am being serious," her mother answered. Her eyes sparkled merrily.

Ava's frustration grew when she saw her mother was fighting not to laugh. Her mood didn't improve any when she saw Stormy spinning around, chasing his tail. She had hit a new low. Now the dog was mocking her, too.

Ava looked at Stormy like he was nuts. "What's wrong with him? What is he doing now? Is he crazy?"

"No crazier than you and me," her mother said with a confident smile. "He's just excited to be here."

"He's out of control," Ava insisted. "He can't stay!"

"Ava, stop being so dramatic. Don't worry. I have everything under control."

This made Ava's anxiety skyrocket even more, because she'd learned at an early age that whenever her mother said "Don't worry," it was always followed by some kind of trouble.

Her mother continued, not missing a beat. "I've hired a top trainer who does Puppy Bootcamps. He was just here meeting with me and Stormy. We've gone over all the details, and everything's settled. When Justin's done with Stormy he will be a little angel, won't you, boy?"

Stormy heard the word *angel* and ran over to the tree, where he tried pulling a crystal angel ornament off a branch. The tree swayed, smacking the decorators, who started spinning again.

Ava rushed up to Stormy. "No! Leave the tree alone! Don't you touch that angel or anything else. Go away!"

Stormy ignored her as he ripped the angel ornament off the tree. As soon as he had the angel in his mouth, he ran over and proudly dropped it at Ava's feet. When the angel hit the floor, its halo broke off.

Her mother clapped with delight. "Look how smart he is. Good boy, Stormy."

"He's not a *good boy*!" Ava snapped. "How can you call him that? He's a four-legged wrecking ball. No wonder he's called Stormy. He's like a perfect storm, destroying everything."

Ava winced as she picked up the angel's halo off the floor. She waved it at her mother. "Look what he did. He just broke this angel."

Her mother shrugged. "Accidents happen. It's not the end of the world. We have hundreds of angels."

"That's not the point," Ava shot back at her mother.

Her mother's eyes narrowed as she crossed her arms in front of her chest. "Okay, then please tell me exactly what your *point* is."

Silence.

Ava gulped. She knew she'd pushed her mother too far.

"We're waiting," her mother said.

Stormy sat down next to her mother and also watched Ava closely.

As Ava looked from her mother, to Stormy, and back to her mother, she resisted the urge to squirm. *Don't show any fear, or you're done*, she told herself. She could see her mother was suddenly in a rare serious mood, and a serious queen was even more dangerous than the fun-loving, impulsive, easygoing queen. She knew her mother was whip-smart. She could outplay anyone, at any game, if she set her mind to it. She was not one to be underestimated, ever.

Her mother locked eyes with her, waiting for her reply.

Stormy barked and wagged his tail. He, apparently, was waiting, too.

She knew it was ridiculous, but she felt ganged up on. It was two against one, even if one was a dog. She took a breath. *Stay cool*, she told herself. *You've got this. Just do what Father would do*. After all, she was the one who was supposed to always be calm, cool, and collected. But her mother always had a way of pushing her buttons, and this was no exception.

She forced a smile, trying to ease the tension. "My point is, it's almost Christmas—"

"Our favorite time of year."

"*Your* favorite time of year," Ava corrected her.

Her mother gave her a blank stare.

"And with everything we have going on right now, with this being my first Christmas charity event to plan, and my upcoming engagement, surely you can understand why we don't have time to take in an unruly, undisciplined, disruptive dog." Ava gave Stormy the side-eye.

Her mother nodded. "I agree."

"You do?" Ava asked, breathing a sigh of relief.

"Absolutely," her mother said. "Right now, Stormy doesn't know how to behave—"

"Exactly!"

"—and that's why I've hired Justin," her mother said with a confident smile. "He's one of the best dog trainers in the world."

"What? Wait. No—"

"Yes," her mother said as she smiled brightly. "Justin will teach Stormy everything he needs to know. You can see how brilliant Stormy already is, so I'm sure he'll learn fast."

Stormy tilted his head as he listened to the queen and started wagging his tail.

At this point, Ava knew she only had one more card to play. She walked over, took both of her mother's hands in hers, and gave her a pleading look. She wasn't beyond begging.

"Mother, please, I need you to understand—"

Her mother smiled gently back at her. "My darling daughter, I do."

Ava had hope. "You know there's no place for a dog in our lives. We're too busy for a dog. We've never had one before—"

"That's because your father was allergic."

Ava fought to keep her voice calm as she continued. "We've gone this long without a dog. We don't need one now." She forced a smile as she hugged her mother. "Thank you for understanding."

Stormy barked and wagged his tail as the queen hugged her back. When they pulled apart, her mother knelt down and buried her face in Stormy's soft fur as she hugged him.

*Good*, Ava thought. *She's saying goodbye to the little trouble-maker.*

But when her mother looked up, Ava was taken aback by her joyful smile. "Stormy is staying. We *do* need him, and he's ours now. Merry Christmas!"

# Chapter 2

As smoke curled up from the chimney of a quaint stone cottage surrounded by a forest of snow-covered trees, the crisp winter air carried the scent of pine and burning wood.

Inside the cottage, Justin was doing what he did best—getting two of his favorite four-legged furry students ready to be dropped off at their new forever homes, or as he liked to say, *furever* homes.

His laugh was rich and full of warmth as he carried Pixie into the living room. The frisky Chihuahua, rocking a red-and-green striped Christmas sweater, wiggled around like she couldn't wait to get put down.

"Okay, Pixie, let's practice the tricks I taught you one more time before you go meet your new family, okay?" Justin asked the excited pup as he set her in front of the fireplace where a crackling fire was going strong.

As soon as Pixie's paws hit the ground, she spun around in circles, barking.

"Calm down, Pixie," Justin said in a stern but friendly voice. "I know you're excited to meet your new family, but first, you need to show me you've learned what you needed to learn before I can take you anywhere. You have to be ready. Do you understand?"

Pixie gazed up at Justin and barked twice.

"Good girl," Justin said. As he knelt beside the spirited pup, he gave a quick hand signal, moving his hand in a circular motion. "Roll over."

Instantly, Pixie dropped to the ground, tucked in her paws, and rolled onto her back and then back onto her feet, completing the motion in one perfect, fluid move.

Justin grinned, giving her a tiny treat. "Yes! Well done. Great job!"

Pixie barked and wagged her tail, waiting for the next command.

"Okay, now up!" Justin said as he raised his hands.

Pixie obeyed instantly, rising onto her hind legs, hopping around to keep her balance.

"Nice!" Justin exclaimed. He patted his chest. "Now jump!"

Like a pro, Pixie, leaped into his arm and started licking his face.

Justin laughed as he cuddled her close. "You did it, Pixie! Nice job. You've come a long way. I wish all my Puppy Bootcamp students were as good as you—"

Justin was cut off when Oliver, an adorable French bulldog, barked as he trotted into the room and joined them at the fireplace.

Justin laughed as he petted Oliver. "Yes, Oliver, don't get jealous. You're one of my star students, too. I can't wait for you both to finally have new homes for Christmas."

Unable to contain her excitement, Pixie leaped from Justin's arms and began jumping back and forth over Oliver's back.

Oliver stood perfectly still, wagging his tail, barking like he was totally in on this circus act.

"Pixie, you're such a show-off," Justin said, loving her even more.

For an answer, Pixie barked and jumped back into Justin's arms, showering his face with kisses.

Charmed, Justin held the squirming pup up into the air before kissing the top of Pixie's head. He knew it was moments like this that he was going to miss the most when he had to return to the States and start working as a full-time vet in his dad's New York City veterinary clinic.

He knew it had always been his dad's dream that he'd join him in the family business. No one had been prouder than his father when he'd graduated at the top of his veterinary class. While he would always be grateful for his parents' unwavering support and encouragement, a volunteer program in Mexico the summer of his sophomore year of college had changed everything for him.

When he'd first heard about the nonprofit animal shelter program in Mexico that focused on finding and caring for stray and abandoned cats and dogs, he'd jumped at the chance to participate. He'd always wanted to do whatever he could to help stray animals, and the fact that this organization was in Mexico had been an added bonus. Traveling internationally had always been at the top of his bucket list. So, this had been a win-win.

As soon as he'd arrived in Mexico, he'd fallen in love with the people and the culture. At first, he'd been overwhelmed by the amount of work that needed to be done and the number of abandoned animals in need, but he'd rapidly found his stride and excelled at what he was doing.

Any time he'd gotten frustrated by how little resources they had to help all the animals, instead of giving up, it had fueled him forward. He'd been able to see firsthand how much he and everyone else could do to make a difference in these animals' lives.

As a first-year volunteer, he'd gotten to help with grooming, feeding, and socializing the animals to prepare them for adoption. That was when he'd found he had a knack for connecting with the animals, especially the dogs.

What had surprised him the most when he'd first started volunteering was how much love the stray dogs and cats had to give. Even though many of them had come from horrible circumstances, they were still eager to find a person to love them and to love.

For some of the animals, trusting took a little longer than for others, but then Justin could relate to that. He wasn't that different. He never immediately trusted someone, either. They had to earn his trust first, and then he was all in.

He knew after just one week of volunteering that he wanted to come back as often as he could, and that was exactly what he did. He returned to Mexico multiple times while he was getting his college education.

As time went on and he gained more experience in school and with volunteering, Justin realized that to give the animals, specifically the dogs, a better chance of keeping their new forever homes, he had to make sure they were the right fit for their families.

Since many of the stray dogs they found had all kinds of "issues," from barking nonstop and jumping up on people, to not getting along with other animals and chewing on everything in sight, Justin knew his biggest challenge would be not only training the dogs so they'd get rid of their bad habits but training them so they would ultimately fit in with their new families.

That was when he'd discovered his secret talent of matching the right dogs with the right families. So far, his success rate was one hundred percent, and that was because he didn't just focus on the dogs. He also took a very close look at the families. If he determined a family wasn't going to take proper care of the dog or had a lifestyle that wasn't conducive to having a certain kind of dog, there was no adoption.

So far, he'd only turned a few families away. While he'd definitely taken some heat from some of the other volunteers who insisted any home was better than no home at all, he disagreed. The last thing he wanted to do was see the dogs he'd come to know and care about—or any dog—be abused and neglected again. So, he often went above and beyond, doing everything he could to make sure and find the right homes for them.

That's why he created his own obedience program, his Puppy Bootcamp, because he felt every dog, no matter how old, *could* still learn new tricks if they were taught with the right encouragement. Part of his bootcamps also included the families, so everyone was involved and working toward the same goals, giving him the reputation of being the ultimate pet matchmaker.

There was nothing he loved more than successfully training stray and abandoned animals to be wonderful pets and matching them with families who would love and appreciate them. Seeing the joy on people's faces when they adopted a new furry family member, and the pure happiness of the animals when they finally got the love they deserved, was what he cared about most.

While he continued to volunteer and do his Puppy Boot-camp during the summer, he finished his education, getting his full veterinary degree and making his dad proud.

While his dad couldn't wait for them to go into business together, Justin had convinced him to let him have a couple of years traveling around the world, paying it forward, helping different animal rescue organizations set up their own versions of his Puppy Bootcamp.

As word quickly grew about how his successful bootcamps and matchmaking prowess were having a positive impact on animal shelters in need, the demand for his services skyrock-eted. This took him to shelters all over the world—and the more he saw, the more he wanted to continue to help train the next generation of volunteers to try and make a difference.

While he'd started out working in mostly third-world countries, as his notoriety grew, so did his client list. Prominent people from academics and politicians to actors and rock stars, started reaching out. They were all more than happy to make generous donations to shelters and get their own perfectly matched and well-behaved pet.

That was how he'd ended up in Skydovia right before Christmas—because one of Queen Kathleen's passions was supporting animal shelters.

Justin could still remember the call he'd gotten from the queen's press secretary asking him to come work with Skydovia's animal shelter and some of the shelters in the surrounding area doing his Puppy Bootcamps and matchmaking pets with families for Christmas.

He'd been thrilled. He had a lot of respect for the queen. It was the opportunity of a lifetime to have a chance to work with her.

He'd first met the queen the summer of his junior year in college when he was volunteering at a shelter in Romania. It was one of the queen's royally funded shelters across Eastern Europe. She had come on other official business, but as always, whenever she visited, she had made a point to stop at the shelter and see how things were going firsthand.

As soon as they'd met, they'd hit it off immediately.

Justin found the queen to be even more charismatic than what he'd seen in the press. She was very approachable, friendly, and down-to-earth, as well as incredibly smart and empathetic to the cause of protecting animals.

She had been following his success with his Puppy Bootcamps and had encouraged him to continue. She'd even made a generous donation to support one of his internship programs and had offered her full support if he ever needed it.

After that, their paths had continued to cross over the years as he'd gotten exclusive invites to high-profile charity events. He was sure the queen had been behind getting him on the list.

While he'd always considered himself more of a behind-the-scenes kind of guy, he'd do whatever it took to get support for shelters and animal clinics, even if it meant putting on a tux and attending events where he always felt very out of place.

He'd been flattered beyond belief that at every event she was at, Queen Kathleen always made a point of seeking him out and getting an update on all he was doing. He admired the way he saw her use her status for good, truly seeming to care about the causes she supported.

So, in hindsight, he knew he shouldn't have been that surprised when he got the call from her team asking him to bring his Puppy Bootcamps to Skydovia. This was one of the biggest honors of his life, and he was determined to make her proud.

From the moment he'd arrived, he'd appreciated how the queen's team did everything they could to make him feel at home, setting him up in a charming cottage where each room was beautifully decorated for Christmas in a clever dog theme. There was even a dog-themed Christmas tree covered with white twinkle lights highlighting different dog biscuits that were hung with shiny red-and-emerald-green ribbons.

At the moment, Pixie was eyeing one of the biscuits, jumping up and down, barking, trying to reach it from the branch it hung off of. She wasn't having any luck, much to her frustration.

But Oliver was smarter. He was slowly strolling around the tree with his big, brown, inquisitive eyes looking for any biscuits that might have fallen off. He was rewarded when he found one and eagerly gobbled it up.

Justin frowned watching them both. "Okay, maybe you two are not ready for your families yet. I need to make sure you don't attack any Christmas trees."

As if understanding him, both pups rushed over to Justin and sat at his feet, looking perfectly innocent.

When Pixie tilted her head sideways and looked up at him with adoring eyes, Justin melted a little. He was really going to miss these two. It was one of the hazards of his job that he was still working on—trying not to get too emotionally attached to any of the pets he trained.

*Good luck with that,* he thought as he picked Pixie up and gave her a hug.

He knew his next big challenge was going to be training the queen's new pup, a rambunctious border collie named Stormy. Justin had met Stormy briefly and saw right away he was too smart for his own good. This one he knew was going to keep him on his toes.

But he was ready.

He'd trained border collies before. He knew how intelligent they were and how crafty they could be to get what they wanted. And what they usually wanted was to play. The danger was if you didn't keep them challenged and disciplined, things could quickly spiral out of control.

But he wasn't too worried. He already had a plan for Stormy. He'd built an agility course in the backyard that he knew Stormy would love. Border collies were famous for winning agility competitions because of their smarts, their speed, and their endurance. The courses pushed them to excel, and they loved pleasing their owners.

He couldn't wait to get started.

"I sure hope the queen's new dog Stormy is as good of a student as you are," Justin said to both dogs. "We don't want to disappoint the queen."

Pixie and Oliver barked, as if offering their support.

Justin laughed, grateful. He needed it. He was confident in his skills, but he'd never worked for royalty before. This was a whole new experience.

He knew for this assignment, all eyes would be on him whether he liked it or not, because when it came to anything royal, the media was relentless.

His goal was to do his job out of the spotlight as much as possible and hope any media coverage that did happen would have the upside of bringing in more donations to help the queen's animal charities and shelters all over the world.

The bottom line was that failure was not an option.

"I'll be fine," he said to the dogs. "I mean, how bad can Stormy be?"

# Chapter 3

Bursting with energy, Stormy barked enthusiastically as he ran circles around the two Christmas tree decorators, literally herding them out of the Grand Hall.

Ava pointed at him, exasperated. "Mother, look at that dog. He's chasing our designers out of here!"

Her mother laughed. "If anyone chased the decorators out of here, it was you by being so picky about the lights on the tree."

"They needed to be done right," Ava insisted. "That's what Father would have done. He would have never settled for less than perfect, and…" Ava's voice trailed off when she realized her mother wasn't listening.

Instead, her mother was trying to put on one of the Christmas tree decorators' harnesses. Stormy ran over to her mother, excited, like whatever she was doing, he wanted to be part of it.

Ava marched over to them. "What are you doing?"

"It's my turn," her mother said with a wide grin as she looked up to the top of the tree. "Get your little remote control and send me up!"

"What? No. Don't be ridiculous," Ava said. "Please put the harness down before you hurt yourself—"

"I'm fine," her mother replied, sounding like a stubborn child. "Come on, let's go. I've been dying to try this out."

"No," Ava said. When she tried to take the harness away from her mother, there was a brief tug-of-war. Their eyes locked. Ava shook her head. "Mother, there is no world that this is going to happen in. Ever."

All the excitement disappeared from her mother's eyes as she let go of the harness. "You're no fun. You're just like your father."

"Thank you," Ava said. "I'll take that as a compliment. That means I'm doing my job like he wanted me to."

Her mother rolled her eyes. "What job is that? Let me guess. Keeping me in line?"

When Ava said nothing…it said everything.

Her mother laughed a little, obviously not offended.

Ava's eyes narrowed as she watched her mother. She knew her casual, nonchalant attitude always spelled trouble. It was one of her mother's superpowers that made her so dangerous. She never got upset. She didn't yell. She didn't scream. Instead, she always pretended everything was *fine*, and then found a way of getting exactly what she wanted one way or another.

Her mother examined the cables that were holding the decorator's harness. "You've changed some things on this contraption you and your father cooked up."

"Yes," Ava said, relieved to change the topic. "I've made it a tension cable system like they use in theaters. Now it can move up and down, *and* side to side, so the decorators won't miss anything."

Her mother nodded, impressed. "My clever engineer. I just wish you'd let me share all your inventions with the world. You could inspire so many children, especially young girls, showing them how cool it can be to embrace math, science, and technology."

And just like that, Ava knew she had to be on her guard again. This was a topic she needed to stay strong on, so she could continue to protect her privacy. She didn't have a lot of things in her life that the paparazzi didn't know about, but the inventions she'd created with her father were among them. So, she chose her words carefully.

"You know Father always wanted to keep all this private. It was our special thing we did together."

Her mother smiled. "Yes, but he was just someone who came up with great ideas and tinkered around a little. For you, this isn't just a hobby. You've taken it to a whole new level. Some of the things you've invented could really help people. I'm so proud of you, and I want everyone to see how brilliant my daughter is."

"And I appreciate that, I really do. But being in this royal family, there's so little that's just mine. Everything we do, the public knows about," Ava said with a hint of sadness in her voice.

Her mother took Ava's hand and gave it a reassuring squeeze. "I do understand, more than you know, and that's why I will continue to respect your wishes."

This time, when Ava smiled at her mother, it was genuine. "Thank you. I really appreciate that."

"But you need to invent something fun for me," her mother added with a sparkling smile. "Maybe something for my closet for my shoes, or hats, or—"

"Whatever you want, just let me know," Ava said.

It was a rare mother-daughter moment when they both were on the same page.

But the moment was shattered when Stormy suddenly pulled a Christmas wreath out of a box and started ripping it apart.

"No! Leave that wreath alone," Ava shouted as Stormy tossed the wreath into the air. When it hit the ground, he started attacking it again. Pine needles were flying everywhere. He barked, excited, and looked like he was having a blast.

"Oh dear," her mother said, grinning at him. "Looks like someone needs a little attention."

Stormy looked back at them with his mouth full of pine needles and wagged his tail.

"This is our fault," her mother said as she headed toward Stormy. "We've been ignoring him, haven't we, Stormy? We're sorry."

Stormy barked twice, wagging his tail.

"No, we're not," Ava shot back. "We've done nothing wrong. He's the one tearing everything apart."

Stormy responded by sitting down and scratching at his glittering Christmas collar.

Her mother frowned. "This collar is too big on you, isn't it? I thought it would be okay, but it's gotten looser."

"Probably because he hasn't stopped running around," Ava grumbled.

"It's okay, Stormy, we'll get you a new one," her mother said. "I'll talk to my jeweler today."

Ava blinked several times in shock. "Our jeweler," she sputtered. "Please tell me those aren't *real* jewels on that collar."

Silence.

"Mother?"

"What?" her mother answered innocently. "You told me not to tell you."

"I…this…I…" Ava didn't know what to say as she anxiously twisted the gold men's watch she was wearing around her wrist.

Her mother raised an eyebrow as she watched her daughter. She left Stormy and approached Ava. "And that watch is too big for you, Ava." Her mother held out her hand. "Here, let me have it. I'll give it to our jeweler when I give him Stormy's collar, and he can resize both of them for us."

Ava grabbed her watch protectively and stepped away from her mother. "No. It's fine just the way it is. I don't want anyone to touch it."

Her mother sighed. "Okay, but if you change your mind—"

"I won't," Ava insisted.

"At least Stormy isn't so hard to help," her mother said.

But when they both turned to look at Stormy…he was gone!

"Where did he go?" her mother asked, worried.

Ava looked around. "He's not in here."

A loud crash from outside the room made them both freeze. Ava groaned.

Her mother was already running for the door. "Stormy, are you okay?" she called out, distressed.

"Is *he* okay?" Ava asked, incredulous, as she followed her mother. "You're worried about *the dog*? I'm sure he's fine, but God only knows what he has destroyed now."

## Chapter 4

Justin had a moment of mixed feelings as he handed Pixie over to her new adopted family. He knew he'd made the perfect match, but it was still hard to give her up.

The Squires were a young mom and dad with two delightful children, eight and ten years old. Pixie was an early Christmas present for the kids. While Pixie had been trained to fit in beautifully with the family, he knew he would miss the feisty pup and how she always kept him on his toes.

An occupational hazard, falling in love with his students.

"Now you be a good girl for the Squires," Justin said as he handed Pixie to the little girl who was eagerly waiting with outstretched arms. "Careful, Pixie can be a little wiggly," he warned her with a smile as he handed Pixie over. But as soon as Pixie was snuggled in the child's arms, she became an angel. No wiggling. No barking. Instead, Pixie licked the little girl's face, bringing laughter and joy to the entire family.

*My job here is done,* Justin thought to himself as the dad shook his hand, thanking him again for making their holiday so special. As he walked back to his SUV, he was grateful for another success story.

When the queen had first asked him to come to Skydovia, he thought he'd only be training her new dog, Stormy. But he quickly learned the queen had several dogs she wanted him to work with and had a list of families who were waiting to meet him. He'd thanked her for the opportunity to help even more dogs and their owners and had immediately gotten to work.

Oliver and Pixie were his last two students, and now that they'd been dropped off at their "furever" homes, he was finally ready to focus all his attention on training the queen's new border collie. Stormy was the last shelter dog on his list before he headed back home to America.

As he made his way back to his SUV, he saw a FaceTime call on his phone pop up from his dad.

"Hey, Dad, what's going on? Is everything okay?" he asked, worried, because he knew with the time change, it was the middle of the night in New York City.

"Everything's fine," his dad quickly reassured him. "We just want to know how everything's going with training the queen's new dog."

"Have you seen the castle yet?" his mom chimed in as she got into frame. "What are the Christmas decorations like? I've been looking it up online and it looks amazing! Be sure to take lots of pictures."

Justin laughed at her excitement. "Mom, I'm here to work. I don't want to look like one of those crazy Americans who are obsessed with the royals and take pictures of everything. They're just regular people—"

Justin's mom smiled brightly. "Regular people don't live in a castle and have crown jewels and wear tiaras and—"

Justin laughed. "Okay, I get it."

"So, have you been to the castle yet?" she asked eagerly.

Justin nodded. "Yes, I was there this morning to see the queen briefly and meet her new dog, Stormy."

His mom's eyes lit up. "Did you meet the princess? I tried looking her up, but there's not much about her in the press. She apparently stays out of the spotlight, but from the few pictures I've seen she seems very pretty—"

"Pretty uptight," Justin finished for her. "She was all stressed out working with some decorators she had strung up on cables—"

"What?" Justin's parents said at the same time.

"I know. It was weird. It's hard to explain," Justin said with a laugh. "I'm just glad I don't have to deal with her. She's not very friendly and really uptight. She's totally the opposite of her mother, the queen, who's supercool."

"A supercool queen and an uptight princess. Sounds like the roles are reversed," Justin's dad said with a laugh. "Just do whatever it takes to get along with everyone. This job is going to be huge for our business. How many people can say they've worked for royalty, for a royal family, huh? No one I know. Especially not Jim Thane and his sons."

"Who?" Justin asked, confused.

Justin's mom leaned closer to the camera. "Your dad's nemesis he's been competing with since college. He just opened up a new veterinary clinic a few miles away with his two sons. They both graduated from Cornell."

"And he never lets me forget about it," Justin's dad said with an eye roll. "Wait until he finds out about what you're doing—"

Justin interrupted quickly. "Dad, remember, I'm not supposed to tell anyone about working for the queen until after

I'm done. I signed a nondisclosure. The NDA is very clear. I can't tell anyone. I shouldn't even be telling you. This is their first royal pet. She's going to announce it at their Christmas Eve charity event. She doesn't want the paparazzi sniffing around, reporting anything about Stormy until I've trained him and he's ready to meet the world. I promised her discretion, so please, both of you, don't tell anyone."

"We won't," Justin's parents said in unison.

"Stormy, what a sweet name," Justin's mom said, smiling.

"I'm not sure if *sweet* was the reason he was named that," Justin said with a laugh. "He's a typical border collie, full of energy. At the shelter, they said he's like an unpredictable storm. You never know what he's going to do next."

"Then aren't you the perfect person to train him?" Justin's mom said with pride.

"Thank you, Mom. I'm going to do everything I can to make this a memorable Christmas for the queen."

Her smile faded a little. "I hate that we're going to miss having you here for Christmas."

Justin's dad put his arm around his wife. "Honey, he needs to do his job. This is very important for us, for the business—"

"And it's important for the queen," Justin added. "She has been very good to me. A lot of the important connections I've made are thanks to her. I know how much having Stormy means to her. She told me she has always wanted a dog but hasn't been able to have one until now. She really wants this to work for her and her daughter. I promise as soon as I wrap things up here, I'm heading home. We can have a belated Christmas."

"And I'll make your favorite Christmas donuts," Justin's mom said.

"The chocolate ones with the peppermint frosting?" Justin asked, excited.

"Of course," his dad said. "That's our tradition."

"It sure is," Justin said. "And I can't wait."

"And then we can finally announce our partnership. Our father and son veterinary clinic, just like we've always planned," Justin's dad said, beaming with pride.

Justin put down his phone for a moment so his parents couldn't see his worried reaction.

"Justin, are you still there? Did we lose you? Justin…"

Justin reluctantly brought himself back on camera. He forced a smile. "Yes, sorry, here I am. I had a bad…signal. I need to go. I'll call you guys later. Go back to sleep."

"We will," his mom said, blowing him a kiss. "Good luck!"

"He won't need it," Justin's dad said with certainty. "He's the best of the best—that's why the queen has him there. Do us proud, son."

"I will," Justin said without hesitation. "Love you guys. I'll talk to you soon."

"We love you, too," Justin's mom said as his dad nodded in agreement.

The forced smile on Justin's face faded the moment he hung up the phone. Dread settled over him as he stared off into the distance, thinking about his future working with his dad.

He drew in a deep breath. He had to pull it together and focus on the present and the job he had to do right now.

The last thing he wanted to do was let the queen down.

# Chapter 5

On a mission, Ava searched the sleek wooden shelves inside the castle's wine cellar for the perfect champagne for the Christmas party. She had a lot to choose from. Their royal wine collection was known as one of the largest and most valuable in Europe.

The cellar itself was equally impressive. A mixture of old-world charm and modern elegance, it was decorated beautifully for Christmas. The stone walls were adorned with gold, glittering garland and festive wreaths that matched.

One of the things Ava loved the most about the cellar was that her brilliant ancestors had made it large enough to host intimate parties.

In the heart of the room was a grand, hand-carved walnut table that was more than a hundred years old. A timeless treasure. You could almost imagine people sitting around the table a century ago, telling stories, whispering secrets, and making toasts with amazing wines. If you looked closely at the table, you could see some telltale signs of its age.

Ava ran her fingers over some faint initials carved into the table that she had been told were done by her rebellious mother when she was a child.

Right now, the table had been transformed into a festive masterpiece. A gold velvet runner that ran the length of the table was covered with fragrant evergreen branches, sprigs of holly, and perfect pine cones. There were gold candelabras with white candles waiting to be lit for the next celebration. Strung across the ceiling were dozens of strands of white Christmas lights, adding to the magical setting.

The Christmas spirit continued with a charming Christmas tree in the corner of the cellar, decorated with cork ornaments that were tied with crimson velvet ribbon, a perfect nod to the royal family's love of fine wine.

Ava scoured the wine racks, thinking of her father's pride in upholding their royal tradition of not just showcasing prestigious vintages but also introducing up-and-coming wineries. This holiday tradition was one of many she was determined to get right. That was why she'd called in reinforcements, Duke Henry of Emberland.

She turned to Henry and saw him texting on his phone. She was grateful to have him by her side for her first time planning the Christmas party.

They'd always been destined to be together.

It was a match their parents had made when they were young children. She'd been raised to understand that marrying Henry was her duty and the best way for the royal family to continue to carry out its legacy. They'd grown up in the same social circles and had a lifelong friendship that was always more of an understanding than a genuine connection.

When she was fifteen, she'd gone through a stage where she thought she had a crush on him. As a teenager, Henry was tall, smart, and good-looking. As he grew up, he became your quintessential modern day Prince Charming with a dazzling smile, thanks to several years in braces. He always carried himself with dignity and a confidence that was admired by his peers.

But in reality, there had never been any real spark between them. She had always hoped there would be, and still thought that maybe after they were married, they would grow to love each other in a romantic way. But for now, she was happy that as the sole heir, she had a partner who was ready to help her rule.

Ava only wished her father was still with them to see her upcoming engagement and marriage. She knew it had been his greatest wish for her to marry Henry, because he had planned out every last detail meticulously, down to announcing their engagement at the Christmas Eve party.

But now, with her father gone, Ava knew it was up to her to carry out his plans. One thing she hadn't been prepared for was her mother's sudden odd behavior about Henry. She didn't know what was going on, but every time she tried to talk about the engagement plans, her mother changed the topic. Something was up, and she needed to get to the bottom of it fast. She knew the sooner the engagement was officially announced, the better, so they could all move on and do the jobs they were meant to do.

Ava walked up to Henry.

He was still texting.

"Henry, thank you again for helping me pick a champagne for our engagement toast at the party. My father always said you had impeccable taste."

When Henry finally looked up from his phone, he nodded, all business. "It's my pleasure."

Ava held up a bottle of champagne. "What about this Bollinger La Grande Année Brut? It's from 2014, and it was one of my father's favorites."

Henry took the bottle and studied it for a moment.

Ava knew everything Henry did was well-thought-out. He was never one to rush a decision. When he nodded, she was relieved.

"Excellent choice," he said. "It's full-bodied, elegant, and beautifully balanced. No one could fault us for this being our choice."

"But do you like it?" Ava asked. "I want it to be something that we both enjoy, because as you know, the champagne we make our engagement announcement with will be the same champagne we will have to use every year going forward at our anniversary parties."

"Yes, of course. I'm aware," Henry said as he handed her back the bottle. "This will be fine."

She would have liked a little more than *fine*, but she let it go knowing this meant there was one more thing she could check off her epic "to do" list of all the things she needed to get done before the Christmas party.

"Is that all?" Henry asked, checking his watch.

"I have one more thing I want to show you," Ava replied, excited. "It's one of my latest inventions that Father always wanted me to finish." She rushed to get a shiny gold wine chiller off a display shelf. She carefully placed it on the table, put the champagne bottle into it, and pushed a button.

The wine chiller silently turned around, making a full turn in about ten seconds. While it rotated, a digital thermometer on the outside showed the champagne temperature dropping from 55 to 47 degrees.

"It worked!" Ava said as she triumphantly took the champagne bottle out of the chiller. "My father always wanted a way to chill a bottle instantly. You know how impatient he was. Well, I finally figured out how to do it by..." Ava's voice trailed off when she saw Henry wasn't paying attention.

Henry was texting on his phone again.

Ava put the champagne bottle down. "Henry, are you listening?"

"Yes, that's great," Henry muttered, still texting.

Disappointed, Ava crossed her arms in front of her chest. One of the things she hated most was being ignored.

"Really?" she said, her voice skeptical. "Because I also invented a wine glass that yells at you when you drink too much. I'm using it at the party."

"Wonderful," Henry said, still staring at his phone.

Silence.

Henry's head jerked up. "Wait, what did you say?"

Ava shook her head, disappointed. "Really?"

"I'm sorry," he said and pulled off looking sufficiently guilty. "I'm trying to finalize a property deal with my cousin before the end of the year."

Ava picked up the wine chiller and tried to show him. "This is the new wine chiller I invented that can chill wine in seconds. Do you want me to show you again?"

"No, it's okay. I believe you, but—"

"But? But what?" Ava asked, not liking the frown on his face.

Henry gave the wine chiller a cynical look. "I'm just surprised you're still tinkering around trying to make things."

When Ava put down the wine chiller with a loud thud, Henry winced.

"*Trying* to make things," Ava repeated. Her eyes flashed a challenge. "I'm not *trying*. I've actually invented a lot of things. This is what I went to school for—"

"Something I never understood," Henry interrupted. "How is this hobby of yours going to help us in the future when we take over the monarchy?"

Ava's eyes grew huge. She opened her mouth to set Henry straight but, like always, controlled herself. She knew it wouldn't do her any good to argue with Henry. Instead, she grabbed the champagne bottle, expertly popped the cork, and poured the champagne into two fluted glasses.

Henry arched an eyebrow. "We're drinking before lunch?"

Ava kept pouring. "I am."

When her glass was full, she took a long sip, savoring the taste as bubbles tickled the end of her nose. She picked up the second glass and offered it to Henry, but he waved it away.

"Has your mother given her official permission yet, so I can propose at the party?" Henry asked.

Ava refilled her glass to the top again. "Not yet."

Henry frowned. "I don't understand what the holdup is. What could possibly be more important than our engagement?"

Ava drank more champagne and set her glass down. "A dog."

Henry did a double take. "What?"

"My mother got a dog from the shelter," Ava answered. "Some rescue dog."

"To do what with?" Henry asked, looking thoroughly confused.

"To keep, apparently," Ava said. She didn't even try to keep the disapproval from her voice. "She just brought him home and announced that we now have a dog."

"Good God, why?" Henry asked. "Is this some kind of publicity stunt for one of her charities?"

Ava shook her head as she continued drinking.

"Is she worried about being alone after we get married?" Henry asked.

Ava laughed. "I doubt it. We barely talk now."

Henry frowned. "I thought you were going to work on getting closer to your mother. A united front is best for the monarchy."

"I'm aware," Ava said. "But it's easier said than done. You know we've never seen eye to eye on anything. My father understood me, but my mother never has and never will…" Ava's voice cracked with emotion. She stared into her champagne glass.

It was as empty as she felt.

She put her glass down, picked up Henry's untouched champagne flute, and started drinking from it.

Henry, looking concerned, took the glass from her. "You're the heir apparent. You need to step up and rein your mother in, just like your father always did. I'll be right by your side helping you."

Out of the corner of her eye, Ava caught a movement and saw her mother hovering at the cellar's doorway, listening. Before Ava could say anything, her mother swiftly walked away.

Ava swore under her breath.

"What?" Henry asked.

"I just saw my mother coming in here. I don't know what she overheard, but she left pretty fast."

"Good, now you have a reason to talk to her about this," Henry said.

Ava gave Henry a look like he was clueless. "That's like going into battle when the other side knows you're coming."

Henry smiled a confident smile. "If you need help, I would be happy to talk to her with you—"

"No." Ava interrupted. "This is something I need to do. I'll be fine."

"You need to talk to her right away," Henry urged.

"Yes, I know," Ava said, trying to keep her patience. "I'll go talk to her right now."

"You're sure you don't need my help?"

"Yes," Ava said, trying look more confident than she felt. "Don't worry, we're getting engaged at the Christmas party just like my father always planned."

# Chapter 6

Ava knew she needed to find her mother fast, because if she'd overheard Henry talking about how he wanted her to *rein her in*, nothing good could come from that.

As she hurried into the castle's elegant Drawing Room, where gorgeous, glittering Christmas decorations added to the grandeur, she found her mother sitting on the couch with her loyal chief of staff, Lydia. The two women were about the same age and had developed a strong bond and friendship over the years. At the moment, they were busy scrolling through a tablet, looking at pictures.

"I love this one of Stormy in the Santa suit," her mother said, excited.

Lydia nodded enthusiastically as she pointed to another picture. "And this one where he's wearing the reindeer antlers. How cute is he?"

"So cute," her mother agreed with a brilliant smile.

Ava froze when she saw her mother's new four-legged obsession, Stormy, lounging by the fire, chewing on an exquisite, hand-embroidered, vintage Christmas stocking.

"Is that a Christmas stocking?!" Ava asked, almost choking on the words.

Her mother gave her a disapproving look "Ava, please, lower your voice."

"Then make him drop that stocking right now!" Ava demanded.

Stormy wagged his tail and kept ripping apart the stocking.

Ava's eyes grew huge as she got a better look at the stocking. "Wait, is that *my* stocking? The one great-grandmother made me?!"

When Ava headed for Stormy, her mother stood up, blocking her path. "Ava, calm down."

Ava lost it. "You're telling *me* to calm down?! What about that…monster dog?!"

"Oh dear," Lydia muttered under her breath.

Stormy, with the stocking still in his mouth, ran over and dropped the soggy stocking at the queen's feet.

"Thank you, Stormy. We need to get you your own stocking, don't we?" the queen asked. "Would you like that?"

Stormy barked and wagged his tail as she knelt down and pet him.

"He's a *dog*," Ava exclaimed.

"Who clearly loves Christmas," her mother said.

"Clearly," Lydia agreed with a wide smile.

Ava shook her head in disbelief. She felt like she was trapped in some kind of alternate universe where four-legged, furry creatures named after natural disasters ruled, and she was being held hostage, helpless to escape the madness.

Stormy barked, grabbed the stocking again, and started running circles around Ava.

"Ah, look. He thinks you want to play with him," her mother said, charmed.

"Oh, I'm not playing," Ava said under her breath in a tone that showed she was done messing around. "Mother, he has to go back to wherever he came from. I'm serious. I have too much going on right now to deal with this. The party. My engagement, Christmas, everything."

Her mother smiled, still watching Stormy. "I've offered to help you—"

Ava laughed.

Her mother tilted her head and studied her daughter. "What's so funny?"

*Careful*, Ava told herself. She could hear her father warning her. *If you upset her, you'll never get what you need from her.*

Ava took a deep breath and tried again. "Mother, please understand. I just want what's best for all of us. I'm already behind planning the party thanks to this…distraction…"

"It appears you've managed to pick a champagne," her mother said. "I know Henry has very strong opinions—"

"About wines, yes," Ava jumped in. "Just like Father had."

"And about other things," her mother said, locking eyes with her.

*Damn*, Ava thought, realizing her mother had definitely heard when Henry told her she needed to control her mother like her father always did. While she was scrambling for something to say to dig herself out of the hole she was in, her mother walked over to Stormy and gently took the stocking out of his mouth.

"Good boy," she said, and then took the stocking back to the stunning stone fireplace and hung it back up where it belonged.

Ava held her breath when her mother turned back to face her.

"Ava, I've listened to your concerns about having a dog, and I've told you that I agree that any pet we have needs to be… well-behaved."

Stormy barked twice and wagged his tail.

Her mother smiled at him. "And that's why I've hired one of the best trainers in the business. Justin is going to pick up Stormy tomorrow and take him to Puppy Bootcamp before I leave for Paris."

Ava shook her head trying to process everything. "Paris? That's not on your schedule."

"We just added it," Lydia said as she stood up. "If you'll both please excuse me, I'm going to go make sure everything's all set for your trip."

"Of course," the queen said with a grateful smile. "Thank you for everything, Lydia." When her mother walked over to the window, Ava tried to follow her, but Stormy got between them and started barking at her.

"What?" Ava asked Stormy, frustrated.

"He's just protecting me."

"From what?" Ava asked, confused.

"I don't know," her mother said. "You tell me." She looked into Ava's eyes and didn't blink.

Suddenly nervous, Ava took a step back. She much preferred her overexuberant, playful mother to the mother who occasionally became quite serious. She was waiting for her to say something about what Henry said, because she certainly didn't want to bring it up.

She felt like they were playing a game of cat and mouse, and she was the mouse about to be pounced on.

"Why are you going to Paris?" she asked, thinking this was a safe topic.

Her mother slowly smiled. "I can't tell you. It's a surprise… for Christmas."

"I don't want a surprise," Ava snapped back before she could help herself. "You know I don't like surprises and this…"—she pointed at Stormy—"was enough. What I want is to make sure our party lives up to its tradition and is the number one fundraiser for local charities. I want this to be the most successful Christmas party we've ever thrown. We owe it to Father, to honor his legacy. You know how passionate he was about all these charities and having everyone come together this time of year to give back and celebrate all we have to be thankful for—"

"Yes, I know. He was very passionate about this party," her mother interrupted. "A party that has been part of my family's legacy for decades. This was a party I always helped my parents organize until I got married…" Her voice trailed off.

"I didn't know that," Ava said, surprised. She waited for her mother to elaborate, but when she was only met with an awkward silence, she continued. "I just think it's a really bad time to go to Paris with everything we have going on. This party needs to be perfect—"

"But you said you don't want my help," her mother replied. Her expression was impossible to read.

Ava hated when her own words were used against her.

"Unless you've changed your mind?" her mother asked. Her voice was hopeful. "Because despite what you might believe, I know a thing or two about Christmas parties and—"

"No—" Ava jumped in to stop her.

The flicker of hope in her mother's eyes faded.

Ava saw her mother's disappointment and felt a pang of regret. The last thing she wanted to do was hurt her mother's feelings, but she knew she had to stay strong and do what needed to be done. That was what her father had taught her, and she couldn't let him or the monarchy down. At the end of the day, she knew this was all going to benefit her mother when the party was a huge success.

"I appreciate the offer," Ava continued. "But I have all of Father's notes. I know what he wanted done. We talked about it. I'm just on a really tight schedule, so I can't afford any more delays or distractions."

When she gave Stormy a pointed look, he wagged his tail and barked.

"Then since you don't need me, there's no reason for me not to go to Paris, right?" her mother asked.

*There it is,* Ava thought. The cat had pounced on the mouse. The mouse was trapped.

"Right," Ava said. While she'd originally come to talk to her mother about giving her official permission for Henry to propose at the party, she knew this wasn't the time to tackle that topic. She needed for things to cool down a bit, because right now, the tension in the room was so thick you could cut it with a knife.

She turned to leave. "I'm going to get back to work."

"Wait," her mother called out. She picked up the tablet she'd been looking at with Lydia. "Before you go, help me decide what Christmas picture to use this year."

Ava turned around, confused. "I thought we already picked one."

"But I think this one will be better," her mother said as she showed her a picture on the tablet that was blown up to cover the whole screen. The picture was of Stormy, who had been photoshopped next to her and her mom by a Christmas tree.

Ava gasped in shock. "Oh my God! You didn't—"

Her mother beamed. "I did, and it's adorable, right?"

Ava shook her head in disbelief as she gave Stormy the side-eye. This madness had to stop.

But before she could say anything, her phone rang. "I have to get this," she said, holding up her phone. "It's Henry."

Her mother nodded, but Ava saw a look of disdain in her eyes before she hurried toward the door and picked up the call. "Henry, hold on a second…"

But Henry jumped right to the point. "Have you talked to your mother yet about our engagement at the party?"

Ava waited until she was outside the room and answered in a hushed voice so her mother wouldn't hear her. "I just got done talking to her—"

"And?" Henry interrupted.

"And…I'm working on it," Ava said with more confidence than she felt. "I have a plan."

# Chapter 7

Ava paced back and forth before going into her mother's bedroom.

When she told Henry she had a plan to get her mother's approval for their engagement to be announced at the Christmas party, it was a bit of a stretch.

The truth was, she wasn't sure how to concoct the perfect plan because she wasn't sure what the problem was with her mother. She just knew they couldn't announce their engagement without her permission. It was one of the royal rules that had been upheld for decades. The ruling monarch always had to give permission before a family member could marry.

All these years, her mother had always been in favor of the marriage, but it seemed like ever since her father had passed away last year, her mother had found all kinds of different ways to avoid the topic.

She hadn't told any of this to Henry because she didn't want to upset him. She knew his top priority was making sure everything stayed on track. Now, with Christmas just a few days away, Ava knew it was a moment of truth, and she needed to make this happen.

Ava took a deep breath. *You can do this,* she told herself. *Just stay positive and upbeat. Let her think it's her idea. Whatever you do, do not upset her*, she could hear her father's voice telling her. It brought her some comfort knowing she was still being guided by his advice.

"Okay, let's go," she whispered to herself. She held her head high as she walked into her mother's bedroom.

The room was a stunning blend of timeless treasures and modern pieces, perfectly reflecting the queen's forward-thinking spirit. While the high ceiling and intricate crown molding honored the past, the stylish jewel-toned emerald-green and silver fabrics on the curtains and bedding added a fresh, contemporary touch. There was also a touch of whimsy as white twinkle lights framed the tall windows, casting a soft glow over the room.

The Christmas tree in front of one of the windows was decorated with ornaments she had made as a child and with ornaments from children all over the world. While the tree was simple, she knew it was her mother's favorite. The room exuded warmth and elegance, just like the queen herself.

A snow-white marble fireplace stood as the room's centerpiece. The mantel was lined with framed photos of Ava and her mother looking happy together. In one photo, Ava was a little girl, and they were cheerfully posing with an old-world Santa by a Christmas tree.

"Mother, do you have a moment?" Ava asked as she nervously twisted her watch around on her wrist.

The queen was surveying stunning cocktail dresses. She gave Ava a bright smile. "Of course. Come in. I'm trying to decide what to take to Paris, but you know I always have time for you."

Ava fought to keep smiling because she never felt like her mother had any time for her at all. She was always too busy being the queen. It was something she'd had to accept growing up. She knew she was very low on her mother's priority list. Thankfully, she'd had her father.

Her mother held up a glittering gold gown. "Which one do you like better? This one, or the red one?" Her mother pointed to an equally spectacular red cocktail dress that was on a rack with a dozen other designer dresses.

But Ava couldn't even see the dresses. She was too busy staring at Stormy, who was sprawled out across her mother's four-poster bed, looking like he owned the place.

"What's the dog doing in here? On your bed?" Ava asked, incredulous.

"Where would you like him to be?" her mother answered as she smiled at Stormy.

"I can think of a million places that aren't here," Ava snapped back.

Her mother covered Stormy's ears. "Don't you listen to her, Stormy. She doesn't mean it."

Ava gave her mother a look that showed she absolutely meant every word. Then she quickly checked herself. She knew this wasn't the time to argue. She had to focus on what really mattered. Right now, that was getting her mother to agree to her Christmas Eve engagement announcement.

She knew she needed to shift gears fast and get them back on a safe topic. She picked up a silver cocktail dress. She knew how much her mother loved fashion. She studied the dazzling dress and smiled. It was stunning. "I like this one, but they're all lovely," she said, meaning it. She'd always admired her mother's flawless sense of style and her ability to look dignified and elegant in royal fashion, while effortlessly staying on trend with designers who matched her vibrant personality.

Her mother smiled as she took the silver dress from Ava. "You're right, this one definitely needs to come to Paris."

"Are you going to a party?" Ava asked.

Her mother laughed. "Of course! There's always a party in Paris."

"Of course," Ava said.

"We should go."

Ava's eyes widened with surprise. "To Paris? You and me?"

Her mother laughed. "Don't sound so shocked. Yes, you and me. It has been forever since we've been to Paris together—"

"I was ten," Ava interrupted, remembering it like it was yesterday. "You took me to my first brunch, and we went on a shopping spree after."

"Yes," her mother said, clapping her hands in delight. "And we got you that pink dress."

"Celine designed it," Ava said. "I remember. I loved that dress."

"I did, too," her mother said. "It was perfect for you."

They shared a rare smile.

"We need another mother-daughter trip to Paris together," her mother continued.

Ava nodded, willing to agree to anything to keep her mother happy at this moment.

Her mother's smile lit up the room. "Wonderful! Let's go in the spring. It's my favorite time of year in Paris."

*Do it now*, Ava urged herself. *Hurry, while she's in a good mood.*

"That sounds great," Ava said, smiling. "And before you go on this trip to Paris, I just needed to confirm really fast that you're good with Henry and me getting engaged at the party like we've always planned."

The queen turned to study several more designer dresses that were hanging on a rack.

Silence.

Ava took a deep breath before walking over to her mother. "We're good, right?"

Her mother held up a forest-green sequined dress and studied herself in the mirror. "Proposals are usually more… intimate and romantic."

Ava, confused, met her mother's stare in the mirror.

"What do you mean?" Ava asked. "Father proposed to you at our annual Christmas party. That's the tradition—"

"We don't *always* have to follow tradition," her mother interrupted.

Shocked, Ava was speechless.

"And for the record, that was always your father's plan, not mine," her mother said as she carefully put down the dress.

"What are you trying to say?" Ava asked. She was done trying to tiptoe around the issue. Something was going on, and she needed to figure out what it was. Now.

Her mother locked eyes with her. "Do you love Henry?"

Ava blinked several times. It was the last question she had been expecting.

"Do you? Do you truly love him?" her mother asked, looking deeply into her eyes.

To avoid her mother's piercing stare, Ava walked over to the window. When she looked out into the royal gardens, everything blurred as her mind tried to process what was going on.

"I don't have time for this," Ava said under her breath.

"What?" her mother asked.

Ava winced. She hadn't meant to say the words out loud.

Her mother crossed her arms in front of her chest in a rare, serious stance. "You don't have time for *love?*"

The disbelief in her mother's voice was the last straw. Ava whirled around and faced her. "No, actually, I don't," Ava said passionately. "Father always said I have one job—to serve our people. Henry's a duke. He understands this life. He'll help me, just like Father always helped you."

Her mother started to say something, then stopped herself.

"What?" Ava asked. "What were you going to say? Tell me. Please, help me understand what is going on. Why are you suddenly making this so hard?"

"I just want you to be happy."

"I am happy," Ava said. "Or at least, I will be once we have this engagement out of the way."

Her mother raised her eyebrows. "Out of the way? That's how you think about one of the most important moments of your life?"

Ava rolled her eyes. "You know what I mean."

"No, I don't."

The tension in the room was palpable as the two women faced each other.

Stormy looked from her mother to Ava and then back at her mother.

Her mother turned back to the dresses.

Ava waited for her to say something, anything, but all she got was silence. She finally gave up, realizing she was getting nowhere tonight, and left the room feeling like a failure.

# Chapter 8

The next morning, as a spectacular sunrise cast a golden glow over the snow-dusted castle, a royal valet put her mother's designer suitcases into a shiny black Rolls-Royce.

Ava, stressed, rushed out the front door and headed straight for her mother.

"Mother, I thought Lydia said you were leaving at nine. It's only seven. I almost missed you…"

"Change of plans," her mother said. "I wanted to get an earlier start. I was going to call you when I got to Paris." She laughed when she saw Stormy run around, sniffing all her bags. "Isn't he adorable?"

Ava bit her tongue from saying what she thought of Stormy as she nervously twisted her watch around her wrist.

She was mentally and physically exhausted. She'd hardly slept. She'd tossed and turned all night. She hadn't just been worried about getting her mother's permission for the engagement. It had been her mother's question, asking if she truly loved Henry, that had really had her head spinning.

She didn't know why she was obsessing so much. Of course she loved Henry. She was kicking herself for not immediately telling her mother that.

She had known Henry her whole life. She'd always known this was the man she was going to marry, because her parents had set it up. She'd never had a problem with the plan. She knew it was her duty. While she knew many people thought an arranged marriage was old-fashioned, she appreciated that there was a time-honored way to make sure a marriage would be a successful partnership, because at the end of the day, especially in a royal family, marriage was an institution, a job—and a job she took very seriously. She had always appreciated that Henry felt the same way.

While she was angry with herself for not immediately answering her mother's question and setting her straight, deep down she knew the real reason why she hadn't spoken up.

And that was what had kept her up all night.

She knew when her mother had asked if she *loved* Henry, she'd really been asking if she was *romantically* in love with Henry, because she knew her mother was a hopeless romantic.

Ava remembered being a young child and discovering her mother's love of romance after finding her watching romantic comedy movies and reading romance novels whenever she had a spare moment. She had called her indulgence her "escape" and said there was no better way to spend your time than surrounding yourself with love, any way you could. When the world got too hard to handle, escaping into a good love story always gave her renewed hope for a happily-ever-after.

She knew her mother believed in fate, grand romantic gestures, stolen glances, and the kind of love that defied all expectations—because for her, romance was more than a fleeting feeling. Love was a commitment to always listen to and follow the heart.

Ava also remembered how her father used to tease her mother about her soft spot for romance. While he was a practical man, duty bound, smart, and steadfast, he'd be the first to tell you a romantic he was not.

Henry was the same way, so it had never bothered her. It was what she was used to seeing. She knew her father had loved her mother, even if he hadn't shown it with romantic, flowery gestures. They'd still had love and that had been what mattered. They'd been partners who complemented each other and made each other better. Ava believed that was what was really important.

And that was what she wanted for her and Henry once they got married and started their lives together. She didn't need silly romantic gestures, candlelight dinners, slow dances, or love letters. She was happy to leave all that nonsense in the movies and romance novels where it belonged.

"I'll call you later," her mother said as she got into the car.

Ava was jolted back to the present. "Wait!" She grabbed the door before the driver could shut it. "I need to—" But the rest of what she was going to say was drowned out by Stormy barking as he tried to jump into the car with the queen.

The queen laughed, charmed. "I'm sorry, Stormy, but you can't go with me this time. You have to stay with Ava."

Ava and Stormy looked equally worried.

"What? No," Ava said. "I can't watch him. I have the party to finish planning—"

"And that's why I'm leaving Lydia here in case you need any help or there's anything else you need," her mother said, smiling sweetly.

"Can she make the dog disappear?" Ava asked, serious.

Her mother ignored the sarcasm. "I told you I can stay if you need me—"

"No," Ava said before her mother could finish. "There's nothing you can do. I've got everything handled." She pointed at Stormy. "But I don't have time to deal with *him*."

Stormy tilted his head, listening to Ava.

"Where's this dog trainer?" Ava asked. "I thought you said he would be picking up the dog before you left."

"He's apparently running a little late," her mother answered.

Ava rolled her eyes. "Maybe he needs to be trained, too."

Her mother smiled patiently. "Justin is a world-class trainer. His Puppy Bootcamps have a huge waiting list. We're lucky he agreed to train Stormy. He's a dog whisperer—"

"A dog *whisperer?*" Ava laughed. "Seriously? Does he read their fortunes, too?"

Her mother ignored the sarcasm and gave Stormy one last hug. "Now you be a good boy." She buried her face in his fur. "I love you. I miss you already. I'll see you soon."

Ava's eyes widened. *This is unbelievable*, she thought. The dog was already getting more affection than she'd ever gotten from her mother.

Ava took a deep breath. "Mother, may I please tell Henry you're going to announce our engagement at the party? We want to follow our royal tradition. It's important to us, and we hope it's important to you as well."

"I've already alerted our press pool that we will be introducing a new member of the royal family on Christmas Eve at the party," her mother said.

"Henry," Ava said, breathing a sigh of relief.

"No. Stormy," her mother corrected her.

All the color drained out of Ava's face. "What?!"

"It's going to be a huge surprised to everyone," her mother said, beaming. "He's our first royal pet."

"What about Henry? Our proposal?" Ava sputtered.

"Valentine's Day would be better," her mother said as she shut the door herself.

"Mother, wait!" Ava cried out. She frantically pounded on the window, but the car took off.

The last thing Ava saw was her mother waving to Stormy.

As Stormy ran after the Rolls-Royce, barking, Ava buried her head in her hands and screamed.

❄ ❄ ❄

Back in the Grand Hall, Ava anxiously circled the giant Christmas tree, waiting for Henry to pick up her FaceTime call.

Stormy followed her, wagging his tail.

When the duke finally popped up on her screen, Ava tried to smile, but it was strained.

"Ava, did we have a call scheduled?" the duke asked, confused.

"No, but I talked to my mother about our engagement announcement—"

"Fantastic. I'll tell my family right away and—"

"Wait..." Ava interrupted.

The duke frowned, waiting for her to continue.

She took a deep breath. "I...um..."

"Is there a problem?" the duke asked. "You said you were going to handle this."

"And I'm going to. I mean…I did," Ava said, talking faster than usual. "But before you tell your family or anyone else, my mother wants to…talk to you first. You know, to officially give you permission. It's royal protocol. She's going to call you."

"Excellent," the duke said.

As Ava forced herself to smile, she felt a bead of sweat trickle down the back of her neck. She was a terrible liar, and her body was rebelling. She hated to lie, but she felt like in this situation, she didn't have a choice. She told herself it was okay, because this wasn't an actual lie if she was just buying herself a little more time to make it the truth.

She just needed to have a proper conversation with her mother, and then she was confident she and Henry would be able to go ahead as planned to announce their engagement at the Christmas party.

Ava's eyes grew huge when she saw Edgar in the doorway watching her.

"Henry, I have to go. I'll call you later, bye," she hung up before Henry could say anything.

Edgar walked toward her.

She cringed. "How much of that did you hear?"

"Enough to know you didn't tell the duke the truth," Edgar said.

"How could I, Edgar? How could I tell Henry my mother has picked a *dog* over him to announce at the party?" Ava asked, as she anxiously twisted her watch around her wrist.

When she spotted Stormy sniffing the Christmas tree, she marched over to him. "Don't you dare touch that," she demanded, hands on her hips.

Stormy barked and wagged his tail, like he was ready to play.

"I mean it," she said sternly. "Don't touch the tree. Don't touch anything. Do you hear me?"

When Stormy barked twice, Edgar tried to hide his smile.

Ava wasn't amused. She walked back to Edgar. "This dog…I just can't.…What was my mother thinking? If my father were here, none of this would be happening." Ava's voice cracked with emotion as a sudden wave of grief washed over her.

That was the way it had been with her. Her sadness came in unexpected waves.

When her father had passed away, she hadn't taken time to grieve. She'd had to step in and help her mother take over dozens of royal duties. Work was her ultimate distraction and she'd been on automatic pilot ever since. Usually, she could handle anything, but every once in a while, like now, she'd say her father's name or think about him, and all her pent-up emotions would come rushing to the surface and the pain would suffocate her.

Edgar put his arm around her. She leaned into him for comfort.

"It's going to be okay," he said gently.

But Ava didn't know if she'd ever feel okay again. What she felt was alone. She fought back tears. "I really miss him," she said softly.

"I know. I do, too," Edgar said. "He would be so proud of all you're doing to pay tribute to him with this party and continuing the tradition of raising money for all the charities."

Ava took a deep breath. "His parties were legendary. It's a lot to try and live up to."

"And if anyone can do it, you can," Edgar told her. "You're the Princess of Skydovia. You can do anything you set your mind to."

Ava looked into Edgar's eyes. "That's what my father always used to say…"

Edgar nodded a knowing smile. "I know. So, believe it."

❄ ❄ ❄

The Library was the room in the castle that had some of the most unique Christmas decorations. That was thanks to her mother, who loved using the Library to try out new trends.

This year, while the Library's floor-to-ceiling bookcases and giant picture windows were trimmed with traditional fresh evergreen garlands, wreaths, and white twinkle lights, it was the Library's Christmas tree that really grabbed attention.

Because this was no ordinary tree. This Christmas tree stood six-feet tall and was made up entirely of books that were expertly stacked on top of each other so they formed the shape of a Christmas tree.

It was a true work of art.

Each book layer of the tree was carefully arranged in a tapered shape to match how a Christmas tree would look. The book covers were all in red and green, with their spines facing out. White twinkle lights were woven between the books, adding to the magic, while a crystal star was perched at the top.

Ava was adjusting one of the books in the middle of the tree when Stormy came running up barking.

He eyed the books, wagging his tail.

"Don't you even think about it," Ava warned him.

Stormy stepped closer to the tree.

"No. Stop!" Ava demanded and tried to grab him.

But it was too late. Stormy already had a book in his mouth.

Ava froze as the tree swayed. She knew if Stormy pulled the book out of the tree the whole thing would come crashing down like dominoes.

Ava begged him in her nicest, most soothing voice. "Please, let go of that book."

Stormy wagged his tail.

"That's right," Ava said, encouraged. "Just drop it. Let it go…"

Stormy let the book go.

Ava breathed a huge sigh of relief…until Stormy grabbed the book again and yanked it out of the tree!

"Nooooo!" Ava cried as the entire tree came crumbling down.

In seconds, all the books that had taken hours to stack up perfectly were scattered all over the place.

Stormy dropped the book he'd pulled out of the tree at Ava's feet, looking very proud of himself.

"What have you done?" she cried out.

Stormy took off zooming around the room as fast as he could, jumping on the couches and chairs.

Feeling totally defeated, Ava didn't have the energy to try and chase after him.

But when Stormy skidded to a stop in front of a display of vintage nutcrackers that were lined up along the fireplace hearth, Ava's heart skipped a beat.

He froze.

Ava froze.

"No…" she pleaded with him. "Not the nutcrackers."

Stormy barked, excited, and raced toward them…

# Chapter 9

Justin was happily humming "Deck the Halls" as he drove up to Vailgate Castle. When he arrived, he parked his SUV next to a van that had an Icescape Catering logo on it. Next to the van, he saw a man he guessed to be in his mid-60s struggling to unload a giant Santa Claus ice sculpture onto a silver cart.

Justin jumped out of his SUV. "Do you need some help?" he offered.

"That would be great," the man said, giving him a grateful smile. "My son usually does all the heavy lifting, but he's on another job right now." He carefully put the Santa sculpture he was holding onto the cart and held out his hand to Justin. "I'm Ted."

"Justin."

They smiled as they shook hands.

"Looks like I came along just at the right time," Justin said as he eyed two more ice sculptures that were still inside the van. There was a beautiful angel with outstretched wings and an impressive reindeer with antlers. "Wow, these are great."

Ted smiled proudly. "Thank you. I hope the princess thinks so. She's a tough one to please."

"I can see that," Justin said, smiling. "I saw her earlier decorating one of the rooms—"

"Terrifying, right?" Ted asked with a laugh.

"I don't know if I'd go so far as to say that—"

"You just haven't spent enough time with her yet," Ted said with a knowing look.

Justin laughed. "Okay. Thanks. It's surprising because I've worked with the queen, and she's so easygoing and nice."

Ted nodded. "Everyone loves our queen."

"But not the princess?" Justin asked, intrigued.

"It's hard to love someone you barely know," Ted answered. "The princess doesn't go out in the public much. I think when she was growing up, her parents were protecting her. Understandable. But I'm not sure what's going on now."

"Really?" Justin asked. "I thought that was a royal's job—to be a public figure and promote the monarchy and all their causes and stuff like that."

"Not this royal family. Prince Fredrick, the queen's husband, was the same way. He avoided the media as much as he could and let the queen get all the headlines."

"Like father like daughter," Justin said.

"Exactly," Ted agreed. "This is the first time I've met the princess, with her being in charge of the big Christmas Eve party. I've heard from some other workers she can be pretty demanding. So, consider yourself warned."

"Luckily, I won't have to deal with her," Justin replied.

"Really? What are you doing for the party?"

"Nothing for the party," Justin said. "I'm just their dog trainer."

Ted's mouth dropped open with surprise. "They have a new dog? Really? Since when?"

Justin winced. "Damn, I wasn't supposed to tell anyone—"

"Don't worry. I won't say anything," Ted assured him. "I'm a vault. I can keep a secret."

Justin laughed. "I hope so, or else you'll have the queen coming after you. Wait, worse, I'll send the princess—"

"No!" Ted shouted in mock horror. "Not the princess!" Ted's phone buzzed with a text. He read it and frowned.

"Everything okay?" Justin asked.

Ted shook his head. "No, my son's having problems with a delivery. He's only a few miles away and wants me to come help him. But I can't be late for the princess—"

"Go ahead and go. I can take the ice sculptures in for you," Justin offered. "Do you want the others that are in the van, the angel and reindeer, too?"

"Yes, all three. That would be brilliant. If you're sure it's okay?" Ted asked.

"It's my pleasure," Justin answered with a smile.

"This shouldn't take long," Ted promised. "I really appreciate this. You're a lifesaver."

Justin was already loading the angel ice sculpture onto the cart. "Don't worry about it. I got you. Take all the time you need."

❅ ❅ ❅

Inside the castle's Library, Ava was muttering to herself as she picked up books from the Christmas tree Stormy had destroyed.

"Is there anything this dog hasn't ruined yet?"

As she was collecting books, she kept one eye on Stormy.

He was on the couch pawing at a Christmas pillow.

"Stop that!" Ava shouted at him.

Stormy barked back at her and wagged his tail.

Ava's grip around the book she was holding tightened. She felt like the louder she talked, the more the dog barked. If she didn't know better, she would have sworn Stormy was doing all this on purpose to torment her.

"Princess, the ice sculptures samples are here," Edgar announced as he entered the Library.

Ava checked her watch and frowned. "They're late," she said, but didn't look up. She was too busy keeping a close watch on Stormy who had now started chewing on the pillow. She ran over to him. "No! Put that down. Give it to me," she demanded.

But when she tried to grab the pillow out of Stormy's mouth, he held on tight and started tugging. Clearly, he thought it was a game of tug-of-war.

But Ava wasn't playing around. She pulled harder. "Let. Go!"

Stormy held on.

She wiggled the pillow to try and get it out of his mouth and tugged harder. "I mean it. Let go!"

Suddenly, Stormy let go, sending Ava flying backward, putting her off balance.

"Whoa!" she exclaimed. Her arms flailed and she felt herself start to fall. That was when she felt two strong arms wrap around her waist, freaking her out even more. "What the—"

"It's okay, I got you," Justin said as he caught her right before she hit the ground.

When she heard a man's voice, she spun around in a panic—sending them both tumbling backward. They crashed into the ice sculpture cart before hitting the floor in a tangled heap.

Ava landed in Justin's lap, and then the Santa ice sculpture face planted in her lap. She flung Santa off her. The sculpture slid across the marble floor.

She batted away Justin's hands that were wrapped around her waist. "Let me go!" Ava shouted as she struggled to get up.

Their eyes met.

"You!" Ava said, confused.

Justin, looking equally shaken, held both hands in the air. "I'm sorry. I was only trying to help. You came flying at me. I was trying to save you from falling."

"I don't need anyone to *save me,*" Ava shot back at him as she stood up, slipping on some ice.

With lightning reflexes, Justin grabbed her right before she fell again. This time, they were face-to-face, their chests touching, their lips just inches apart.

For a moment, time stood still as they stared into each other's eyes.

Ava's heart raced. She felt tingling all over, from the top of her head to her toes, confusing her even more.

"Are you okay?" Justin asked.

For a moment, she could only stare at his lips. He was saying something else, but her heart was pounding so hard that it was all she could hear. She hastily backed away from him. "No, I'm not okay," she said as her heart raced. "Look what you've done," she said as she pointed at all the busted up sculptures that had fallen during the cart crash.

"Me?" Justin flung back at her. "Uh, you were the one who caused all this, attacking an innocent dog!"

"What?!" Ava shook her head, because she couldn't believe what she was hearing. "I wasn't *attacking* that dog. He's the one who's been wrecking everything."

"I didn't see him crash into the cart," Justin said as he tried to pick up what was left of the sculptures.

Stormy was pawing at the Santa and trying to lick his face.

Ava's eyes narrowed as she watched Justin. "Wait, you're a decorator. I saw you yesterday with the wreaths, and you're also doing ice sculptures? You're doing two jobs, and obviously not doing either very well."

Justin's eyes widened. "I beg your pardon?"

"No," Ava said.

Justin laughed. "No, what?"

"No, I will not pardon you," Ava said emphatically.

Justin blinked several times. "Oh my God, are you serious?"

The look Ava gave him said she was dead serious. "Yes, I'm *serious*," Ava insisted. "You left earlier before I could approve your wreath and now you bring in these subpar sculptures—"

"Subpar?" Justin sputtered.

"Yes," Ava said as she traipsed around the cart studying what was left of the ice sculptures. "These are all wrong. The reindeer looks like a horse, and the angel needs much bigger wings." Ava glanced over at the melting Santa and pointed at it. "And I never asked for a Santa Claus, so I don't know why you brought him."

"Are you kidding?" Justin jumped in. "Everyone needs Santa!"

Ava mouth dropped open. She was not used to being spoken to like this. She locked eyes with him.

"Are you trying to get fired?" she asked.

He grinned back at her.

Ava's eyes narrowed. "You think I won't do it?"

Justin laughed. "No, I'm sure you'd *love to* fire me, but you can't do it, because you didn't hire me. The queen did."

"My mother?" Ava asked, confused. She shook her head. "No, she has nothing to do with planning this party and…" But her voice trailed off when she saw Justin walk over to Stormy. He petted him and held out his hand. Stormy immediately put his paw into Justin's hand, and they shook.

"Good boy," Justin said as he petted him some more.

Stormy barked and wagged his tail.

Ava's eyes widened with understanding. "You're the dog trainer."

"Yup, I'm the dog trainer."

"So, you're not a decorator?"

"Nope," Justin said. "When I was here yesterday meeting with your mom, I heard Christmas music playing, so I followed the music and…"

"Came in with the wreath decorators," Ava finished for him.

"If you say so," Justin agreed with a boyish smile.

"But if you're not the ice sculptor, what are you doing with all these?" Ava asked.

"I was trying to help out Ted—"

"Ted?" Ava asked, growing more confused by the second.

"Yeah, you know, your ice sculpture guy," Justin said. "Don't you know the name of the people you hire?"

Ava answered him by not answering him.

"I met Ted outside. He had a family emergency, so I brought these in for him. He should be here any minute."

"And then you'll have to explain to him how you destroyed all his hard work," Ava said.

"You did this, not me," Justin said. "Didn't she, Stormy?"

Stormy barked twice, wagging his tail in agreement.

Ava shook her head in amazement. "You both are unbelievable."

"Thank you," Justin said, proudly.

"That wasn't a compliment," Ava fired back at him.

Justin shrugged and kept smiling.

"You said my mother hired you? How do you know her?" Ava asked, in a tone that was far from friendly.

"I met her in Romania at a fundraiser for one of the animal shelters she supports," Justin replied. "I've also worked with her when she was in New York with some other veterinarians."

"You're American."

"Guilty," Justin said with a smile.

"And a veterinarian," Ava stated, sizing him up.

"Technically, yes, but right now, I'm focusing on training shelter dogs and matching them with the right families—or, as we like to say, *furever* homes. You know, fur—"

"Yes, I understand. I'm familiar with the term."

Justin arched an eyebrow. "Really? Then why haven't I ever seen you at any of the charity events with your mom?"

"Because that's my mother's passion, not mine," Ava said.

Justin studied her. "So, what cause do you support? What are you *passionate* about?"

Ava was taken aback. She couldn't remember the last time anyone had asked her what she really cared about. Right now the only thing she was focused on was trying to protect the monarchy and her family's legacy.

"This isn't about me. It's about you," Ava said, refocusing the conversation before it got completely out of control. "If you're a dog trainer you better be a good one because that dog," Ava pointed to Stormy, "needs a lot of training."

"And so do you," Justin shot back at her.

Ava recoiled. "Excuse me?!"

"I don't just train the dog. I also train the owners," Justin explained. "If the dog has a problem, it's usually tied to one of them."

Ava marched toward Stormy. "He's not *my dog*. I don't even want him here!"

Stormy dropped his head, looking sad.

Justin smile disappeared. "Stop, you're hurting his feelings."

Ava threw up her hands. "Seriously? You, too? Now I see why my mother likes you. He's a *dog*. He doesn't understand what I'm saying."

"That's not true," Justin corrected her. "You can't talk to a dog like that."

Ava opened her mouth to say something, but then shut it quickly. She was tired of arguing. "Can you just take him away before he wrecks anything else?"

"It's not like he did it on purpose," Justin said. "He's a dog."

"Oh, now you say he's just a *dog*." Ava laughed. "That's convenient."

"What's your point?" Justin asked.

As Ava stared back at Justin, he had her so confused she didn't know what her point was anymore. "Just take the dog and don't bring him back until he's…fixed," Ava said, flustered.

"That's already been taken care of," Justin said with a cheeky smile.

Ava cringed. "I wasn't talking about *that*. I didn't mean… Just take him, please. Now."

"Gladly," Justin said. "I'm happy to get him away from someone who obviously doesn't understand him. Come on, Stormy."

But when they both turned to Stormy—he was gone!

Ava looked around frantically. "Where did he go? What is he demolishing now?"

Justin walked around the room. "Stormy, come on. Time to go."

Ava started to panic. "He's not here."

Justin headed for the door. "I told you not to talk to him like that."

"Where are you going?" Ava called out after him.

"To find *your* dog," Justin answered.

"I told you, he's not my dog!" Ava yelled back, but it was too late. Justin was already gone.

# Chapter 10

As Ava and Justin searched the Grand Hall looking for Stormy, she was trying not to panic.

"He's not in this room either," Ava said with a sigh.

Justin shook his head, frowning. "He's obviously upset."

"You blame me for this, don't you?" Ava asked. "You think this is all my fault?"

"Dogs are highly empathetic. They're impacted by the energy in the room."

Ava lifted her head high. "I have great energy."

Justin gave her a skeptical look.

"I do," Ava insisted.

"I warned you not to talk to him like that," Justin said as he headed for the door.

"Now where are you going?" Ava called out after him, but this time Justin didn't answer back.

✳ ✳ ✳

In the grand entryway of the castle, delivery men were bringing in life-size nutcrackers for the Christmas party. Ava greeted them as she continued to look around for Stormy.

"Can you please put all the nutcrackers in the Grand Hall with everything else?" Ava told the men. "Thank you, and did any of you see a black-and-white dog running around outside?"

They all shook their heads as they passed her.

"It was a friend's dog," Ava quickly added. She knew she had to be very careful to make sure no one knew there was a new royal dog, and that at the moment, that dog was missing.

"If anyone sees him, please let me know," she added.

Behind the last nutcracker coming through the door was Justin.

Ava looked behind him. "Did you find him?"

"No," Justin said, looking just as stressed as she felt.

"I haven't had any luck either," Ava said. "I've been asking all the delivery people and decorators that have been coming and going, getting ready for the party, and they haven't seen him, either. I'm telling everyone he's a friend's dog, because no one can know we have a dog until my mother makes the official announcement.

"I know. I get it," Justin said. "You've said that several times."

"Because it's important."

Edgar and Lydia walked in and joined them. They looked equally concerned.

"The staff has looked everywhere. Stormy's not in the castle," Lydia said.

"I need to call the queen," Edgar added.

Ava panicked and grabbed Edgar's arm. "Edgar, wait! Please don't call her yet. We're going to find him. You know how upset she'd be. There's no reason to worry her. He couldn't have just disappeared. He has to be somewhere. He's probably just in here hiding, destroying more decorations. We just need to keep looking—"

Justin pointed to the open door. "I think this is our problem. You said people have been coming in and out all day. He could have easily slipped outside. Dogs love being outside. That makes a lot more sense than him hiding out somewhere here. He's not the kind of dog who hides. He's the kind of dog who runs."

Ava's frown deepened. "Well, that makes me feel much better, thanks."

"I'm just telling it like it is," Justin said.

When Edgar looked even more worried, Ava took his hand. "Please, Edgar, just give me a little more time to find him. I *will* find him. We have to find him…"

Edgar looked at Lydia. "What do you think?"

Lydia hesitated. She looked at Ava and then back at Edgar. "I think we can wait a little while longer, but if we don't find him in the next hour or so, the queen will need to know."

"And I'll tell her myself," Ava said. "I promise."

Edgar and Lydia exchanged a look and nodded.

"Okay," Edgar said.

Relieved, Ava hugged him and then hugged Lydia. "Thank you, Edgar, thank you, Lydia."

"What about me?" Justin asked with a teasing smile. He held out his arms for a hug.

When Ava ignored him, Edgar, Lydia, and Justin all laughed.

"But seriously, we need to find Stormy fast," Justin said. "The longer he's gone, the less chance we have of getting him back. He hasn't been chipped and doesn't have any dog tags yet. I was going to do all that today."

"So, what do you suggest?" Ava asked as they all turned their attention to Justin. "You're the dog expert. How do we find him?"

"We could post some flyers online and in the village with his picture," Justin said.

"But remember, we can't tell anyone he's ours," Ava jumped in. "Can you see the headlines? 'Princess loses the first royal pet.' The press would have a field day with that."

Lydia stepped forward. "I can say that Stormy is mine and give out my information for people to contact. That way, no one will find out anything."

"That's a great idea, Lydia. Thank you," Ava said, relieved.

"I'll go make the flyer right now," Lydia said.

"I'll help," Edgar added, as they left together.

Ava turned to Justin. "And you'll keep looking outside?"

"Yes, as soon as you're ready," Justin replied. "It's supposed to snow. You won't get very far in those shoes."

They both stared down at Ava's designer heels.

"Me? No." Ava laughed. "I'm not going anywhere. I have a Christmas party to plan, and I'm already so far behind now."

Justin gave her a blank stare.

She rushed to continue. "It's our annual Christmas party we host ever year. It's the event of the season, to raise money for charity. I'm sure you've heard of it—"

"No."

"Well, it's what we're known for. Everyone looks forward to it all year. My father started overseeing all the planning when he married my mother. He enjoyed working closely with the decorators and the caterers to create something unique and special. Year after year, people would wait with anticipation to see what he would do next. He always said our Christmas party reflected who we were as a royal family and set the tone of the new year." Ava paused when she noticed Justin didn't look impressed. "Trust me. It's a big deal, and this is my first year taking over. Everyone's counting on me, so—"

"So, you think you're too busy," Justin finished for her.

Ava smiled and breathed a huge sigh of relief that he finally understood. "Yes, *so* busy."

Justin nodded. "Then I'll just call your mother."

Ava's smile disappeared. Her eyes narrowed. "You wouldn't."

The charming smile Justin flashed her assured Ava that he most certainly would.

Ava shook her head in disbelief as they stared each other down.

She knew she was trapped.

She took a deep breath. "Fine," she said through gritted teeth. "What do you want me to do?"

# Chapter 11

A light dusting of snow covered the royal stables. Twinkling lights framed the arched windows, and garlands of evergreen were draped over the stable doors, while icicles clung to the eaves like nature's own holiday decorations.

Ava inhaled the scent of fresh pine and hay that lingered in the crisp winter air as she entered the stables with Justin. She had changed into her riding gear that included a red wool cape and polished black boots. As she confidently headed for a beautiful black stallion, Justin hesitated in the doorway.

"I still think we should drive," he said, looking uncomfortable.

"We can cover more ground and go off the roads this way," Ava insisted as she expertly adjusted a saddle on the proud stallion. Her voice and demeanor softened as she lovingly stroked the horse's silky neck. "Are you ready for a ride, Midnight?"

Midnight affectionately nuzzled Ava and whinnied.

Justin shuddered and took a quick step back.

Ava gave him a questioning look. "You've ridden horses before, right?"

Justin laughed. "Yes, of course."

"Okay, then you can take Shadow," Ava said as she pointed to a fiery stallion who snorted and pawed at the ground.

Justin gulped.

When Ava tossed him a bridle, he almost dropped it.

Shadow snorted again and tossed his mane.

Justin took a few steps back. "You know, Shadow doesn't really look too into this…"

Shadow pawed at the ground again.

"What are you talking about?" Ava asked. "Shadow is great."

Justin pointed to an older mare who was sleeping in her stall. The name on the stall was Daisy.

"I think we should take this one instead," he said.

❄ ❄ ❄

Ava and Justin rode side by side across the snow-covered castle grounds, the landscape looking like something from a winter postcard. While Ava happily took in the scenery, Justin shifted uneasily in the saddle, scanning for any sign of the missing dog.

"I love being out here when it's like this, don't you?" she asked. When Justin didn't respond, she glanced at him and saw him holding onto Daisy's reins for dear life. He was off balance in his saddle, fighting not to fall.

Ava frowned. "You're sure you've ridden before?"

"Yes," Justin said. "It has just…been awhile."

Ava gave him a skeptical look. "How long?"

"Don't worry about me. I'm fine," he insisted.

"Okay," Ava said. "Then let's get moving. We have a lot of ground to cover. Come on Daisy, let's go, girl."

When Daisy started trotting, Justin freaked out.

"Whoa! Hold on. Wait," he said, bouncing around in his saddle.

"You're the one who said we needed to find this dog fast," Ava said as Midnight took off in a gallop.

Daisy started galloping, too, but in the wrong direction!

"Daisy, no! Heel! Stop! Heeeelp!" Justin cried out.

Ava's eyes grew huge when she looked over her shoulder and saw Daisy galloping away with no signs of stopping, and Justin looking like he was about to fall off her at any moment.

"Oh no. Daisy, stop! Stop!" Ava shouted as she raced after them. "Justin, hold on. I'm coming!"

❄ ❄ ❄

As Ava guided Midnight in a slow walk down the snowy path, Justin sat behind her, clinging to her waist.

Daisy followed them. Her reins were secured to Midnight.

"Why didn't you just tell me you couldn't ride?" Ava asked.

"Because I thought I could do it," Justin said with a sigh. "Apparently not."

"You look terrified."

"Yup," Justin said, sounding embarrassed. "That about sums it up."

"Are you afraid of horses?" Ava asked.

Silence.

"You are," Ava answered for him. "That explains a lot. They can sense when you're afraid, and then they take advantage of you."

"Sounds like some of my other relationships," Justin mumbled.

"What?" Ava asked. Even though she'd understood him perfectly, she wanted him to elaborate.

"Nothing," Justin said. "And I'm aware of how horses work. Remember, I am a vet—"

"A vet who's afraid of horses?"

"Yes, okay, I'm afraid of horses," Justin said. "Are you happy now?"

Ava frowned. "No, not at all. I think that would be terrible. Horseback riding is one of my favorite things in the world. Midnight is my best friend. You have no idea what you're missing."

"Well, thanks, but I'll pass. I thought I was going to be thrown and break my neck."

"That would have been unfortunate," Ava said.

Justin laughed at her matter-of-fact tone. "Very."

As they rode in silence for a few minutes, the only sound they could hear was the horses' hooves crunching through the snow, each step landing with a soft thud.

When Midnight snorted, Ava felt Justin shudder. As much as she loved giving him a hard time, she couldn't help but feel a little bad. His fear was real. She placed her hand over his where it rested on her waist and gave it a reassuring squeeze.

"It's okay," she said softly. "You're safe with me. Midnight would never do anything to hurt us." Ava smiled a little as she felt Justin relax.

"And I thought Daisy was a great choice, but clearly, she's the wild one," Justin said.

Ava laughed.

"What's so funny? What are you laughing about?"

"The thought of Daisy being wild. She mostly sleeps all day. She's as gentle as they come," Ava said.

"Humph, well, not with me," Justin muttered.

"She was just having a little fun with you. Right, Daisy?"

When Daisy whinnied, Ava felt Justin tense up.

"Yeah, well, I'm going to stick with dogs," Justin said. "And right now, all I care about is finding Stormy."

"Once we do find him, how long will it take you to train him?" Ava asked.

Justin shrugged. "It depends. He's obviously crazy smart—"

"Or just crazy," Ava added.

"The smart ones can either learn really fast or be a handful," Justin continued.

"Let me guess which category you think this dog is in," Ava replied.

"Honestly, I don't know yet. I won't know until I can spend more time with him."

"And that's one thing we don't have—time," Ava said. "My mother wants to introduce him at the Christmas party."

"I know," Justin said. "She told me. She's very excited about it."

"So, once we find him you'll need to train him fast. We can't have a royal dog running around causing chaos," Ava said.

"No guarantees," Justin said. "But I'll do my best. Besides, things that really matter are worth the wait, right?"

Ava shook her head vehemently. "No. Things that really matter should happen right now. No one has any time to waste. Come on, Midnight, let's go." As they picked up their pace, Justin gripped her waist even tighter.

❄ ❄ ❄

Outside the royal stables, Ava and Justin watched the stablehand take the horses inside.

Ava shook her head, frustrated. "I can't believe none of the stablehands or anyone else has seen that dog."

"And we didn't see anything, either. No footprints, nothing," Justin said. "I'm starting to get worried…"

"What do you mean?" Ava asked sharply.

"I really thought he got outside, and we'd find him playing around the castle," Justin said. "I hope he's okay." Justin raked his fingers through his hair, stressed. "I can't believe I've lost the queen's first pet."

Ava's eyebrows shot up with surprise. "So, now you're blaming yourself? I thought this was all my fault."

"Oh, you yelling at him definitely had something to do with him taking off," Justin said. "But this isn't just on you. We were both arguing, raising our voices. I should have known better. I know how sensitive border collies are. They're people pleasers. The last thing they want to do is upset people. I should have taken him away from you as soon as I saw how much you didn't like him."

Ava blinked several times, taken aback. "It's not that I don't like him—"

Justin stopped her with a look.

"Okay, so, maybe I was a little harsh," Ava conceded. "I've never had a dog before, and when my mother brought him home, it was such a shock. She didn't talk to me or warn me beforehand." Ava took a deep breath. "But if she finds out I lost her dog, she'll never forgive me. The media can't find out either. I can't be known as the princess who lost her mother's beloved pet."

"And I can't be known as the dog trainer who lost the queen's dog," Justin said. "I'd never work again. We both have a lot to lose here."

Ava nodded. "We do. I should've had more patience with him, but right now, I'm under so much pressure—"

"Clearly," Justin agreed.

Ava frowned. "What do you mean by that?"

"Just that it's obvious you have a lot going on, because you're wound up so tight."

Ava gave him a blank stare.

"You know, tense, stressed—that's what I meant," Justin clarified.

"You make me sound so lovely," Ava said sarcastically.

"I'm sure you can be, but maybe just not right now," Justin offered.

Ava wasn't sure if she should take that as compliment or not.

"With dogs, it's more the tone of your voice and your body language they pick up on," Justin explained.

"Really? A dog can sense all that?"

"Yup," Justin said. "Just like people can."

"Really?" Ava asked, unconvinced. "Then tell me what my body language and tone is saying right now to you."

When Justin studied her closely, she felt herself blush.

"It's saying…desperate…"

"What?!" Ava sputtered, shocked. She had never been called *desperate* in her life.

"To find Stormy," Justin added.

When Ava gave him a searching look, his expression was impossible to read. He was staring at the stables. "Maybe Stormy didn't come here because he doesn't like horses, either."

"Seriously, what happened to you?" Ava asked. "There has to be a reason you're afraid of horses. Usually everybody loves horses."

Justin laughed. "Yeah, well, not me, not since a county fair when I was eight and tried to get a ride on a pony, and it bit me!"

"What?" Ava asked surprised. "What did you do to it?"

Justin frowned. "Why do you assume this was my fault and that I did something wrong?"

Ava rolled her eyes. "Really? So, you're blaming a poor little pony?"

"How do you know it was *little*?" Justin shot back at her.

Ava laughed. "Because it was a pony at a fair."

"Okay, fine, maybe it was…small. I don't remember because I was just a kid, and I was too traumatized after getting bit."

Ava waited him for to continue.

He didn't.

They stared at each other.

"You're not going to let this go, are you?" He sighed.

She shook her head. "No. I want to know."

"Okay, fine," he relented. "I was picking out what pony I wanted to ride, and this white one looked good, so I tried to make friends by feeding it an apple—"

"And it accidentally nipped you," Ava finished for him. "That can happen. It's not the pony's fault. You didn't know how to do it right—"

"Well, it got me good," Justin said as he held out his hand and showed Ava a faint scar.

When Ava touched the scar and traced it with her finger, their eyes met. A jolt of electricity shot through her, and a shiver ran down her spine that wasn't from the cold. She swiftly pulled her hand back, confused by the unexpected spark between them.

"So, now you believe me?" Justin asked.

"Yes," Ava said, not meeting his stare. She started walking. "But it still wasn't the pony's fault."

A chuckle escaped Justin as he caught up with her. Without a word, they matched each other's pace.

Finally, Ava spoke first. "How can a vet be scared of horses?"

"Not all vets work with them, you know," Justin answered. "I never have, and I never will."

"Ever?" Ava asked, surprised.

"Ever," Justin responded with conviction.

Ava glanced at him. "Did you always know you wanted to be a vet?"

Justin hesitated before answering. "My dad is a veterinarian. He's always expected me to go into the family business with him. My grandpa was also a vet. So, they say this is my legacy."

Ava nodded. "I understand that very well. Following in your family's footsteps. But you don't sound too excited about it."

Justin's jaw clenched as he stared straight ahead.

"You don't want to do it," Ava said. It was a statement, not a question.

When Justin looked over at her, she could see the guilt in his eyes.

"No," he answered. "I don't. I love my dad, but I don't want to be a full-time vet right now."

"What do you want to do?"

Justin's face lit up. "Exactly what I'm doing right now— travel around the world saving and training shelter dogs and matching them with families. There's nothing more rewarding than finding these dogs a new home and seeing how much love they bring to people who want to add a pet to their family."

"I've heard that a lot of people adopt the wrong pets and then end up returning them to shelters," Ava said. "Like at Easter, I've read about hundreds of bunnies that are adopted and then returned the next day."

Justin nodded sadly. "Just like puppies and kittens at Christmas. It's an impulse purchase. People don't do the research and understand how important it is to have the right match so a pet can fit into their lifestyles."

"And that's where you come in, matching dogs to their owners?" Ava asked.

"Exactly," Justin said. "It's a lot harder than you might think, especially when someone falls in love with a pet that has a lot of behavioral problems. It's my job to train them to make sure they can be part of the family forever, not just a quick purchase to be returned like a purse someone doesn't want."

Ava couldn't help but be impressed. "You're clearly very passionate about what you do. My mother says you're the best of the best."

"Your mother is very kind," Justin said. "But this job for her, with Stormy, is my last job before I have to head home and start working for my dad."

"Can't you just tell him how you feel?" Ava asked.

Justin shook his head. "It would break his heart. I'm sure there are things you'd like to tell your mom but can't."

Ava nodded. "You feel it is your duty to work with your father."

"Exactly," Justin said. "Your legacy is to be the queen someday. My legacy is to take over my dad's business someday. We might come from two very different worlds, but our paths aren't that different when you really think about it."

"We're both doing what we were raised to do," Ava agreed. "But my situation is a lot different from yours."

"Because I'm not royal—"

Ava shook her head. "No, because you don't want to take over your family business."

"And you do," Justin said.

Ava nodded. "Of course. I'm ready to step in as queen whenever I'm needed. I was born to do this. I love what I do—at least, most of it. It's an honor and a privilege to serve our people. I've always taken this role very seriously. Every choice I've made in my life up to this point has been to protect my family's legacy, our people, and the monarchy."

Justin raised an eyebrow. "Wow, that's not what I expected."

"What did you expect?"

"I thought all royal children secretly wished they could escape their blue bloodlines and be regular people," Justin said. "I thought you might want to break free from all the royal rules and obligations and escape all the pomp and circumstance."

Ava shook her head. "All those things make up who I am. The royal rules, traditions, and obligations are my identity. I wouldn't be anything without them."

"I know some of the royal protocol, but your mother… When I've seen her, she seems to break some of those rules. She's more…modern."

Ava frowned.

"And you see this as a problem?"

"I believe if you bend one rule, then you bend another," Ava said. "Then pretty soon, you're not following any rules and things are just…"

"Natural."

"Chaotic," Ava said, correcting him.

"You know, I've met your mother multiple times and—"

"You think she's chaotic?"

Justin laughed. "What? No. I think she acts like she's in touch with what is happening in the world. She's relatable and approachable. She doesn't seem to put herself on any high pedestal above anyone else. She's just…real."

Ava's eyes flew to his face. "Are you saying I'm…fake?"

"No," Justin replied. "You two are just…different."

Ava continued walking in silence for a moment, choosing her words carefully. "My mother is not your typical royal. She has a very exuberant personality. My father used to call her a 'free spirit.' It was his job to keep her feet on the ground and on the right track."

"And what did your mother think about that?"

Ava thought about it for a minute. "I don't really know, but I imagine she was grateful. My parents balanced each other out perfectly. Now that my father is gone…" Ava's voice trailed off. It was still so hard to say those words out loud. She shook herself mentally, squared her shoulders, and lifted her chin higher. "Now that he's gone, it's my job to take over where my father left off."

"Helping to run your country," Justin said.

"Helping to manage my mother," Ava corrected him.

"If you ask me, the queen doesn't strike me as the kind of woman who would like to be *managed*—"

"Did I ask you?" Ava asked.

Their eyes met.

"No, you didn't," Justin said. "I'm sorry. What do I know? It's none of my business."

Ava felt a sudden rush of apprehension. She didn't know what had come over her. She never talked about her family like this and especially not with a stranger. She knew more than anyone how careful she had to be, because she couldn't afford for anything she was saying to end up online in the tabloids.

She anxiously twisted her watch around her wrist. "I shouldn't have said any of this about my family. My mother had you sign an NDA, correct? Because everything I've said is off-the-record and confidential—"

"Of course," Justin reassured her. "You don't have to worry about me saying anything to anyone."

Ava breathed a sigh of relief. "Good. Thank you. Because if any of this ends up in the press, you'll be hearing from our legal team—and trust me, you don't want that to happen."

Justin blinked several times, surprised. "Wow, that was an easy jump for you."

"What *jump*?" Ava asked.

"From us talking about our families to you threatening me with legal action."

"I wasn't threatening you," Ava said.

Justin's worried expression softened a little.

"I was promising you," Ava said. "I'll do whatever it takes to protect my family."

Justin held up both hands like he was surrendering. "And the shots just keep coming. Don't shoot. I'm innocent."

Ava frowned. "You think this is funny?"

"No, it's not funny," Justin answered. "It's sad that you think you can't trust anyone."

Before she could answer, Justin walked ahead of her.

"Stormy! Stormy! Where are you?" he called out. He turned back to her. "Are you coming?"

"Where are we going?" Ava asked.

"You tell me," Justin said. "You know Stormy loves people. He'll go where they are. Any ideas?"

Ava suddenly smiled as an idea hit her. "Yes! I know where he might be!"

## Chapter 12

The entrance to the royal Christmas tree farm glittered with thousands of twinkling lights.

Justin looked around, impressed. "You're right, this is exactly the kind of place Stormy would love. Look at all the people."

"This is where everyone loves to come this time of year," Ava said with a proud smile as they strolled by a hand-carved wooden sign that said *Skydovia Christmas Tree Farm.*

The farm was buzzing with holiday cheer. You could hear Christmas carolers singing in the distance. Excited children tugged their parents toward a jolly old-world Santa who was wearing a long, fur-trimmed crimson cloak with black boots. His snow-white beard looked as real as the twinkle in his eyes. He was waving to everyone, belting out a heartfelt "Merry Christmas!"

"Merry Christmas!" Justin happily answered back, waving to Santa.

Ava grabbed Justin's arm. "Can you please not attract attention."

"I was just saying hello."

"Why are you obsessed with Santa?" Ava asked.

"Why aren't you? It's *Santa,*" Justin shot back. "Is there some royal rule against him?"

Ava, stoic, stared straight ahead. "When I was eight, my father told me Santa wasn't real and that it was time for me to grow up. He was right. Now, can we please focus on finding the dog?"

Ava looked around. She nervously flipped up the hood on her red cape and put on a giant pair of sunglasses, trying to go incognito.

Justin did a double take. "Are you afraid someone will recognize you?"

"Yes," Ava said emphatically. "No one can know I'm here."

"Okay, whatever you say," Justin said. "But—"

"But what?" Ava asked.

"It just that cape and your sunglasses—don't you think it's a little…dramatic? I don't see anyone else here wearing a cape and—"

Ava stopped him with a frosty look.

Justin shrugged. "Okay, forget I said anything.

"Already forgotten," Ava said as she took in her surroundings.

The scent of fresh-cut pine filled the air as eager villagers wandered past beautiful, lit-up Christmas trees. Their laughter mingled with the sound of jingling bells from passing horse-drawn sleighs. It all brought back a rush of memories for Ava.

"Things haven't changed much since I was here last," she said softly.

"Do you come here very often?" Justin asked.

"I did, when I was little," Ava said, smiling as she remembered. "My parents would bring me here every Christmas to pick out our family Christmas tree that we'd get to decorate…"

"So, you didn't use your fancy decorators I saw hanging from the ceiling earlier?"

"No, we did everything ourselves," Ava said proudly. "My father was the expert in putting up the Christmas tree lights. He used to put me on his shoulders so I could decorate the top of the tree…"

"What about your mom?"

"She was always in charge of getting out all our favorite ornaments. She would lay them out on the table so we could decide where each one should go on the tree. Most of them were things I'd made, or my parents had made with me. They weren't anything special or valuable."

"But they were special to you," Justin said.

Their eyes met. "Yes, they were."

"That sounds like a very cool tradition," Justin added.

Ava's smile faded. "It was until the paparazzi started stalking us."

"What do you mean?" Justin asked.

"I mean, they would come here and follow us around everywhere we went and take pictures and videos of everything we did. Then they'd blast them all over the media with made-up, scandalous stories that weren't true."

"That sounds horrible. Couldn't you stop them?" Justin asked. "I mean, you're the royal family, and this is your Christmas tree farm—"

"But it's open to the public," Ava said. "Because we wanted everyone in the village to have access to enjoy it. This is for them—"

"So, that gives the paparazzi access, too."

Ava nodded sadly. "Yes. We used to have an agreement with the media of what they could cover and when they would let us have our privacy, but times changed, and everything became fair game. When we became like hunted animals, that's when we had to stop coming.

My father wanted to protect me, so I stopped doing a lot of things in public."

"I'm sorry. That really sucks," Justin said as he gave her a sympathetic look.

"It's even worse now," Ava said. "Since the photographers don't get many photos of me, any pictures or videos they do get bring top dollar, making the paparazzi even more aggressive."

Ava shuddered just thinking about it. She adjusted her red knit scarf to cover even more of her face.

"Don't you have your own royal photographers who can take pictures you can approve and put those out there so the demand is not so high?" Justin asked.

"We do, but I've been burned so many times that I don't trust anyone anymore," Ava said.

Justin glanced around the crowd and back at Ava. "And shouldn't you have a bodyguard or a security team or something for your protection?"

"Yes," Ava said. "I have several teams."

"So where are they?" Justin asked. "I don't see anyone around."

"Because I don't have anyone here," Ava said. "No matter how hard they try and blend in, the paparazzi are trained to spot them. I couldn't risk them blowing my cover and the media finding out that Mother has a new dog and that I've lost it—"

"*We've* lost Stormy," Justin interrupted. "You're not in this alone, remember? I got you."

Ava felt a mixture of gratitude and trepidation as her heart fluttered. While she had to admit it was comforting to know Justin was going to help her, his presence made her feel… nervous. There was something about the way he looked at her and their banter that sparked something deep inside her that she'd never felt before. While she rarely trusted anyone, she knew right now Justin was her best bet, her only bet, when it came to finding Stormy before her mother found out he was missing.

"Okay, where do you want to start?" Justin asked, looking around. "This place is huge."

"Two hundred acres," Ava said. "But most of the people will be right around here to look for their trees."

Justin pointed to a path leading to a field of Christmas trees that had a lot of people on it. "Looks like the Norway spruce is a popular pick."

"Always," Ava said. "The needles stay green for a long time."

"That's a good thing—"

"But," she continued, "Norway spruce also tend to drop their needles, so it depends on how long you need it to last. For people getting trees right before Christmas, it's a great choice."

"But if you get it too early, you could end up with a skinny, naked tree," Justin said.

Ava bit back a laugh. "I never thought about it that way, but yes, I guess you're right. It could get pretty…skinny."

"And we can't have a naked Christmas tree for a royal family. That would be very scandalous," Justin said, grinning back at her.

Ava rolled her eyes. "Do you always make jokes about everything?"

Justin looked surprised by her question. "Yes. Life is too short to take anything too seriously."

"That sounds like something my mother would say."

"And that's why I've always liked your mother," Justin said. He walked over to one of the trees and inhaled the fresh pine scent. "It smells just like—"

"Christmas," Ava finished for him.

"Exactly," Justin said with a smile.

"That's why we always get real Christmas trees," Ava said. "It's one thing my mother always insisted on, even though my father thought it would be more practical to get artificial trees that would be perfect."

Justin shook his head. "I'm with your mom. Perfect is no fun. What's your favorite kind of Christmas tree?"

"Of course, as a royal family, we can't have any official favorites. We have to be very careful about things like that."

"Okay, so *unofficially*, what's your favorite?" Justin asked with a twinkle in his eyes. "If you tell me yours, I'll tell you mine."

Ava laughed a little. She found his enthusiasm infectious and his charm impossible to deny. At first, she'd been taken aback and insulted when he didn't treat her like a princess. That had never happened to her before. She found it both disarming and fascinating when he treated her like a regular, normal person.

"So?" Justin asked, waiting for her answer.

She gave in. "A lot of royals choose the Nordmann Fir. They're very popular, especially here in Eastern Europe. They're considered a luxury Christmas tree."

"I don't know if I've ever seen one," Justin said.

"I can show you one here," Ava offered. "They have a symmetrical shape with these soft, dark green, glossy needles that don't shed."

"So, they don't get naked?"

Ava blushed. "No, they don't."

"So, is that your favorite?" Justin asked.

Ava shook her head. "No. My favorite is…the Douglas fir, but you can't tell anyone."

Justin crisscrossed his heart with his hand. "Cross my heart."

Ava gave him a confused look.

"Sorry." Justin laughed. "It's an American thing. When we promise something, we say, 'Cross my heart and hope to die, stick a needle in my eye.'"

Ava cringed. "Well, that sounds very unpleasant."

Justin laughed heartily. "And that's why we don't lie. Why do you like the Douglas fir the best?"

Ava smiled, thinking about it. "Because I love how fragrant, fluffy, and full they are. The needles are really soft, so they don't prick your fingers when you're hanging ornaments. They also won't drop too many needles if you take care of them properly."

"Like, of course, you do."

"Of course," Ava said.

"The Douglas fir is my favorite, too."

"Really? No. You're just saying that," Ava said.

"No, seriously, we've always had a Douglas fir. I don't really know any other Christmas trees. They're really popular in the States. I think it's what most people buy. There are these other trees that only have a few branches that a lot of designers use, but I think they always look—"

"Naked," Ava finished for him.

Justin's eyes lit up. "Exactly. See, 'naked' is a great way to describe Christmas trees—"

"The ones we don't want."

Justin nodded. "Because who wants a tree you can barely put any ornaments on?"

"Agreed," Ava said.

They shared a laugh.

"Wait, did we just agree on something?" Justin asked, surprised.

Their eyes met.

"I think maybe we did," Ava said.

Justin grinned back at her. "Then there's hope for us yet."

Ava looked away so Justin couldn't see she was smiling, too. She kept her eyes on the ground looking for Stormy. *Just focus on finding the dog,* she told to herself. When she picked up her pace, Justin kept up.

"You know, I thought Douglas firs were mostly grown in North America," Justin said. "I didn't know they grew in this part of the world."

"Traditionally, they don't," Ava said. "But my father always loved them, so we imported some young trees and had them grown here at the farm. The Christmas tree we're using this year for our party in the Grand Hall is a Douglas fir. It's a very special tree. It's a tree my father planted and watched grow all these years. He always said he was waiting for the perfect Christmas to feature it. I wish we had used it last year before he…" Ava couldn't finish the sentence.

"I think it's the perfect way to remember him this year," Justin said.

Ava nodded. That was exactly what she was hoping to do. She twisted her watch around on her wrist.

"Nice watch," Justin said.

"Thank you," Ava replied as she held up her wrist. "It was my father's. He wore it every day to remind him of what truly matters most." She carefully took off the watch, turned it over, and showed Justin so he could read the inscription on it.

*Time for Duty.*

Justin read the inscription out loud. "'Time for duty.'" His eyebrows rose. "That's what he thought was most important?"

Ava smiled and nodded. "Yes. Duty before everything else. He taught me so much. He was the one person who understood me."

"What about your mom?"

Ava blinked, surprised. "My mother? We couldn't be more different if we tried. I'm more behind the scenes. She's always the life of the party. My father always handled her…now I have to…"

She cringed, cutting herself off. "I shouldn't have said that."

"The whole 'never complain, never explain?' thing?" Justin asked.

"Wrong royal family, but right idea," Ava said.

Justin nodded. "I guess it doesn't matter if you're royal or not, parents are—"

"Complicated," Ava finished for him.

They shared a look of mutual understanding.

Ava walked over to one of the Christmas trees and checked its water container.

"What are you doing?" Justin asked as he joined her.

"Checking my Tree Tender."

Justin laughed. "Your what?"

"It's something I invented to make sure Christmas trees always have enough water that doesn't freeze."

"Really? You made this?" Justin asked, impressed. "Have you invented anything else?"

"A lot of things," Ava answered. "It's just a hobby. It's not a big deal," she said, echoing the words Henry had said to her earlier.

Justin held up his hand to high-five. "It's a huge deal. You're an inventor. That's really cool."

Ava hesitated, then gave him a quick high-five.

She had to admit she was both surprised and pleased by Justin's reaction to her being an inventor. It was certainly different from what she was used to getting from her doubting duke. That's what she secretly called Henry when he gave her a hard time about her inventions. He'd never been impressed with anything she invented.

She gave Justin a nervous look. "But no one knows, so…"

"Your secret is safe as long as you invent something for me," Justin said with a grin.

"What do you need?" Ava asked.

Justin thought about it. "To clone myself so I can help more people and their pets."

Justin moved a branch out of Ava's way as they stood up. "And since you're the genius, you also need to invent something to track down our runaway royal."

"If I could, I would," Ava said. "Because my mother will never forgive me if we don't find him. That dog is all she cares about."

# Chapter 13

Paris in the winter was magical.

At the Christmas market lining the Champs-Élysées, snow glittered on the rooftops of charming wooden stalls filled with handcrafted holiday gifts and festive treats like delicious pastries, spiced cider, and mulled wine.

Across from the Christmas market, in the window of a chic Parisian designer boutique, a glittering gold couture gown was displayed next to a lavish gold-themed Christmas tree. Underneath the tree were dozens of beautiful gold-wrapped presents, tied with crimson bows, promising even more treasures.

Inside, the boutique was just as opulent with floor-to-ceiling mirrors reflecting dozens of stunning, elegant gowns.

Sipping a glass of champagne, the queen sat back on a plush white velvet couch, studying three models as they paraded before her.

Each model wore a different dazzling red cocktail dress.

Celine, the designer, refilled the queen's glass. "Your Majesty, what do you think of the dresses? I followed the design ideas we talked about. I can make any changes you want or need."

"These are all amazing," the queen said with a bright smile. "As always, Celine, you did a phenomenal job. These are even more spectacular than I imagined."

Celine smiled back at the queen. "Thank you. I'm so glad you're pleased. It has been my honor to create original gowns for you and the princess for your special occasions. Which dress do you think she'll like best for your Christmas party?"

Celine motioned for the models to do another spin in front of the queen.

"First of all, to the models, you are all perfection," the queen said as she tipped her champagne glass to them.

The models beamed. Their smiles lit up the room. As they continued to twirl slowly, showing off the dresses, it was clear they were in awe of the queen.

As the queen sat back and studied the girls, she thought it was very smart of Celine to use models who looked similar to Ava. This way, she could truly imagine how the dresses would look on her. One model had her hair down and the two others were wearing their hair up, so you could see what options would be best for each dress.

"This is a very hard choice," the queen said.

"Is there one dress that stands out more than the others? One that catches your attention?" Celine asked.

The queen took another sip of champagne as she thought about it. "Our Christmas party is the event of the season. I know Ava wants everything to be perfect, including herself. This is why I came to you. You always do such spectacular work. But when it comes to Ava…honestly, I never know what she'll like the best."

Celine nodded.

The queen's smile grew. "So, I'll take all three. Ava can decide."

"Brilliant. I think that's a wonderful idea," Celine said. She motioned for the models to leave the room.

As soon as the models were gone and they were alone, the queen stood up and gave Celine a heartfelt hug. All the formalities were gone.

"Thank you for doing this, my dear friend. I've missed you," the queen said.

Celine hugged her back. "I've missed you, too. How are you holding up?"

The queen took a deep breath and forced a smile that didn't quite reach her eyes. "I'm...okay. Losing Fredrick has been devastating, especially seeing what it has done to Ava. I'm worried about her and her future."

"Is she still planning to marry Duke Henry?" Celine asked.

The queen rolled her eyes and finished her champagne. "Yes. Unfortunately. Since her father arranged it years ago, she feels it's her duty."

Celine gave the queen a knowing look. "An arranged marriage—something you understand well."

The queen set down her glass. "Too well, and that's why I want more for Ava. I don't want history to repeat itself...again."

"Have you ever talked to her about your marriage, what it was really like?" Celine asked.

The queen shook her head. "No. She loved her father so much. He was everything to her. How could I tell her I never really loved him, at least not in a romantic way? When we were first married, I hoped we would grow to love each other. But as you know, our marriage was never more than a business merger. Before I was with Fredrick there was someone I cared deeply about, but he wasn't an aristocrat, so my family didn't approve. Then, when my father died suddenly and I was only twenty, and had to take over the monarchy, I was matched with Fredrick. He was a lot older and came from a distinguished noble family. He was well-versed in the traditions and expectations of royal life. He understood the weight of duty and the responsibility that came with the crown a lot more than I did at the time."

The queen paused…remembering.

"I was still shell-shocked from losing my father. I felt like I didn't have a choice. I had to marry Fredrick because I was terrified of ruling our country alone."

Celine nodded.

"After Ava was born, Fredrick basically took over raising her," the queen continued. "He molded Ava into everything he wished I could be but never was. She became a mini version of him. Stoic, driven, dedicated, and above all else, duty bound."

"All honorable traits," Celine said.

"Yes, Fredrick was a very honorable man," the queen agreed. "But there should be more to life than just following a checklist of rules, even a royal life."

"So, tell her that," Celine said.

The queen put down her champagne and wrapped her arms around herself, like she was giving herself a much-needed hug. "But Ava doesn't have to marry a man she doesn't love. She has choices. She can marry whoever she wants. I want her to have everything I didn't have."

"So, what are you going to do?" Celine asked. "I'm sure you have a plan."

"Oh, I do," the queen said, her eyes sparkling with determination. "But it's risky…"

❄ ❄ ❄

As a sleek black Rolls-Royce navigated its way through Paris traffic, the queen sat in the backseat, talking to Edgar on FaceTime.

"Edgar, I've tried calling Ava several times. She's not answering. Is everything okay?"

"Yes, everything is just fine," Edgar said with a tight smile.

The queen's eyes narrowed as she looked at Edgar closer. "Edgar? I know you. What's going on? What aren't you telling me?"

Edgar cleared his throat. "The princess has been working very hard on the Christmas party—"

"And you're worried about her," the queen finished for him. She knew how protective Edgar was of her daughter, and she was thankful for it.

Edgar sighed. "Yes, I am."

"Do I need to come back and help?" the queen asked.

"No!" Edgar blurted out, then instantly backpedaled. "You know Ava—she wants to prove she can do this on her own."

The queen sighed. "Yes, I know. But tell me the truth, do *you* think she can do it?"

Edgar nodded. "Yes, I think she can."

"Okay, then please have her call me."

Edgar looked relieved. "I will."

"And how is Stormy?" the queen asked.

Edgar gulped.

"I miss him already. He's gone with Justin, the trainer, right?"

Edgar hesitated. "Stormy is definitely...*gone.*"

The queen sat back, pleased. "Wonderful! Thank you, Edgar. I always know I can count on you. I'll talk with you soon."

Edgar nodded.

After she hung up, she happily scrolled through dozens of photos of Stormy on her phone. He was already bringing her more joy than she had ever imagined.

Her whole life, she had dreamed of having a dog, and now, finally, that dream was coming true. As a child, her nanny had a border collie named Bandit. She was allowed to play with him a few times and fell in love. She'd never forgotten him. She had begged her parents for her own dog—any dog—but despite countless promises, it had never happened. They would always tell her, "*It's not the right time.*"

She hated that phrase.

When she married Fredrick, she'd thought she'd finally be able to get the dog she'd always wanted. But after he'd suddenly developed an allergy to dogs, that had never happened. Fredrick had declared no dogs, ever.

After giving up hope of ever having her own dog, she'd focused her energy instead on setting up royal charities to support animal shelters and pet adoptions. While it was one of the causes she was most passionate about, she never dreamed that someday it would lead her to finding Stormy.

She smiled, remembering the first time she had seen the rambunctious pup during a fundraising event at a shelter. He had been playing outside and when he'd spotted her, he'd raced toward her, barking like crazy, as if to say, "Take me home!"

The horrified shelter staff had chased after him, but not before he'd jumped up on her, his muddy paws ruining her white designer dress.

But instead of being upset, she'd been instantly charmed. When she had knelt down to get a better look at him, he'd wagged his tail and licked her face, delighting her even more. But it had been when she had looked into his soulful brown eyes that she'd known without a doubt that he was meant to be hers and Ava's.

When she'd found out his original owners had been forced to give him up after being transferred overseas, she had been thankful she could step in and offer him a stable home.

She had been warned about his discipline issues, but that hadn't deterred her. After meeting Justin and hearing so many people sing the praises of his Puppy Bootcamps, she'd known he could also work his magic on Stormy and help make him the perfect addition to the royal family.

As she zoomed in to get a closer look at an adorable selfie she'd taken with Stormy, she couldn't understand what Ava's problem was. *Who couldn't love this face?* she thought.

Granted, she knew they hadn't had the best first meeting with Stormy wrecking all the Christmas decorations, but she needed to find a way to get Ava to give him a second chance. She was confident that once Ava had some quality time to spend with Stormy, she'd fall in love with him, too.

At least that's what she hoped would happen.

The queen sighed, because while she was certain Stormy would be good for the both of them, these days she felt like anything she tried to do for her daughter was wrong. She hated that the distance between them, now that Fredrick was gone, was even greater than before. She felt like any connection she'd had with her daughter had been lost years ago. It broke her heart, because there was nothing more important to her than her daughter.

And yet, she knew Ava didn't feel the same. She had known this for a very long time.

In the early years, they had been the picture-perfect family—creating traditions, making memories. But once the paparazzi had invaded their lives, Fredrick had insisted Ava be kept out of the public eye. At first, the queen had agreed. She would do anything to protect her daughter.

She hadn't realized it would last into Ava's adulthood.

Over time, Ava and her father had become a team, bonded in ways that never included her. Fredrick had always reminded her that she was the queen. She had a different role to play, a country to rule, a legacy to uphold.

But all she had ever wanted was to spend time with her family.

Now that she had a second chance with Ava, she wasn't going to let it slip away. As for Ava marrying the duke, she knew she had to tread carefully. She blamed herself for putting her daughter in this position. She should have never agreed to the arranged marriage. But at the time, it hadn't been a promise. It had been just something to consider for the future, despite what Ava believed.

She'd always wanted the choice to be Ava's. If she and Henry had a spark, if they fell in love, wonderful. But she never agreed to anything that would trap her daughter into a loveless marriage.

She had fought with Fredrick about it, time and time again, but it was one of the few things she hadn't backed down on. Little did she know that he would have such control over their daughter that Ava would do whatever it took to honor his wishes, like she was doing now.

The queen cringed thinking how Fredrick had believed marriage was a merger, a partnership, and something that should benefit the royal family. He had thought love was unpredictable, uncontrollable, and messy—something that could distract someone's focus from what really mattered most.

He had been adamant about how duty and responsibility should reign supreme, and that nothing in their family should matter more than upholding tradition, preserving their legacy, and fulfilling their royal roles with unwavering devotion, even at the cost of personal desires.

Now that Ava was following in her father's footsteps, the queen knew she had her work cut out for her, and time was running out. She knew how committed Ava was to making this marriage happen.

She took a deep breath and willed herself to stay calm. "How long until we're there?" she eagerly asked her driver.

"About fifteen minutes, Your Majesty."

"Perfect," she said as she sat back in her seat, smiling.

❄ ❄ ❄

When it came to jewelry, the queen had flawless taste, and that's why Vallmount Luxe, one of the most sought-after jewelry boutiques in Paris, was her choice to commission something very special for Ava.

Coco Vallmount, the designer and owner of Vallmount Luxe, was a force to be reckoned with. Smart, fresh, fun, and creative, she'd infused new energy into her decades-old family business, earning the queen's attention and respect.

From the first piece the queen had commissioned Coco to make for the royal collection, a modern take on a tennis bracelet using star-shaped diamonds, the designer had gone above and beyond to impress.

Now, as the queen settled into one of the jeweler's elegant private rooms, she knew she'd made the right decision to trust Coco with creating this one-of-a-kind Christmas gift for Ava.

Coco entered the room like a model strutting down the runway. Her confidence made her even more beautiful, but it was the platinum jewelry box she was holding that captured the queen's attention.

"Your Majesty, you are looking as radiant as ever," Coco said.

The queen smiled brightly. "I was just going to say the same about you. You look stunning, as always. Thank you for making time to see me during this very busy time of the year and helping me surprise my daughter."

"It is always an honor to work with someone who has such exquisite taste," Coco said as she sat down next to the queen. She held out the jewelry box like it was the most precious thing in the world. "Are you ready to see it in person?"

The queen's heart raced. "I am. The pictures you've sent have been stunning."

"But they are nothing compared to what you are about to see," Coco promised.

The queen held her breath as Coco slowly opened the jewelry box, revealing a jaw-dropping platinum watch surrounded by flawless diamond and blue sapphires.

The queen inhaled sharply, touching her heart. It was one of the most beautiful things she had ever seen. She could already envision Ava wearing it.

When Coco carefully took the watch out of its case and presented it to the queen, the gemstones caught the light and dazzled even more.

The queen was in awe. "It's…perfection."

"Just like your daughter," Coco said. "We are calling it Étoile Brillante—"

"Bright star," the queen said, nodding her approval. "I love that, because Ava will always be my bright, shining star."

Coco smiled. "And you can see how we incorporated the diamonds and sapphires from your royal collection, as you requested."

The queen gently ran her fingers over the delicate crafts-manship. It was exactly what she had asked for—the perfect balance of tradition and modern refinement. "You have done a wonderful job. Thank you so much."

"I'm so pleased that you're happy," Coco said, smiling back at the queen. "I must say, this is one of the most beautiful custom pieces I've ever created, and it's an honor to know the princess will be wearing it."

"My daughter loves to live by her schedules. She must look at her watch a hundred times a day. Now, every time she looks at this, she'll be reminded of what's really the most important thing in life." The queen handed Coco an envelope embossed with the royal crest. "This is what I'd like the engraving to say."

"Of course, Your Majesty," Coco said. "We will take care of this for you right away."

"Wonderful. And please thank your entire team for making this possible in time for Christmas. I know Ava is going to be so surprised and will love it so much."

# Chapter 14

As Ava walked through a trail of sparkling Christmas trees with Justin, all she could think about was how much time they'd wasted searching for Stormy. She knew they must have walked at least three miles, and still there was no sign of him.

When she glanced over at Justin, she saw he was equally frustrated.

"It doesn't look like he's here," Ava said, disappointed.

"At least not where we've looked," Justin agreed. "I really thought he wouldn't be able to resist a Christmas tree farm with all these people." He pointed at a sign that said *Cocoa Hut*. "Do you want to go get something to drink and warm up?"

Ava looked around nervously and shook her head. "No, I can't. Someone might recognize me."

Justin's eyes widened. "With your hood on and those sunglasses, no one can even see you, much less recognize you."

"No, thanks," she said. She wasn't going to take any chances.

A call from Edgar on FaceTime popped up on her phone. Ava hesitated before answering it. She sucked in a deep breath and plastered on a smile. "Hello, Edgar."

"Have you found Stormy yet?" Edgar asked.

Ava forced herself to keep smiling. "Not yet, but...we think we know where he is."

When Justin gave her a surprised look, she quickly turned away from him.

"Really?" Edgar asked eagerly.

Ava nodded. She hated herself for lying…again.

"Well, I just talked to your mother," Edgar said.

"Oh no. You didn't say anything, did you?" Ava asked in a panic.

"Not yet, but I can't keep this from her much longer. She has a right to know."

"Of course. I agree," Ava said. "Just give me a little more time, please."

"You need to call her," Edgar said.

"Who?"

"Your mother."

Ava looked surprised. "Why?"

"Because she said you're not answering her calls. You don't want her getting suspicious, do you?"

"No! Of course not," Ava said.

"So, call her."

Ava nodded. "Yes, I will. I'm just trying to find Stormy first."

"Then you better hurry," Edgar said. "If I don't hear from you soon, I'm calling her."

"I understand," Ava said. "Thank you for giving me a chance to find him first. I'll call you soon." She hung up, feeling more depressed than ever.

"What's wrong?" Justin asked. "Who was that?"

"Edgar. He called to warn me my mother wants to talk to me. She's called me a couple of times, but I haven't answered," Ava said.

"Why not?"

"Because she can read me like a book, and I'm a terrible liar. He also told me he can't put off telling her much longer."

Justin shook his head, looking upset. "He can't tell her."

"Try stopping him," Ava said. "He's nothing if not loyal. I don't blame him. I know I've put him in an impossible position, and I hate that."

"But you'd hate having your mom find out you lost her dog more," Justin said.

"Exactly," Ava agreed. "I'm going to text Lydia to see if she's had any luck with the flyers."

"Good idea. Hopefully she's gotten some leads, because so far, we're striking out here," Justin said. "But let's check out the food stalls again. They're usually dog magnets."

As they walked off together, Ava started texting Lydia. But before she could send her text, a little boy came racing around the corner, straight for her...

"Princess! Watch out!" Justin hollered as he pulled her out of the child's way just in time, preventing the collision.

In all the commotion, Ava's hood fell down, and her sunglasses slipped off.

The little boy's mouth dropped open and his eyes grew huge as he stared at Ava like he couldn't believe what he was seeing.

"Princess?" the little boy asked under his breath.

Ava scrambled to put her hood and sunglasses back on.

The excited child started yelling at the top of his lungs. "The princess is here! The princess is here!"

Ava tensed as people around them started to hurry over and get their phones ready to take pictures and videos.

"Oh my God, no," Ava said as she frantically looked around for a way to escape. Her panic grew when an older woman, who looked like she was in her eighties, took the first picture of her. Ava froze like a trapped animal, then sprang into action, rushing past Justin. "We have to go now!" she said as she passed him. She wanted to run, but she knew that would draw even more attention to herself. She needed to stay calm, cool, and collected, and get the hell out of there fast!

As she hurried off, she heard people firing questions at Justin.

"Was that the princess?!"

"That was her, wasn't it?!"

Then she heard Justin laugh.

"What? No! Are you kidding?" he asked. "Me with the princess, that would be the day."

Ava frowned. Even in her panic, it annoyed her to hear Justin say that.

❄ ❄ ❄

When Ava burst into the greenhouse and shut the door behind her, she looked out the window to make sure no one had followed her.

The coast was clear.

Once she was sure no one was coming after her, she was able to catch her breath and look around the greenhouse. It was filled with gorgeous red and white poinsettias. On the wooden counters, there were baskets filled with sprigs of holly and mistletoe tied with red ribbons.

Under different circumstances, she might have appreciated how festive it looked, but right now, all she cared about was making sure no one had any pictures of her.

She quickly texted Edgar the details of what happened and what the woman looked like who had taken her picture and told him it was a code red.

He called her immediately without FaceTime.

"Edgar, hi, I'm sorry," she said as soon as she picked up his call. "But I think it was only one person that got anything."

"Our security team is on it," Edgar said.

"Oh no!" she whispered into the phone when the door of the greenhouse swung open. "Someone's coming in," she said as she ran and hid under a table.

"Are you okay?" Edgar asked, worried. "Where are you? I can send in security right now!"

"I'm at the gree—" Ava stopped talking when she saw Justin. "Never mind, Edgar, it's only Justin." She stood back up. "Please let me know when you find that paparazzo who took my picture and be sure any pictures she has of me are destroyed. I'll be home soon."

Frazzled, Ava hung up and was met with Justin's surprised look.

"Who were you talking about on the phone?" Justin asked. "I didn't see any paparazzi."

Ava gave him a shocked look. "You didn't see that woman taking pictures of us?"

Justin laughed. "That grandmother?"

"The paparazzi have all kinds of disguises," Ava said, dead serious. "And how could you yell out 'princess'? What were you thinking? That's like waving a red flag to have everyone look at me—"

"I know, and I'm sorry," Justin said. "That little boy was about to run into you, and I was just trying to protect you both and—"

"It doesn't matter," Ava said. "The damage is done. Can you please just take me home?"

"What about finding Stormy?"

"Don't you understand? My cover's blown here," Ava said in a high, thin voice. She sounded more scared than upset. "I can't be here. You're going to have to find him."

"That's not what we agreed to," Justin said, disappointed.

A text alert from her phone saved Ava from having to respond.

When she read the text, her eyes it up. "It's Lydia. They found Stormy!"

"Yes!" Justin, excited, pumped his fist into the air. "Where is he? Is he okay?"

"Yes," Ava said, as relief flooded through her. "He's been running around our Christmas market. See? Lydia sent a picture."

Ava showed Justin a picture of Stormy sitting next to a candy cane booth.

"That's him!" Justin shouted, excited. "Let's go!"

# Chapter 15

Ava was grateful that, true to his word, Justin got her out of the Christmas tree farm without anyone recognizing her.

Still, her anxiety grew as they pulled up to the Christmas market to get Stormy. She adjusted her so-called "disguise" in the mirror. She made sure all her hair was tucked into her hood, and that her scarf covered most of her face. She put on her sunglasses but could still feel her heart pounding with fear.

She twisted her watch around her wrist.

Justin watched her. "You okay?"

She nodded but didn't trust herself to say anything because she'd started shaking. She hated that she was reacting like this. Having people recognize her had triggered a lot of pent-up anxiety she'd never dealt with over the years.

"Then let's go get him," Justin said as he swung his door open, got out of the SUV, came over, and opened her door for her.

Ava hesitated. The only place in Skydovia that had more people than the Christmas tree farm was the village's annual Christmas market. She stared at the ground as she wrung her hands together.

Justin studied her. "You're not okay, are you? Look, you stay here, and I'll go."

Ava's eyes flew up to meet his gaze. "Really? Thank you. I'll let Lydia know you're on the way."

"No problem. You just relax. Lie low, and I'll be right back," Justin said and shut her door.

"Thank God," Ava whispered to herself as she watched him walk away. She glanced around the parking lot. It was full. She sunk down lower in her seat, trying not to think about the close call she'd just had at the Christmas tree farm.

She got out her phone. She really wanted to talk to Henry. He was always so in control that no matter what was happening in her life, she felt she could count on him to be calm, the voice of reason, just like her father had always been.

She sent Henry a quick text.

*Can we talk?*

Henry answered immediately.

*Not now. Call later.*

Disappointed, Ava stared at her phone. She couldn't help but compare Henry to Justin. Henry was her soon-to-be-official fiancé, but he never checked in on her. Where Justin was always asking if she was okay. She knew they were two completely different personality types. She felt a little better telling herself that if Henry knew she *really* needed him, he would be there for her.

She cringed thinking what his reaction would be if she told him about Stormy. She might have been imagining it because she was under so much stress, but lately, she felt like he was growing more impatient with her. She wasn't sure what she was doing wrong. She knew he was upset that they hadn't gotten the official green light yet for announcing their engagement at the party, so she could only imagine what he would say about her losing her mom's new dog.

"And that's why I'm not telling you," she said out loud to herself. Henry was someone who was all about solutions, not problems. While he had a lot of strong opinion, she couldn't even remember the last time they fought. If they ever disagreed with each other and things got too heated, he always seemed to know what to say to either divert the conversation or end it entirely.

She thought about how, over the years, she'd walked away from more than one conversation with him wondering what had just happened. She'd start with something specific she wanted to discuss, but somehow, the conversation always got derailed, and she never ended up addressing what she truly wanted to say.

Her reminiscing was interrupted when Justin suddenly flung open driver's side door of the SUV and jumped inside.

Ava's hand flew to her heart. "Oh my God. You scared me to death. I didn't see you come up—" She abruptly stopped talking when she saw the distressed look on his face. "What is it? What's wrong? Where's the dog?" Ava looked out the window for Stormy.

Justin shook his head, visibly upset. "He got away."

"What?!" Ava cried out. "No! How?"

"Lydia put him on a leash, but somehow he pulled out of his collar and ran off," Justin said as he held up Stormy's bejeweled Christmas collar.

Ava squeezed her eyes shut with frustration. "Because it was too big for him. I can't believe this is happening. Didn't they chase him down?"

"They tried to look for him," Justin said. "But he slipped away before anyone knew he was gone."

Ava groaned. "So he could be anywhere."

Justin nodded. "But the good news is everyone's still looking, and we know he's okay—"

"But we still don't have him!" Ava interrupted him. She dropped her head into her hands, distraught.

"Look, I'm going to take you home, and I'll come back and continue the search," Justin said. "We're going to find him. He was just here."

"He's probably running around the market destroying all the decorations," Ava said.

"And that means we'll catch him," Justin said, sounding optimistic. "The candy cane booth owners said they found Stormy chewing candy canes off the wreaths."

Ava rolled her eyes. "Of course he was."

Justin chuckled. "At least we know he's okay."

"But I'm not going to be when my mother finds out about this," Ava said. Nothing about this was funny to her. It was a nightmare. "She's going to think I lost him on purpose." She turned to stare out the window.

Justin shook his head. "What? No, she wouldn't think that..."

"Yes she will," Ava said, twisting her watch. "She knows I didn't want him. I told her she had to take him back to the shelter, that we couldn't keep him. Then, she has me watch him for a few hours while we're waiting for you to pick him up and I lose him? A coincidence? No. Trust me. She won't think so."

Ava continued to stare out the window feeling worse by the second. "Can you just please take me home?" she asked in a small voice.

"Okay," Justin said, as he started the SUV.

As they pulled out of the parking lot, Ava stole a glance at him. She frowned a little, realizing he was even more handsome in his profile, because it accentuated his chiseled jaw. She jumped when he turned and caught her staring at him.

As she blushed, she scrambled for something to say. "I'm sorry I can't help you search the Christmas market. If the paparazzi found out about any of this, God knows what kind of lies they'd make up this time—"

"It's okay. I got you," Justin said as he turned his attention back to the road.

Ava's phone rang. "What now?" she sighed. When she saw it was her mother, her blood went cold. She promptly declined the call and started taking deep breaths to try and calm herself.

"Who was it?" Justin asked. "Edgar? Lydia?"

"No, my mother."

"So, why didn't you answer it?" Justin asked.

"Because I'm not ready to talk to her," Ava said. "I need to prepare myself for exactly what I'm going to say to her."

"Are you going to tell her about Stormy?"

"Not unless Edgar makes me," Ava said. "Hopefully, he'll give us more time now that he knows we just had him and we're so close. You said we would find him. You still believe that, right?"

"Yes," Justin answered without hesitation.

"Then why worry her?" Ava said with conviction. "They'll probably track him down before you even get back there," Ava said, forcing herself to sound more confident than she felt.

"Right," Justin said.

But when Ava looked over at him, she saw his hands on the wheel tighten. *You're not fooling anyone*, she thought. *You're just as worried as I am.*

❄ ❄ ❄

The sun set as Justin walked Ava up to the front door of Vailgate Castle.

"You didn't have to walk me to the door," Ava said.

"What kind of gentleman would I be if I didn't?"

Ava arched one eyebrow. "Are you trying to say you're a *gentleman*?"

"Are you trying to say I'm not?" Justin shot back with a sexy smile.

Ava shivered all the way down to her toes. His smile was lethal. She doubted anyone could resist it, so she knew she shouldn't feel bad when her pulse quickened and a rush of excitement swept over her.

She pulled herself together. "I don't have time for your witty banter."

Justin's smile grew. "You think my banter is *witty*."

"I didn't say that."

"Uh, I think you did," Justin said, grinning back at her. "You must be feeling better if we're going at it again. You were so quiet on the drive back here that I was starting to get worried."

"Very funny," Ava said.

"I'm not kidding. I know today was rough on you."

Ava was surprised that he wasn't joking around anymore. He was being genuine. She held out her hand. "May I have your phone, please?"

Justin looked surprised but intrigued as he handed her his phone. "Sure, but what for?" He watched as she filled out a new contact form, putting in a phone number under the name Holly.

"Holly?" he asked confused.

"That's the code name my father gave me. Please only use that name for me going forward. Don't ever call me 'princess' again in front of anyone, anywhere."

Justin saluted her. "Yes, ma'am." When Ava frowned, he rushed on. "Sorry, I meant 'yes, princess.' No wait, I'm not supposed to call you the 'P' word. How about Your Royal—'"

"Stop, just call me Holly. That's it. No other names. Got it?" Ava asked.

Justin grinned back at her. "Got it. So, wait, no last name?"

"Seriously?! You're impossible."

"But I'm witty, so at least I have that going for me," Justin said, flashing another smile.

Ava gave him a look like she wasn't amused, but when she turned to open the door, the corner of her lips twitched with a smile that she couldn't help. "Call me on that number if you find out anything. I don't care how late it is. Please keep me updated. I'll keep looking around here in case he comes back." She stepped into the castle, then turned around and faced him. "Thank you for not giving up."

"On Stormy or you?" Justin asked.

"Both," Ava found herself saying before she could help herself.

Their eyes met.

"We're going to find him," Justin said.

She nodded. "We have to. Goodnight, Justin."

"Goodnight…Holly," Justin said with a wink before he headed back to his SUV.

When Ava shut the door, she leaned on it for a moment, inhaling a deep breath. Her mind and heart were colliding with emotions she wasn't used to having. The only way her practical mind could make sense of how she was feeling around Justin was to tell herself she was just exhausted, emotionally and physically, from all the stress of losing Stormy. She told herself that had to be why every one of her emotions right now seemed topsy-turvy, turned upside down and inside out.

She knew there was only one thing that would make her feel better.

Work.

She stood up straighter, squared her shoulders, and headed for the Grand Hall. As she picked up her pace, she started going through a checklist of all the things she still needed to do to get ready for the Christmas party.

She was worried about what she would find when she entered the Grand Hall. She'd left instructions on how she wanted all the decorations finished, but who knows what had happened without her supervision. She was pleasantly surprised when she walked into the room and saw it was now completely decorated for Christmas.

A canopy of white twinkle lights was strung across the ceiling, casting a magical glow over the entire room. Glittering gold garlands and wonderful sparkling wreaths added to the festive flair, while a collection of life-size vintage nutcrackers brought a touch of whimsy.

Ava smiled with relief when she saw the star of the show. Their massive Douglas fir Christmas tree now had perfectly placed lights. She could tell even from a distance that each row of lights was exactly five inches apart, just as she'd instructed, and just like her father had always done.

Ava turned when she heard someone enter.

"You're back," Edgar said as he entered the room.

"Without the dog," Ava said sadly.

"Yes, I know. Lydia informed me," Edgar said, looking disappointed.

Ava jumped in before Edgar could say anything more, because she saw the concerned look on his face and knew what was coming. "Edgar, I know you want to call my mother and tell her I lost her dog—"

"I wasn't going to say anyone *lost* him. I was going to say he ran away and is missing," Edgar said.

"Edgar, I appreciate you trying to protect me, but at the end of the day, he was my responsibility. He disappeared on my watch. This is my fault. I know my mother will see it the same way. You know things have always been…difficult for us. I feel like after this, she'll never forgive me."

"Your mother loves you very much."

Ava shook her head. She wished she could believe that. "What she loves right now is that dog." She took Edgar's hand and looked into his eyes. "Edgar, I promise you we're going to find him. We just had him an hour ago. We know he's okay and at the Christmas market. He couldn't have gone too far. Justin will find him. He's a dog trainer. He knows what to do. Remember, my mother said he's the best of the best, right?"

"Yes, but—"

"So, let's give him a little time to find him," Ava pleaded. "This way, I don't completely ruin my relationship with my mother, and we don't have to upset her."

"She would be very upset if she knew he was missing," Edgar agreed.

"Exactly," Ava said. "It's not like we don't know where he is. It's just a matter of Justin tracking him down and bringing him home. So, can we have a little more time? Please?"

Silence.

Ava held her breath as she watched Edgar consider the idea. What she knew of Edgar was that he was always reasonable and made smart decisions solely based on what he ultimately believed was best for the family.

When Ava saw a flicker of doubt in his eyes, she tried one last thing. "You know my father would always keep upsetting things from my mother so she could concentrate on being the queen while we would troubleshoot from behind the scenes. That's all I'm asking you to do now. What my father would do. If he were here, he would ask you to do the same thing, don't you think?"

Edgar took a deep breath then nodded his head slowly. "Yes, your father probably would be doing the same thing."

"So, you'll give us a little more time?" Ava asked, her voice filled with hope.

Edgar didn't look happy about it, but he nodded again. "Okay."

Overjoyed, Ava hugged him. "Thank you! Thank you so much!"

Edgar stood stiffly, surprised by the hug. "But—"

Ava stepped back quickly. Edgar's tone worried her. "But what?"

# Chapter 16

Edgar took a moment before he continued.

Ava nervously waited, shifting from one foot the other.

"I can give you tonight, but if we don't find Stormy by tomorrow morning, I'll have to tell your mother. It's her dog. She loves him so much already. She needs to know. I'm sorry…"

When Ava saw how miserable Edgar looked, she fought off the panic growing inside her so she could comfort him. "It's okay," she said, even though she was thinking this was anything but *okay*. "I understand."

And it was true. Even though she didn't like it, she did understand where Edgar was coming from. She knew Edgar had already left his comfort zone by not telling her mother immediately. She didn't want to put him in a compromising position any more than she already had. She knew she needed to be thankful for any extra time he would give her.

"You will let Justin know?" Edgar asked.

"Yes, I will text him right away," she answered.

Edgar's eyebrows raised. "You have his number? You gave him yours?"

Ava blushed. "Only so we could stay in touch during the search."

Edgar nodded thoughtfully. "I see."

Ava jumped in. "There is nothing to *see*. This is just so we can stay in touch about the dog. This is only about the dog. Nothing else. Just the dog." She was feeling more flustered by the second.

When she searched Edgar's expression to see what he was thinking, his expression gave nothing away.

"Thank you for giving me this extra time, Edgar. I won't let you down."

"There's only so much you can control," Edgar said.

Ava frowned. "I know, and that's what I'm the most worried about. I feel so helpless. I just don't understand how my mother could, on a whim, bring home some stray, wild dog, without even talking to me about it, without any warning, and right before Christmas when I'm trying to plan the biggest party we've ever had."

"I'm sure she had a very good reason," Edgar said.

Ava gave him a skeptical look. "Edgar, come on. You know my mother often acts impulsively without thinking things through. You also know that's why my father always had to step in and keep her from going completely off the rails. Now that's my job, and I feel like I'm already failing. If my father were here right now, what do you think he would do about this dog situation?"

"Your father would have never allowed a dog in the first place," Edgar answered with conviction.

"Exactly!" Ava said, feeling better that she wasn't the only one who thought her mother was way out of line. She rubbed one of her throbbing temples. The stress was getting to her. "I just need to think like my father and figure this all out."

"I'm sure you will," Edgar said.

To try and calm her frazzled nerves, she started walking around the Grand Hall, surveying all the decorations.

"While Justin finds the dog, I need to get back to concentrating on something I do have control over—our Christmas party. It looks like things in here have really come together.

"We tried to follow your instructions exactly down to every small detail."

Ava gave him a grateful smile. "And you all did an excellent job. Thank you so much for doing all this while I was gone."

"So, you approve?" Edgar asked, looking pleased.

"Yes," Ava said. "Overall, but—"

Edgar's smile faded.

"Of course, there are a few things that need to be... adjusted," Ava continued.

"Of course," Edgar agreed as he watched her walk over to one of the life-size nutcrackers and try to move it. It was bigger than she was and started to tip over.

Edgar rushed over to help her. "Please, don't hurt yourself. We can move anything you like."

"It's okay, I've got it," Ava said as she struggled to move the nutcracker a few feet to the right. "These guys are heavier than I thought."

"Please let us handle this. You don't want one crashing down on top of you," Edgar said.

Ava stepped away from the nutcracker. "You're right. We've already had enough decoration disasters to last a lifetime."

She reluctantly gave up on the nutcrackers and headed over to a dazzling display of Christmas wreaths that were each individually suspended from the ceiling by small silver cables. They were lined up perfectly about seven feet from the ground.

Ava got out her phone and tapped an app that had a wreath on it. All the wreaths suddenly lit up and started rotating 360 degrees, showing off every angle.

Ava smiled proudly. "This looks even better since I added more lights. You know what father always said—"

"You can never have too many Christmas lights," Edgar finished for her.

They shared a smile.

"Exactly."

"Your Wreath Rotator invention is still one of my favorites," Edgar said with admiration as he stepped closer to the wreaths, watching them slowly spin around. "How you come up with all these things I will never know."

"Almost all my inventions solve problems," Ava said with a bright smile. "Like, for example, these wreaths. I never understood why you'd have beautifully decorated wreaths that you only see one side of when you hang them on your door or the wall. So, I thought 'Wouldn't it make much more sense to have a way to display them where you can see *all* of the wreaths?' And that's how the Wreath Rotator was born. I designed this one specifically for in here, but I'm also working on one you can use with just a single wreath."

"Sign me up for one of those," Edgar said.

Ava smiled back at him. "You will be at the top of my list."

"It's very impressive."

"And practical," Ava said. "The best inventions usually are." She started walking down the line of wreaths. One by one, she meticulously adjusted each plush gold velvet bow so it was perfect. She stood back to survey her work.

"What do you think?" she asked.

"I think they all look exquisite," Edgar said. "The entire Grand Hall has never looked more festive. I know your father would be very proud of you."

When Ava turned back to Edgar, there were tears in her eyes. "That's the best compliment you could ever give me."

"It's true," Edgar said. "Believe it. What you've done here to help raise money for our local charities and honor your father's memory is very commendable. I know your mother will also approve."

Ava laughed. "That's only because my mother loves a party, no matter who plans it."

Edgar nodded with a discreet smile. "It has been wonderful to see how excited she has been to introduce Stormy at the party. I haven't seen her this happy in a very long time."

Ava's smile faded.

In that moment, she realized it wouldn't matter how spectacular a party she planned. If the dog was still missing, her mother would be crushed, and Christmas would be ruined.

She knew what she had to do. She headed for the door.

"Where are you going?" Edgar called out after her.

"To find the dog before tomorrow morning," Ava said with determination.

❄ ❄ ❄

Under the glistening moonlight, Ava stood in front of a spectacular fountain in one of the royal gardens as she called Justin. The garden was glistening with Christmas lights.

He picked up on the first ring.

"Did you find him?" Justin asked before even saying hello.

"That's what I was calling to ask you," Ava answered. "So, I'm guessing this means no."

"Nothing yet," Justin said. "Lydia and I have been looking everywhere. We even split up to cover more ground. She's been handing out flyers to everyone and telling them to call her if they see Stormy."

"And nobody has seen him? How is that possible?" Ava asked, frustrated. "He's a dog running around a Christmas market. Surely somebody must have seen something."

"We haven't been able to find anyone who has yet," Justin said, sounding tired. "But don't worry, I'm going to keep looking. I won't give up until we find him."

Ava started pacing. "Our time is running out. I just talked to Edgar. While I was able to buy us a little more time tonight, if we haven't found the dog by tomorrow morning, he's going to tell my mother. He says he can't wait any longer."

"Oh God."

"I know," Ava said as she glanced over at her horse, Midnight, who was tied up to a tree, waiting for her. "That's why I'm going to keep looking tonight, too."

"What? Where?"

"I've been riding around to all our different gardens to see if he might be there. We have more than a dozen of them on the property. They're all decorated for Christmas, so I thought maybe he'd go there. We know he loves to destroy Christmas decorations. I don't know, but I had to do something, and we didn't get to search the gardens earlier because you—"

"Freaked out about riding," Justin finished for her.

"Yes."

"But it's dark out," Justin said, sounding concerned. "Should you be riding alone at night?

"No," Ava replied. "That's why I'm taking six security guards."

"Six?" Justin asked, surprised. "Really?"

"No," Ava shot back. "That would be ridiculous. I'm only taking three."

Silence.

Ava looked at her phone. "Justin, are you still there?"

"Yes, I'm just in shock."

"About?"

"You, joking around. This is a first," Justin said, sounding impressed.

She frowned. "You make me sound so…boring."

Justin laughed. "Boring? No. That the last thing you are. Maybe a little serious…"

"Well, one of us has to be."

"Ouch," Justin said with a chuckle. "But seriously, maybe you should have someone riding with you to keep you safe."

"Are you offering to go riding with me?"

Justin laughed loudly. "Me? Oh, hell no! That wouldn't be keeping you safe at all. But call if you need me. I'll be up all night looking, too."

"I'll be fine," Ava said. "Call me if you find him or find out anything."

"I will. Be careful."

Ava looked up at the stars in the sky. "We have to find him, Justin."

"I know," Justin said. "We will. Your mother trusted me with Stormy. I'm not going to let her down."

"I wouldn't advise it," Ava said.

"Another joke—"

"No," Ava said, dead serious. "Trust me. You don't want to disappoint my mother."

# Chapter 17

After Justin hung up with Ava, he continued searching for Stormy at the Christmas market. Even though all the vendors had closed up for the night, he knew Stormy could still be around, because there was so much for a curious dog to explore.

When he first entered the Christmas market to pick up Stormy at the candy cane stall, he had been surprised and impressed by how large it was for such a small, quaint village. During the day, it had been filled with people and was a truly immersive holiday experience.

The market was set in the heart of the village where cobblestone streets sparkled under twinkling white Christmas lights. Wooden stalls lined the village square. They all had matching gold awnings trimmed with fresh evergreen garlands and wreaths. The air had been filled with the scent of roasted chestnuts, cinnamon-spiced cider, and fresh-baked gingerbread.

He'd loved how all the vendors greeted shoppers with warm smiles and how they couldn't wait to share their stories about the traditional items they were selling.

There were handmade ornaments, candles, knit scarves, mittens, hats, intricate lacework, and carved wooden toys. There were also stalls filled with all kinds of Christmas treats, from Skydovia's famous dark chocolate sea salt fudge and

Christmas butter balls to an assortment of fresh-baked Christmas cookies, cakes, and pies.

The candy cane stall where Stormy had been found earlier featured another Skydovia traditional favorite—dark chocolate–dipped candy canes—that he couldn't wait to try.

At the heart of the square stood a towering Christmas tree decorated with hundreds of twinkling white lights, yards of gold velvet ribbon, and sparkling red and gold glass ornaments.

This was where Justin had watched villagers gather all day, laughing and catching up with friends and family, while Charles Dickens–inspired carolers strolled through, singing classic Christmas songs.

He thought Skydovia's Christmas market was a scene straight out of a storybook, where old-world charm and royal traditions made everything feel even more magical.

But right now, Justin wasn't seeing any kind of *happily-ever-after* storybook ending in his future unless he could find Stormy before the sun came up.

For the fifth time, he walked over to a giant gingerbread house that was at the entrance to the market. It seemed like the kind of place Stormy would love.

"Stormy! Where are you, Stormy?" he called out.

He rubbed his hands together, wishing he'd worn some gloves. Once the sun set, the cool, crisp winter air had a real bite to it.

"Stormy. Come on. Help a guy out here. I'll give you anything you want. A steak. A candy cane. A Christmas wreath to destroy. Anything!"

Justin knew he was getting desperate if he was trying to bribe a dog with a candy cane. The stress was obviously getting to him.

As much as he'd given the princess a hard time for Stormy running off, his own sense of guilt was overpowering. He was the dog trainer. The dog expert. Something like this should never have happened, no matter what the princess said or did. The queen had hired him to take care of Stormy, to protect him, because that was what he did. He didn't lose people's beloved pets.

He shuddered just thinking about it.

Nothing like this had ever happened to him before. Things were only made more complicated by the fact that he was working with a royal family.

He had to find a way to make this right. He had to find Stormy. The only thing that gave him any peace of mind was that he was told Stormy had been fine earlier when they'd found him. He wasn't hurt or sick or anything like that. He was just being a royal renegade, probably thinking this was all a big game.

As he was circling the gingerbread house, lost in thought, he almost ran into a man coming from the other direction.

"Whoa, sorry!" Justin said. "I wasn't paying attention…" His voice trailed off when he recognized Ted, the guy he had helped earlier with the ice sculptures.

"Hey! You're the dog trainer!" Ted said merrily.

Justin laughed. "And you're the ice sculpture guy."

"What are you doing here?" they both asked at the same time.

Justin laughed again. "I thought I was the only one still left here tonight."

"No, I'm working on a new ice sculpture over at the park. An angel. She's a beauty," Ted said.

"That's really cool," Justin responded.

Ted pointed at him and smiled. "Was that an ice joke?"

"No," Justin said. "But if you like, we can go with that."

Ted laughed. "Oh, I've heard them all. What are you doing here? Did you lose one of the dogs you're training?"

Justin froze. "What?"

Ted patted him on the back as he grinned ear to ear. "Just kidding. Apparently, my jokes aren't so good. Of course you'd never lose one of your dogs, right?"

Justin forced himself to smile. "Right. Who would ever do that?"

"So?" Ted asked. "What are you doing here?"

"I'm…uh…waiting for a friend," Justin finally got out. "She was supposed to meet me for dinner at the…candy cane place."

Ted's eyes widened. "You're eating candy canes for dinner?"

"Uh, no," Justin stumbled. He was a horrible liar. "We were going to have them for…dessert."

"Before dinner?" Ted asked.

"Yes," Justin said, scrambling. "You know the phrase, 'eat dessert first, life is short…'" *Now just shut up, before you really say something stupid*, he told himself.

"Well, you've missed dinner and dessert. Everything's closed down here," Ted said.

Justin stuffed his hands into his pockets. "Yeah, I see that now. I must have gotten the time wrong."

Ted slung his arm around Justin. "Don't worry, you can come with me, and we'll grab a beer. I owe you one for helping me today."

"Oh, I can't. I really need to keep looking…"

"For what? Your friend who's not showing up?" Ted asked. "No, what you *need* is a drink. Come on!"

Before Justin knew what was happening, Ted was leading him away from the gingerbread house.

"But I thought you said everything was closed," Justin said, trying to think of a reason to escape so he could keep looking for Stormy.

Ted grinned at him. "Not everything."

❄ ❄ ❄

As Justin sat inside a lively, festive pub, he drained almost his entire beer in one long, thirsty gulp.

"Whoa! Slow down," Ted said, laughing. "What's the hurry? Unless you have a pretty lady waiting for you."

Justin laughed. "Who has time for that?"

"Trust me, if it's the right one, you make the time," Ted said.

"Then I guess I haven't found the *right one*," Justin said as he stared at his beer.

"Why not?" Ted asked. "You're a good-looking guy with a good job. You seem like a catch."

Justin laughed. "Well, thanks, Ted. I'm hiring you as my personal PR person. But seriously, I've met some great women, but the relationship never gets very far."

"Why? What's wrong with you?" Ted asked, only half joking.

"I travel a lot, all over the world," Justin explained. "So I'm not around very much to give them all the attention they want."

"Because you're giving all your attention to those dogs you train," Ted said.

Justin nodded. "Yeah, I guess you could say that. They're definitely my first love."

"What kind of dog do you have?" Ted asked.

Justin shook his head, sadly. "I don't have any for the same reason. I travel too much. It wouldn't be fair to them. I've seen firsthand what happens to pets who are always left behind when their owners leave, and my job is not conducive to me bringing my own pet along."

"Yeah, that wouldn't work," Ted said and took a swig of his beer.

"What about you?" Justin asked.

Ted grinned back at him. "I have two dogs, a Labrador and a golden retriever."

"Those are great dogs."

Ted nodded. "Ben and Jerry. Besides my wife, they're my best friends."

Justin smiled, thinking about how great it would be to love someone who was also your best friend. "How long have you been married?"

"Thirty-five years," Ted said proudly. "I knew as soon as I met Sue that she was the one for me. She's smart, funny, kind, honest, and a real looker, too, if you know what I mean."

Justin laughed.

"She was also the only one who didn't think I was nuts for wanting to be an ice sculptor. She was dating a doctor before me, so you can imagine how disappointed her parents were." Ted chuckled. "But I found a way to win them over."

"I have no doubt of that," Justin said and meant it.

Ted suddenly got very serious. "But now everything is riding on me getting the princess some ice sculptures she'll approve of for her big Christmas party. That could really change everything for us. Right now, I'm mostly doing small, private parties, some weddings, a few events here and there, but with a royal stamp of approval, I would be in high demand, and I could save up enough money so my son could take over the business and Sue and I could retire."

Justin cringed. "Well, I certainly didn't help anything there with destroying all your samples."

"It wasn't your fault," Ted said. "It was an accident."

"Still, I'm sorry I messed up your first meeting."

"You were just trying to help, and I appreciate that. At least she's giving me another chance to bring her some new samples to check out. We'll see if I can impress our Picky Princess—that's one of the nicknames some of the other designers have given her because she's been hard to please planning their big Christmas party."

"She definitely has some strong opinions about things," Justin said.

Ted nodded. "Lucky for her, she found her match years ago."

Justin's head jerked up. "What do you mean?"

"She's marrying a duke," Ted said. "It's not official yet, but they've been promised since they were kids. Two powerful families coming together. They're the perfect match."

Justin felt like someone had just punched him in the stomach. His reaction confused and upset him. He knew he had no business feeling anything for the princess. This news about some duke shouldn't bother him a bit.

But it did.

"A duke," Justin finally got out. "Well, good for her." He stood up from the bar. "Thank you for the beer, Ted, but I really have to go. Next one's on me."

"Good luck with the dog you're trying to train, for *you know who*," Ted said with a wink.

"Thanks, I'll need it," Justin replied as he headed for the door.

## Chapter 18

Ava was sick with worry as she led her horse, Midnight, back into the royal stables. The proud stallion was limping.

"We're almost there, Midnight. It's okay. We're just going to keep taking it slow," Ava whispered into his ear.

One of the royal stablehands came rushing to meet them and took the reins from Ava.

"Your Highness, please, let me help you."

"Thank you, Timothy," Ava said, her voice thick with emotion. "I don't know what happened. One minute, we were riding and everything was just fine, and the next minute, he slowed down and started limping. It's his left front foot. I checked his hoof. The sole is sensitive, and it seems like it's getting worse."

"Our veterinarian is on the way," Timothy said.

Ava gently ran her hand down Midnight's neck. Her voice was soft and reassuring as she pressed her forehead against his. "You're going to be okay," she whispered and then wrapped her arms around his neck, willing him to feel how much she cared.

Midnight pressed his warm muzzle against her shoulder, leaning into her touch.

She looked into his eyes. "Don't worry. I'm not going anywhere. I won't let anything happen to you. I promise."

✳ ✳ ✳

As the sun rose on a beautiful, clear, crisp, winter morning, a fresh blanket of snow covered Vailgate Castle.

Inside the royal stables, Ava was sleeping next to Midnight until he stirred, waking her up. She sat up, groggy. "Are you feeling better this morning, Midnight?"

When he snorted, stood up, and put weight on his left foot, she sighed with relief. "Look at you this morning. You are doing so much better!"

She, on the other hand, felt stiff and tired from spending the night in the stables making sure Midnight was okay.

After their vet, Dr. Regina Tyler, had checked him out and diagnosed him with a bruised left hoof, promising he would be fine, Ava had split her time between keeping an eye on Midnight and continuing her search for Stormy on foot around the property.

The last thing she remembered before falling asleep was sitting down next to Midnight to text Justin and give him the unfortunate update that she hadn't found the dog. She hadn't meant to fall asleep but apparently her exhaustion had gotten the better of her.

She checked her phone and found a string of Justin's texts throughout the night and this morning.

They were all short and to the point and said the same thing.

*Still haven't found him. I'll keep looking…*

As she stood up and stretched to try and ease her aching muscles, she saw Edgar and Lydia enter the stables.

"I can't believe you stayed out here all night," Lydia said, sounding concerned.

"I was fine," Ava insisted. "The stalls are heated and in between keeping an eye on Midnight and looking for the dog, it just made more sense to stay here."

"We're worried about you," Edgar added. "You haven't eaten anything. You haven't slept—"

"I'm fine," Ava said.

"And Midnight is still doing okay?" Lydia asked.

Ava ran her hand down Midnight's silky neck. "He's doing great, aren't you, boy?"

Midnight whinnied softly as he nuzzled Ava's neck.

"Ah, I love you, too," Ava said. She had been so worried about him last night until she found out his hoof was just bruised, probably from stepping the wrong way on something that had been hidden underneath the snow when they were riding.

"You need some rest," Edgar insisted, sounding like a protective parent. "And something to eat right away."

Ava shook her head. "No, what I need is to find the dog before you call my mother this morning."

Edgar and Lydia exchanged looks.

Ava panicked. "What? You didn't tell her already, did you?"

Edgar looked offended. "No, of course not, because you said *you* wanted to be the one to tell her."

Ava frowned. "I did say that, didn't I?"

Lydia and Edgar nodded.

"How much time do I have before we have to tell her?" Ava asked.

"She always calls after breakfast to check in," Lydia said.

"That would be the best time," Edgar agreed.

Ava let out a deep, shaky breath. "Okay, then after breakfast it is." She got out her phone and texted Justin.

*Any luck?*

Justin texted right back.

*No. You?*

Ava's frown grew as she texted.

*No. Edgar says I have to tell my mother after breakfast.*

Ava was surprised by Justin's next text.

*I'll do it with you. What time?*

"I can't believe it," Ava said as she read the text again.

Edgar stepped forward. "Is everything okay?"

Ava nodded. "I was just updating Justin that I have to tell my mother after breakfast, and he's offered to come over and tell her with me."

"That's very honorable," Edgar said, looking impressed.

"Very," Lydia agreed.

Ava texted him back…

*At 10. Thank you!*

She looked up from her phone at Edgar and Lydia. "Thank you both for giving me more time. I really thought we were going to find him."

"Me, too," Lydia said sadly.

"As soon as the call is over, I'll keep looking and I know Justin will, too. We will find him."

"Once your mother finds out Stormy is missing, I'm sure she'll return immediately," Edgar said.

"Yes, I know," Ava said, already dreading it.

"She may cancel the Christmas party," Edgar said.

Ava's eyes grew huge. "What? No! She wouldn't do that. Above everything else, this party is a fundraiser and a beloved royal tradition. All the invitations have gone out. People have been planning on this for months. It can't be canceled now."

Edgar gave Lydia a questioning look. "What do you think?"

Lydia shook her head, looking worried. "Honestly, I don't know what she'll do."

Ava covered her face with her hands with growing fear and frustration. "I can't believe all this is happening. Everything was fine until she brought that dog home. If she wanted a new pet she should have gotten…another horse—"

Midnight interrupted by letting out a loud snort.

"See? Midnight agrees," Ava said. "A horse, I could have handled."

"Everything is going to be fine," Edgar said.

Ava gave him a look. "Do you really believe that Edgar? You saw how much my mother loves that dog."

"This is going to be very hard on her," Lydia said.

"So hard," Edgar agreed, making Ava feel even worse.

❄ ❄ ❄

As Ava sat at a massive dining table, she pushed eggs around her plate, not taking a single bite. She eyed her favorite cream cheese chocolate croissant. She tore a piece off, but then dropped it back on her plate. Normally, breakfast was her favorite meal, but with her stomach tied in knots over calling her mother, she couldn't eat a thing.

While eating was out of the question, at least she felt good about how she looked.

She was wearing one of her favorite traditional red power pantsuits. Whenever she felt like she had a big job to tackle, she always felt more confident if she looked her best. For this critical phone call with her mother, she had taken the time to meticulously do her makeup and hair. She didn't want her mother seeing any stress on her face before she had time to carefully tell the story about what had happened.

She had to stay calm, cool, and collected, and act as if everything was under control. She needed to downplay the fact that the dog was missing and emphasize that they were about to find him any minute. She was determined to present this as a small problem she was handling to try and convince her mother there was nothing to worry about.

*Good luck with that,* she thought. She knew her mother would see right through her fake confidence.

Her hand shook as she picked up her water glass, taking a small sip to ease her dry throat. She set it down and anxiously twisted her watch around her wrist.

She worried this was going to be the last nail in the coffin of the strained relationship she already had with her mother. After this, she feared there would be no going back and redeeming herself in her mother's eyes.

She let out a deep breath as she picked up the white linen napkin off her lap. She folded it neatly and set it on the table to the left of her plate. She checked the time on her watch.

It was nine-thirty.

Edgar entered the dining room.

Ava didn't wait for him to say anything. She pushed her chair back and stood up quickly. She lifted her chin high and put her shoulders back. "I'm ready."

"Justin's not here yet," Edgar said. "We still have a half hour."

"That's okay," Ava jumped in. "I don't want to wait. I want to get this over with."

She'd thought about it, and while she appreciated Justin's offer to be there for moral support, she found that the longer she waited, the more anxious she became. She needed to be clearheaded and concise when she talked to her mother, so the sooner she got the call over with, the better.

"Let's make the call. Now," Ava said, summoning up all the courage she had inside her.

"Wait!" Lydia shouted as she ran into the room. "You don't have to call the queen! I just got a text. Someone found Stormy at the bakery! He's safe. See?" Lydia showed Ava a photo of Stormy inside the bakery, eyeing a counter of pastries.

Ava grabbed the table, weak with relief. "That's him!"

"Yes." Lydia nodded enthusiastically. "The owner of the bakery told me they found Stormy outside the bakery when they opened this morning. He was eating gingerbread cookies off of their Christmas tree."

"Of course he was," Ava said, laughing. At this point she didn't care what the crazy dog did as long as he was okay, and she didn't have to call her mother.

When Edgar's phone rang, all eyes flew to him.

"Is that—" Lydia, wide-eyed, started to ask.

"Yes," Edgar said, breathless. "It's the queen. She's calling early."

Ava rushed over to plead with him. "Edgar, please don't tell her anything. I'll go get the dog now, myself, and bring him right back here. He's fine. Look at the picture—"

Edgar gave her a stern look. "We have to tell her. We can't pretend this never happened."

"Why not?" Ava blurted out before she could help herself.

After seeing the looks on Lydia and Edgar's faces, she regretted the outburst immediately and backpedaled. "I just mean, of course we'll tell her, but let's tell after we have him back here safely, so she doesn't worry. If we tell her right now, when we don't actually have him yet, she's still going to panic. I'll tell her the whole story after we get him. I promise."

Ava looked from Edgar, who didn't look convinced, to Lydia, who looked like she was softening to the idea. Ava saw her opportunity and turned her attention to Lydia.

"Lydia, you know my mother—don't you think this is the better idea?"

Lydia hesitated before answering, as if she was considering her answer carefully. "The priority is to get him back here safely—"

"Agreed!" Ava exclaimed.

Lydia turned to Edgar. "I don't think it would hurt waiting a little longer to tell the queen. I'll go with the princess to get him."

Edgar's phone rang again.

"I have to get this," Edgar said apologetically.

"Wait…" Ava urged. But it was too late. Edgar had answered the call.

As Ava held her breath, Lydia took her hand and gave it a reassuring squeeze as they listened to Edgar talk to her mother.

"Your Majesty, good morning," Edgar said and then listened to whatever the queen was saying.

Ava squeezed Lydia's hand tight.

"Yes, everything here is…going as planned," Edgar finally said.

Overjoyed, Ava ran over and hugged Edgar, almost knocking the phone out of his hand.

"Sorry." Ava laughed.

Edgar took a step away from her. "Yes, that was Ava. She's with me right now. She didn't call you last night…"

Ava bit down hard on her lower lip, looking guilty.

"That was because we had a bit of a scare with Midnight," Edgar continued.

Ava perked up, giving Edgar two enthusiastic thumbs up.

"Oh, please don't worry, Your Majesty, he's doing just fine. There's no need for you to rush home. We called in the vet, and it was only a bruised hoof. Dr. Regina fixed him up and said he'll be ready to ride again in no time. Ava was with him. She took great care of him, and she has everything under control."

Ava did a little victory dance and then high-fived Lydia.

When Edgar walked away to start talking about some other matters the queen needed taken care of, Ava texted Justin.

*We found him! We need to pick him up.*

*Meet me at the village bakery!*

# Chapter 19

Keeping her word to Edgar, Ava hurried out of the front door of the castle to go pick up Stormy.

But before rushing off to the bakery, she had run upstairs to change out of her red power suit into something more casual. Her goal was to try and blend in a little more and look less conspicuous, less like a princess.

The only problem was she didn't own anything casual, so she'd had to borrow some things from her mother, who always had an outfit for any occasion.

As she jumped in a silver Range Rover, she hoped what she'd picked would work. She was now wearing a pair of designer jeans, a red cashmere sweater, and a simple, classic, ivory wool peacoat. She also had on her mother's fur-lined winter boots that were the same ivory color as her coat, and had added a matching red knit scarf and hat to help hide her identity. The giant sunglasses she'd worn before, she also brought along.

Lydia was waiting for her inside the Range Rover and did a double take when she saw Ava.

"Do I look okay? Will this disguise work?" Ava asked nervously. "I raided everything from my mother's closet."

"When was the last time you wore jeans and dressed like this?" Lydia asked.

"Uh…Never."

"It will work," Lydia said with conviction.

Ava felt more confident as she settled into her seat, and they drove off.

❄ ❄ ❄

When they pulled up to the village bakery, the first thing Ava noticed was all the clever, culinary-themed Christmas decorations. The next thing she noticed was all the people coming and going from the bakery.

"I didn't think there would be so many people here," she said under her breath.

"Yes, I imagine everyone is picking up their pastry orders for Christmas," Lydia said as she opened her door.

Ava nervously adjusted her sunglasses, hat, and scarf.

"Are you ready?" Lydia asked.

Ava braced herself. She was about to get out of the Rover when she got a FaceTime call from her mother. She panicked. "No, no, no…"

"What's wrong?" Lydia asked.

Ava held up her phone. "It's my mother. I can't get this. She'll see me dressed like this and will know something is up, but if I don't answer again she'll also know something is going on. I've been avoiding her calls."

"It's okay," Lydia said. "Hand me your phone."

When Ava did, Lydia hung up on her mother.

"What are you doing?!" Ava said, grabbing her phone back.

"Just take a breath and call her back without FaceTime so she can't see you," Lydia said. "Say you got disconnected or have a bad signal. Your mother does that to people all the time when she doesn't feel like talking on camera."

"Wait, she's done that to me," Ava said.

"See?" Lydia said with a smile. "You stay here and call her back, and I'll go get Stormy."

"How about I stay here and not call her back?" Ava tried.

"That's not one of the options," Lydia said with a smile. "Call her now. You know how much she hates to be kept waiting."

"Yes, I know," Ava said, but she still was worried.

"Keep the call short—say you're right in the middle of something, but you'll call her back in an hour once you're back home."

Ava smiled at Lydia. "You're really good at this."

"I've had a lot of practice, working for your mother."

They shared a smile.

"Now, go, call her. I'll be right back with Stormy." Lydia shut the door before Ava could respond.

Ava looked around at the crowd of people around the bakery and slid down in her seat so no one could see her. She dialed her mother, making it a regular call without any video.

The queen picked up on the third ring. "There you are! I thought I was going to have to send out the Royal guard to find my missing daughter."

Ava forced herself to laugh and to try and sound like she wasn't freaking out. "I'm sorry. Edgar told me I needed to call you. It's my fault. I've just been so busy trying to…get ready for the Christmas party and everything else."

"I heard about the big scare," her mother said.

"What?!" Ava exclaimed, almost dropping her phone. "Edgar told you?"

"About Midnight, yes," her mother said. "I'm so glad he's doing okay."

Ava breathed a huge sigh of relief. "Yes, Midnight, he's doing fine. Everything's great. I'm getting everything done. Everything's good. We're just looking forward to…having you home."

Her mother laughed. "I haven't heard you sound this positive in a long time. Maybe I need to go away more often."

"Yes, that'd be great," Ava said, distracted. She was staring out the window waiting for Lydia and Stormy to come out of the bakery.

"What?" her mother asked sharply. "You want me to be gone more?"

Ava snapped back to attention. "What? No. I'm sorry, what did you say?"

Her mother laughed. "Nothing. You're obviously very distracted. Is that why you haven't called our press office yet?"

Ava frowned, trying to keep up. "About what?"

"Stormy," her mother answered. "They told me they haven't heard from you yet about how you want to introduce Stormy at the party, and you know time is running out…"

*Oh crap*, Ava thought to herself as she scrambled to find an answer.

"Ava? Are you still there?"

"Yes, I'm here," Ava said, trying to stay calm. "I'll contact them today."

"With your plan?"

"Yes," Ava answered. "With my plan."

"That you'll run by me first," her mother said sweetly, but Ava knew she wasn't kidding.

"Yes, of course."

"Good, because you know how important this is to me."

"Yes, Mother. I know," Ava said, rolling her eyes. "Right now, I'm right in the middle of something. Can I call you back in about an hour?"

"That would be wonderful," her mother said. "I look forward to it and—"

Ava cut her off when she saw Lydia exit the bakery with a distressed look on her face. "Sorry, Mother, I have to go. I'll call you later." She hung up, got out of the Range Rover, and rushed over to Lydia.

"Lydia, what's wrong? Are you okay?"

Lydia shook her head, distraught. "No, I'm not. Stormy got away again. I'm so sorry."

Ava felt like she had been hit by a freight train. "What?! No…" She clutched her stomach, feeling like she was going to be sick. "What happened?"

"They think he ran out the back of the bakery when a delivery was made a few minutes ago," Lydia said, upset. "The delivery man had his hands full, so when Stormy ran out the door, he couldn't catch him. He also didn't know Stormy would take off and run away again. By the time he told the bakery owner what had happened, it was too late. Stormy was gone." Lydia's voice cracked. She was fighting back tears. "I'm so sorry. I can't believe this happened again."

Ava took Lydia's hand. "Lydia, stop. None of this is your fault..." Her voice trailed off when she saw Justin's SUV pull up to them.

Justin jumped out holding a dog leash. He gave Ava a surprised look. "Wow, you look so...normal."

Ava wasn't sure if she should take this as a compliment or an insult, but at this moment, she didn't care.

"Where's Stormy?" Justin asked as he looked around.

"He ran away again," Ava answered, her voice simmering with frustration.

Justin laughed. "You're kidding, right?"

Ava shook her head. "No."

"I wish we were," Lydia said with a sigh. "The last time anyone saw him, he was running toward the park."

Ava threw up her hands in frustration. "This is insane! All this dog does is run away. Of all the dogs, why in the world did my mother pick *this one*—" Ava stopped venting when she noticed people were starting to stare at Lydia and then they started to look at her. "Oh no," she said, panicking. To try and hide her face she rushed over to Justin and started nuzzling his neck.

"Uh, what are you doing?" Justin asked, surprised.

Ava whispered into his ear. "People are recognizing Lydia because she's always with my mother. If they recognize her, they could recognize me. Just play along." She hugged him, buried her face in his chest, and muttered, "Pretend we're a couple. They'd never expect me to be with someone like you. No offense."

"Uh, some taken," Justin replied with a laugh as he pulled her closer and wrapped his arms around her. "How's this? Does this feel like a loving boyfriend?"

"It's fine," Ava said as she kept her face hidden. Actually, if she was being honest with herself, it was more than *fine*. Having Justin cuddle her close made her feel cherished and safe and all warm inside, despite the frigid winter weather. When he asked if it felt like a *loving boyfriend*, she didn't know. Henry had never held her like that.

When she looked up at him, their eyes met, and for a moment, everything else melted away like they were the only two people who mattered. Her pulse skipped a beat when she saw a flicker of something in his eyes that confused and excited her all at the same time.

"That was close," Lydia said, jarring Ava back to reality. "Now that people have figured out I'm not with the queen, they've lost interest."

Ava cautiously looked around and saw that Lydia was right. The crowd of curious people was gone. She slowly stepped away from Justin. "Okay, I think the coast is clear."

"Are you sure?" Justin asked as he draped his arm around her and pulled her in closer. "I mean we can't be too careful, right, Honey Bear?" He kissed Ava on her cheek.

Ava, startled by the kiss and her racing heart, pushed Justin away from her. "Stop that. You can't kiss me."

When Justin laughed, his eyes twinkled with mischief. He was clearly enjoying himself. "Why not?" he asked. "Is there some *royal rule* about that?"

Ava, all business, locked eyes with him. "Yes, as a matter of fact, there is."

Justin laughed louder. He turned to Lydia. "She's kidding, right?"

When Lydia shook her head, Justin's smile faded. "Seriously?"

Ava crossed her arms in front of her chest. "Yes, seriously, so you need to…watch yourself."

Justin's eyebrows rose. "Me? I didn't do anything. You're the one that suddenly threw yourself at me, hanging all over me, acting all lovey-dovey—"

"Lovey-dovey?" Ava asked, confused. "What are you talking about?"

"Okay, I guess it's an American term. It means that *you* were flirting with me," Justin said. "You told me to play along, so I did. So, if anyone broke any *royal rules*, it was you."

Ava was shocked speechless.

Lydia put her hand over her mouth, hiding a smile.

When Ava saw Lydia watching them with curiosity, she knew she needed to put an end to whatever was going on between them, fast.

"Can you please stop joking around for once?" Ava asked, staring at Justin. "This is serious. We're just wasting time. We need to go after the dog right now."

"Another order?" Justin asked. "Who knew a princess could be so…bossy?"

Lydia playfully raised her hand then promptly put it down again when Ava gave her a look.

Ava lost it. She locked eyes with Justin. "You know what you are? You're—"

"Charming, funny, smart…" Justin offered with a grin.

"Infuriating!"

Lydian winced. "Someone needs to get over to the park right away to find Stormy. Are you two going to be okay to work together?"

"What choice do I have?" Ava said, avoiding Justin's stare. "I can't go anywhere with you, Lydia. You attract too much attention."

"And no one will pay any attention to me," Justin jumped in. "Isn't that what you said?"

Ava ignored the jab.

"We'll be fine," Justin told Lydia. "We can take my SUV. Don't worry, I can handle this. I've handled some of the most difficult dogs in the world."

"Are you calling me a…*dog*?" Ava was so upset, she choked on her words.

Justin smiled his sexy smile. "I was talking about Stormy."

"Were you?" Ava's eyes narrowed. She wasn't buying it.

Lydia stepped forward. "Time out. Both of you. You need to go to the park and get Stormy, or Ava, you need to come home with me right now and call your mother."

Ava pulled herself together. "We're going right now. Right, Justin?"

Justin saluted her. "Yes, boss."

Ava gritted her teeth but didn't engage. She turned to Lydia. "What about Edgar? When he finds out we lost Stormy again, he's going to call my mother—"

"It's okay," Lydia interrupted. "Leave Edgar to me."

Ava gave Lydia a curious look.

"He thinks we're picking up Stormy now. He can wait a little longer for an update. But you need to move fast. I can't hold him off for long…"

Ava gave Lydia a quick, grateful hug. "Thank you."

"Don't thank me," Lydia said. "Go get Stormy, so we don't have to worry about Edgar."

"Let's go, Honey Bear," Justin said with a huge grin as he held the SUV door open for her.

Ava flashed him her own dazzling smile. "Call me that again, and I'll throw you in the dungeon."

Justin laughed, turning to Lydia. "She's hilarious."

Lydia didn't blink. "She's not joking."

Justin's grin vanished. Without another word, he got into his SUV and shut the door.

# Chapter 20

Skydovia's park, less than half a mile from the village square, looked like a winter wonderland with dozens of trees glittering with Christmas lights. In the center of the park was an impressive display of life-size sculptures. There was a spectacular snow angel, a perfectly carved Christmas tree, a snowman, and a Santa with a bag of toys. One of the most impressive sculptures was a five-pointed star that sparkled from every angle.

As Ava and Justin hurried toward the sculptures, they looked around everywhere for Stormy. Ava nervously adjusted her so-called disguise. She lowered her hat, covered more of her face with her scarf, and made sure her sunglasses were secure. She was trying to be as unrecognizable as possible.

Justin glanced over at her. "Don't worry, no one is going to recognize you."

"How can you be so sure?"

"Because I *barely* recognized you," Justin said with a laugh.

"But you *barely* know me," Ava said.

"Does anyone really know you?" Justin asked. "But seriously, you're a hard person to forget, but in that outfit, you look almost like a regular person."

"Almost?"

"Those giant sunglasses are still a bit…dramatic."

"They hide most of my face," Ava said as she picked up her pace. "Let's find this dog and get out of here."

"Yes, boss."

Ava shot him a look. "Please, stop calling me that."

"There are so many names I can't call you. I can't use the 'P' word. Oh, that's right, I can call you Holly. Is that your code name because you love Christmas?"

"Can we please just focus on finding the dog?"

Justin frowned. "Why are you always calling Stormy *the dog*. He has a name—"

"Because I don't care what his name is," Ava fired back. "All I care about is finding him before Edgar calls my mother."

Justin shook his head, looking disappointed. "So, you just care about not getting in trouble with the queen? You don't care about Stormy at all."

"I didn't say that."

"Yeah, you did," Justin said. "I just didn't want to believe it."

Ava glanced at him and saw that this time, he wasn't kidding. She could feel his disappointment and disapproval. She wasn't sure which bothered her more.

*Why do you care what he thinks?* she asked herself.

*Because I do*, a nagging inner voice answered.

She didn't know what was happening to her, but she felt like with Justin, she was all over the place. She usually prided herself on being in control of her emotions, but right now, she couldn't think clearly. One minute, she thought she had him all figured out, and the next, he'd say or do something that forced her to completely reevaluate everything she was thinking about him. And now at this moment she knew *he* was reevaluating her, and not in a good way, and she hated that.

Being around him was unnerving—exhausting, even—because she'd never felt like this before. The way he could turn on the charm and become utterly irresistible at any moment was dangerous. She hated feeling like she wasn't in control of her own emotions. And yet, as much as he frightened, flustered, and fascinated her, something about him kept pulling her in.

"I don't see Stormy anywhere," Justin said, looking around.

Ava had stopped to check out the angel sculpture. *Not bad*, she said to herself as she studied the angel's intricate wings. She was leaning in to get a closer look when a teenager, coming from the other direction, bumped into her, sending her sunglasses flying through the air.

Justin scrambled to pick up her sunglasses for her. "I got them." As he was picking them up, he saw a group of photographers heading straight for them. "Oh God!"

"What's wrong? Are they broken?" Ava asked as Justin ran toward her.

Before she knew what was happening, Justin pulled her into his arms and started kissing her!

For a moment, she froze.

Then, as the kiss rocked her to her core, her body surrendered, melting into his as she kissed him back with a passion she hadn't known she had.

As they deepened the kiss, she wrapped her arms around his neck, pressing herself even closer to him, longing for things she hadn't even known she wanted.

Time stood still as her desire consumed her.

Until a dog started barking.

Justin pulled away first, leaving her breathless and dazed. "Stormy?"

But when they both looked over to where the barking came from, they saw a terrier playing in the snow.

Justin raked his fingers through his hair. "I thought that was Stormy."

Ava nodded, touched her lips, and smiled. She was still trying to process the best kiss she'd ever had.

"That kiss…" Justin started.

Ava felt like she was in a dream. "It was—"

"To protect you from all the photographers."

Ava's smile disappeared. She shook her head, confused. "What?"

"There was a group of them headed straight for you," Justin said. "I didn't want them seeing you or taking pictures or anything, so I ran up and kissed you. Like you said, no one would ever expect you to be with someone like me, right?"

Ava couldn't find her words as she stared at him.

"I'm really sorry," Justin said. "I was way out of line. I should have handled that differently. I promise it will never happen again. It was a mistake. Please don't send me to the dungeon," Justin finished with a laugh.

As Ava stared back at him, his voice echoed in her brain, crushing her heart.

*It was a mistake. It was a mistake. It was a mistake.*

She felt like someone had just tossed a giant bucket of ice water over her. Moments ago, she'd been lost in the most amazing kiss of her life—only to be told it was fake, a mistake, an accident, something that would never happen again. She knew she should be relieved to hear the kiss wasn't real, because that would have been highly inappropriate. But all she felt was a crushing sense of loss—and that upset her even more.

She felt her cheeks burn red thinking about the way she'd passionately kissed him back. She knew she needed to pull herself together and do damage control fast.

"I saw them, too," she said swiftly. "The photographers."

Justin looked surprised. "Really? How did you see them? They were behind you."

Ava scrambled for an answer. "I, uh, I thought I saw someone…in front of me. That's why I kissed you back, so no matter where they were, they saw it."

*Stop talking now,* she warned herself. She knew she wasn't making any sense.

Justin looked around, worried. "Why are there so many photographers in the park?"

"Maybe they're hoping my mother will show up," Ava answered. "She's always attending public events. I think she's even judged this local ice sculpture contest before. She's all about being involved in the community."

Justin continued to look around. "Well, it looks like we're good now. I don't see them anymore. I'm sorry, I panicked."

Ava forced herself to smile. "I did, too. But it worked. It looks like we fooled them."

Their eyes met.

Ava thought she saw of flicker of something in Justin's eyes, but in a second it was gone.

"That was a close call," Justin said, still looking around. "Luckily, no one else was around. Here you go." He carefully started to put her sunglasses back on. "Keep these on, and we should be fine."

As Ava adjusted her glasses, their hands brushed, sending another spark through her, stealing her breath.

Justin frowned, taking both her hands in his. "You're freezing. Your hands feel like ice cubes. We need to get you warmed up."

Ava's pulse jumped. She yanked her hands away, stuffing them into her coat pockets before he could completely turn her brain to mush. "I'm fine," she said, a little too quickly. "We need to find the dog. We've had enough…distractions."

"If you get frostbite, we won't be doing anything. Come on," Justin said. Not taking no for an answer, he took her hand and started walking off.

"But wait…" Ava tried to protest but gave up when he only tightened his grip and picked up their pace.

❄ ❄ ❄

Next to the park, Ava paced outside a festive, holiday-themed wine bar named Mulled and Merry, waiting for Justin. He'd run inside to make sure there weren't any photographers and that it was safe for her to come inside.

She rubbed her ice-cold hands together and blew on them to try and warm them. Justin was right. She was freezing. The one thing she'd forgotten to wear was gloves. She was twisting her watch around her wrist when Justin opened the bar's door.

"We're good to go," he said as he waved for her to come in. "No photographers."

Ava hesitated. "We really should keep looking—"

"We're not going to stay long. I just want to make sure you're okay."

"Why?" Ava asked. She snapped her mouth shut. *Damn,* she thought, annoyed with herself. She hadn't meant to say the words out loud, but she was baffled. Why was Justin always acting like he actually cared about her well-being?

She knew if she were with Henry, the first thing he'd do would be to ask why she hadn't brought along gloves in the first place. Henry wasn't exactly known for his patience or empathy.

Justin walked over to her and held out his hand. "Come on."

Ava grasped her hands together and locked eyes with him. "Your number one concern right now should be finding this dog and saving your reputation and your career, *not* me being cold."

"You don't like people helping you, do you?" Justin asked, catching her off guard.

Ava thought about it for a second before answering. "I don't like asking people for help when I'm perfectly fine handling things on my own—"

"But what if someone offers to help, like I'm trying to do?" Justin asked.

"Then I wonder why," Ava answered.

Justin arched an eyebrow. "You don't trust someone is just trying to be…nice?"

Ava shook her head. "No, because in my experience usually when someone is trying to be, as you say, *nice*, they are only doing it because they want something from me."

"Wow, that's dark," Justin said.

"It's the truth," Ava said.

Justin took a deep breath. "Okay, let's start over here. I get that you don't know me very well, but I can promise I want nothing from you. But if we're going to find Stormy, we have to work together. We're running out of time."

"Agreed."

"And I don't know Skydovia. I need your help," Justin continued. "And you're not going to be much help to me if you're frozen like a popsicle. So, can we please go inside for a few minutes for you to warm up? Then I promise you I'll do everything I can to help you find your mom's dog. Okay?" Justin held out his hand again to her.

"Fine," Ava finally said. She walked past his outstretched hand, opened the door herself, and went inside the bar.

As she entered the bar, she knew he'd been right. She needed to warm up. *So why did I make such a fuss?* she asked herself. It wasn't like he'd been asking her to jump off a cliff. While she'd like to blame her paranoid behavior and hazy mind on the cold, she knew what the real problem was, and it was even more dangerous than getting frostbite.

It was the damn kiss!

She blushed just thinking about it. Since she'd grown up knowing she was promised to Henry, he was the only person she'd ever kissed. They'd always had a more intellectual connection than a physical connection, and while she always thought their kisses were *nice*, they were nothing like the kiss she'd just had with Justin.

That kiss was on a whole different level.

There was nothing *nice* about their kiss. It was full of passion, want, and need. Or at least, those were all the things she had felt…

*Stop it!* she scolded herself. *That kiss was a mistake. You heard him say it's not going to happen again. Ever. So get a grip. Forget about it!*

But she knew one thing for certain. She would never forget her kiss with Justin.

And that was a problem. A big problem…

❄ ❄ ❄

As Ava sat at a table with Justin, warming her hands by the fire, she felt self-conscious still wearing her sunglasses inside. But the wine bar was crowded, and she didn't dare take them off, because she knew someone could recognize her.

It wasn't just the official paparazzi she was afraid of. She also had to avoid what she called the "unofficial paparazzi," consisting of regular people who all had cameras on their phones. She knew anyone who saw her would be eager to snap a picture, because it was a well-known fact you could practically sell any photo of her to the press and make a fortune.

Justin frowned when she continued to fiddle with her glasses. "What's wrong? Are they broken?"

"No," Ava quickly reassured him. "It just feels strange wearing them inside."

"You're fine. You just look…cool," Justin said with a bright smile.

"I've never been called *cool* before, unless *Ice Princess* counts."

"Let me guess, because you're a great ice skater?" Justin asked, with a cheeky grin.

Ava couldn't help but laugh. "No, but thank you for saying that. I wish that was why they call me that."

When he took her hands and rubbed them between his, her heart skipped a beat.

Their eyes met.

"You're finally warming up," he said, smiling. "Are you feeling better?"

"Yes, thank you," she said as she smiled back. She was finally relaxing until she heard—

"Ava?!"

Ava jerked her hand away from Justin as she looked up and saw Henry marching toward them. "Oh God…"

Henry, fuming, stopped in front of Justin, glaring at him. "Who is this?" he demanded. He looked around. "Ava, where is your security?"

"Henry, it's okay," Ava said, standing up to face him.

Justin stood up, too. "Ah, this must be your duke." Justin smiled and held out his hand to Henry. "Hi, I'm Justin."

Henry ignored Justin as he locked eyes with Ava. "Ava, what are you doing here?!"

She cringed. Henry was glaring at her like she'd just kicked a kitten.

Justin held up his hand to try and stop Henry's tirade. "You might want to keep it down. She's trying not to draw any attention to herself."

This triggered Henry even more. "Who the hell are you?!"

Ava stepped between them. "Justin, please, can you give us a minute?"

Justin gave Henry a look and then glanced back at Ava. "Are you sure?"

"Yes, she's sure," Henry finished for her.

Ava pleaded with Justin with her eyes.

Justin nodded. "Okay, you know how to reach me if you need me."

"What the—" Henry stepped forward.

Ava stopped him by putting her hands on his chest. "Henry, please…"

Justin held up both hands like he was surrendering. "I'm going. Just…calm down."

"Thank you." Ava mouthed the words to Justin behind Henry's back. The last thing she needed was for Henry to cause a scene. She knew he was just trying to be protective of her. She needed a minute alone with him to explain because she knew Henry was nothing if not reasonable.

As she sat down, she watched Justin leave the bar.

Henry waited until Justin was gone and then sat down next to her. "Okay, do you mind telling me now, what is going on?"

Ava leaned closer to him and whispered. "Please, keep your voice down."

Henry's eyes flashed with frustration. "Who was that man? Why are you here, and why are you dressed like that?"

"How did you recognize me?"

Henry pointed at her black leather purse that was sitting on the table. "I had that purse custom-made for your birthday. You're wearing your mother's coat, the one she wears when she goes on her walks in the garden—and I don't know where you got that hideous hat and scarf. Does your mother know you're here?"

"Oh, God, no!" Ava exclaimed.

Henry's eyes narrowed.

Ava rushed on, "Because I'm here getting her…Christmas present." She turned to face the fire, knowing Henry could read her like a book.

"You're getting her present, here, in the village?" Henry asked, sounding skeptical. "No. I'm not buying that. You never come to the village. Ava, what's really going on?"

When Ava turned to face him, she saw people were starting to recognize Henry. "Please don't call me Ava," she whispered.

His eyes widened. "What?"

When Ava saw several people whispering, pointing, and getting out their phones, she jumped up from her chair so fast, she almost knocked it over. She knew once they recognized Henry, it wouldn't take long for them to put two and two together and figure out who she was. "I have to go."

"What?" Henry asked, incredulously.

"I'm sorry, but I'll explain everything later."

She rushed out of the bar without looking back.

As soon as she got outside, she tried to call Justin.

He didn't pick up.

Afraid Henry was going to follow her, she hurried off, texting Justin.

*Where are you?*

# *Chapter 21*

Ava was out of breath when she finally found Justin by the park's live nativity scene. He was looking for Stormy around the wooden stable display where fresh hay was scattered on the ground. The two people playing Mary and Joseph were dressed in period costumes, kneeling beside a manger. There were also three wise men standing nearby, next to some sheep and a donkey.

"There you are," Ava said, relieved. "Any luck here?"

"Not yet," Justin said. "I thought he might like being around other animals, but no."

"Why did you take off like that?" Ava asked.

Justin shot her a surprised look. "You're the one who asked me to go."

"I just meant for you to give me a minute, not to disappear."

"Did you see the look on your duke's face? He looked like he wanted to duel."

"He's not *my* duke, and he only duels at dawn."

Justin's eyes widened. "Seriously?"

Ava met his questioning stare. "What do you think?"

"Honestly, I have no idea what you royal types do or don't do. You're living in a whole different world," Justin said. "I just know he was upset, and I didn't want to cause any trouble."

"Henry was just worried about me."

Justin laughed. "Oh, I'm sure he was."

Ava's eyes narrowed. "What is *that* supposed to mean?"

"Can we just get back to looking for Stormy? Or do you need to go back with your duke?"

Ava crossed her arms in front of her chest. "I told you he's not *my* duke."

"Aren't you two engaged?"

Ava blinked several times, caught off guard. "Where did you hear that?"

"Does it matter?" Justin asked as he looked into her eyes.

"We're not engaged," Ava quickly corrected him.

Justin smiled. "Really?"

"Not officially. That's supposed to happen at the Christmas party."

Justin's smile faded. As he turned away from Ava, he backed into the donkey, and it started chewing on his jacket. "What the—!" When he tried to pull his jacket away from the donkey, it took another big bite. "Stop that," Justin said as he tugged on his jacket, looking freaked out.

The donkey took another bite.

"Fine, take it!" Justin exclaimed as he yanked off his jacket and ran away from the furry, four-legged thief.

Ava laughed. "You're afraid of donkeys, too?"

"Wow!" Justin shot back. "You really know how to kick a guy when he's down."

"I'm sorry," Ava offered. And she really was. She marched up to the donkey. "You're going to give me that coat right now!"

The donkey ignored her and kept chewing on the sleeve.

She leaned closer. "Do you know who I am?" She lifted her sunglasses and looked into the donkey's big brown eyes. "Drop it."

The donkey immediately dropped Justin's jacket.

"Thank you," Ava said as she picked up the jacket. She brushed off the snow and held it up. "Here you go."

Justin made his way back over to her, avoiding the donkey. "Thank you," he said as he put it back on. "But now it has donkey slobber on it."

Ava laughed. "I don't think that's a real thing."

"Hey, I'm the vet," Justin said, playfully puffing up his chest. "It's real if I say it's real."

All Ava could do was laugh more.

Justin joined in. "Thank you for coming to my rescue."

"Anytime," Ava said without thinking. When she saw Justin's raised eyebrows, she continued. "Anytime, while we're doing this search. Together. Now. Today…You know what I mean."

Justin grinned. "No, but okay."

When Ava's phone buzzed with a text, her face lit up when she saw it was from Lydia.

*Stormy's at Skylight Restaurant!*

Ava sent a text back.

*Lock him in a room!*

Another text from Lydia popped right up.

*They already did!*

"Yes, yes, yes!" Ava exclaimed as she did her version of a victory dance, spinning around and then shimmying her shoulders, pumping her fist into the air.

Justin laughed, shocked. "What are you doing?"

"Celebrating, because we found Stormy, and this time, he can't get away!"

"Are you serious?"

"Yes! He's at the Skylight Restaurant."

"In the village?" Justin asked.

"No, but it's only a couple of miles away, and this time, I'm driving!"

"Wait, what? Why?" Justin asked, confused.

But Ava was already rushing ahead, and Justin had to run to catch up with her.

❄ ❄ ❄

In a snow-covered forest, by a sign that said *Skylight Trailhead*, Justin and Lydia stood next to a shiny, candy-apple-red, pro-level, top-of-the-line, snowmobile. Its high-performance suspension and reinforced skis were built for speed and control.

It was a beast.

Ava was sitting in the driver's seat, wearing a red snowmobile suit that matched Justin's. "Come on, Justin, get on!" she called out to him before she gripped the handlebars and revved the engine.

*VROOM!*

She smiled ear to ear as the growling sound cut through the frosty air and the snowmobile rumbled to life beneath her. She loved feeling in control of all this horsepower.

Justin clutched his helmet to his chest, looking nervous. "Are you sure this is the only way to get there?"

"This or the restaurant's sleigh, but it only runs a few times a day," Lydia said.

"And this will be much faster," Ava chimed in as she revved the engine again.

*VROOM! VROOM!*

Lydia turned to Justin. "Don't worry. She knows what she's doing. She grew up snowmobiling. She knows all the trails around here like the back of her hand."

Ava grinned back at them. "I sure do, now come on. Hurry up." She patted the seat behind her. "Get on. Lydia can't hold Edgar off much longer."

Justin checked a weather app on his phone. "We're supposed to get a snowstorm tonight."

"Right," Ava said. "And that's why we need to move. Now."

Justin walked over to the snowmobile to check out the pet carrier that was attached to the back. "And you're sure this thing will hold Stormy?"

"Yes," Ava said. "I told you. I made it for Edgar's golden retriever, and it works great. Would you stop worrying about everything? Trust me that I know what I'm doing."

"She does," Lydia agreed as she handed Ava a helmet. "And I know you'll be careful."

"Always," Ava said, giving Lydia a bright smile. "Thank you for helping to set this up so fast."

"You've always been one of Bobby's best customers. He was happy to help," Lydia said.

"Who's Bobby?" Justin asked.

"He owns the snowmobile store in Skydovia," Lydia answered.

"We've been getting our snowmobiles from him for years," Ava added. "And this one's a beauty." Ava revved the engine again.

*VROOM! VROOM! VROOM!*

"Let's go!" Ava shouted as she put on her helmet, adjusting the fit.

Justin reluctantly put on his helmet as well and tentatively sat down behind Ava.

Ava tested the helmet's built-in microphone. "Can you hear me?" she asked Justin.

"Yes," he answered. "But I didn't touch anything. How do I turn this on and off?"

"You don't have to worry about it," she explained. "The mic's voice-activated. Just talk normally, and it picks up everything."

"Testing one, two, three," he tried.

"Perfect," Ava replied. "Ready to go?"

Justin hesitated. "I don't know…"

"You can't be afraid of snowmobiles, too."

"Snowmobiles, no," Justin said. "You on the other hand—"

*VROOM! VROOM! VROOM! VROOM!*

Ava drowned out anything else he was going to say. She gripped the handlebars. "Ready?"

Justin gave Lydia a worried look.

Lydia smiled and gave him two thumbs up.

Justin took a deep breath. "Are you sure I can't drive? I've done a lot of snowmobiling, and I'd feel more comfortable if I was driving—"

*VROOM! VROOM! VROOM! VROOM! VROOM!*

Ava drowned him out again.

He finally gave up. "Okay, I'm ready. Let's go."

"Then hold on!" It was the last thing she said before she gunned the throttle.

The snowmobile roared to life, kicking up a cloud of snow as it rocketed forward.

# Chapter 22

As Ava expertly maneuvered the powerful snowmobile through Skydovia's forest, she felt Justin's arms around her waist, his body pressed against her, sending a warm, tingling sensation through her.

"How are you doing back there?" she asked.

"Do you always drive this fast?" Justin replied, sounding nervous.

Grinning, Ava accelerated, going even faster.

This was her happy place—racing through the snow-covered trees. She smiled, remembering the first time she had gone snowmobiling with her parents. She was five, and they had given her a snowmobile suit and helmet for Christmas. It was the best present she'd ever gotten.

On that first ride, and every ride after, she rode with her father because he said her mother was too wild of a driver. He wasn't wrong. She had often watched her mother veer off-trail, searching for new places to explore, while her father stuck to the marked paths, riding at a more cautious pace.

Secretly, Ava had always wanted to ride with her mother because it looked like more fun, but she'd never told her father that. She hadn't wanted to hurt his feelings.

When she was finally old enough to ride solo and went off-trail for the first time, she instantly understood why her mother loved it so much.

Snowmobiling gave her a true sense of being free. She was able to do whatever she wanted and go wherever she wanted, something that was very rare in her perfectly planned royal life.

Now, being on a snowmobile again felt exhilarating. This last hectic year, she hadn't had the time, so she was determined to make the most of it now.

The view was spectacular as they climbed the mountain up a steep and winding trail.

"Isn't it beautiful up here?" Ava asked Justin.

Ava felt Justin's arms tighten around her. "Uh, right now all I'm looking at is how close you're driving next to the cliff—"

"Relax. I've got this," Ava said with a laugh. But as she turned a sharp corner, she was caught off guard by a tree branch, heavy with snow, that was hanging over the trail.

"Branch! Duck!" she shouted as she swerved to miss it.

They both ducked and narrowly missed it smacking them in the face.

"That was close!" Justin shouted.

"Sorry," Ava said, laughing. She was having a blast. She was still laughing when she took another sharp turn and out of nowhere, a deer suddenly jumped in front of them.

"No!" she screamed as she swerved to miss it, sending the snowmobile skidding toward the cliff.

"Stop!" Justin shouted.

"I can't!" Ava hollered back. "Jump! JUMP!"

They both jumped off the snowmobile right before it plunged over the cliff.

It slammed into a tree and burst into flames.

Then there was nothing but silence.

A few feet down the cliff, a mound of snow suddenly shifted. Then—whoosh!—Ava's arms shot out, breaking through the heavy powder. Gasping, she sat up, yanking off her helmet. Her breath came fast as she gulped in the frosty air. She frantically looked around for Justin.

"Justin? Justin!"

Panicking, Ava fought to dig herself out of the snow so she could stand. "Justin! Where are you? Oh my God. Please be okay. You have to be okay—"

"I'm okay!" Justin's voice rang out from above.

She whipped her head up to see him standing at the top of the cliff, covered in snow. Overcome with relief, she dropped to her knees. "Thank God. I didn't see you," she said as tears started to fall. "I thought…"

"It's okay. See? I'm right here," Justin reassured her as he fought through the snow, making his way down the cliff. "You said jump, so I jumped. I didn't need anyone to tell me twice."

Ava laughed through her tears as Justin made his way to her.

"Wow, you're way down here," Justin said. "Looks like you should have jumped earlier. Hold on, I'm almost there."

Ava looked below her to where the snowmobile was still burning. A tremor ran through her. The reality of what had just happened was sinking in fast. "I could have killed us both," she whispered, her voice cracking.

"It wasn't your fault. That deer came out of nowhere," Justin said as he finally reached her.

She met his eyes. "You don't have to let me off the hook. I was going too fast."

Justin gently wiped away one of her tears. "I'm good. You're good. That's all that matters." His gaze shifted skyward, his expression turning serious. "But the snow's coming down harder. Looks like that storm is hitting early."

Ava glanced up and was instantly blinded by the swirling snowflakes that stuck to her lashes. "We need to get off this cliff. Now."

"Come on," Justin said, taking her hand and guiding her over a deep snowbank. "You go ahead of me."

"Why?"

"Because if you slip, I can stop you," Justin said.

Ava shot him a look. "Or I'll take you out, and we'll both go down. No, let's do this side by side."

"Together," Justin agreed. "Okay."

They took a deep breath, then carefully started climbing, one slow, deliberate step at a time.

When Ava slipped, Justin caught her.

When Justin slipped, Ava grabbed him.

They were a team, and slowly but surely, they made their way up the cliff…together.

When they got to the top, breathless and shaken, they stood shoulder to shoulder, clutching their helmets, staring down at the smoking wreckage below.

Ava squeezed her eyes shut. She felt like she was in a nightmare she couldn't wake up from. She couldn't believe how close they'd come to the unthinkable.

If anything had happened to Justin, she knew she'd never forgive herself. She shivered, remembering the moment the snowmobile went airborne…

"Are you okay? Are you cold?" Justin asked.

Ava studied him through the swirling snow. Even after she'd almost killed him, he still looked genuinely concerned for her.

"You really continue to surprise me," Ava said.

"How so?" Justin asked.

"By being so…nice. You should want to throw me over the cliff."

Justin looked over the edge. "I'm not saying I haven't thought about it, but then how would I get out of here?"

Ava laughed softly. She brushed some snow off his shoulders. "The snow is really starting to come down hard."

"And it doesn't look like it's going to let up anytime soon," Justin said. He got out his cell phone and frowned when he saw he couldn't get a signal.

"There's no cell service up here," Ava told him.

"Okay, so that doesn't leave us a lot of options, does it?" he asked.

"Only one," Ava said. "The only way out of here is to walk."

Justin's frown grew. "How far are we from the restaurant?"

"Not far, about two miles," Ava said, trying to stay positive.

Justin's eyebrow arched. "That might not be far on a snow-mobile, but on foot, in this snow, fighting this wind, it's going to take us a while."

Ava nodded. "I know, but we don't have any other choice. Let's check to see if our helmet mics are still working."

They both put on their helmets.

"Testing, testing, can you hear me?" she asked.

"Yes," Justin said. "You're a little faint, but I got you."

Ava took her helmet off, and Justin did the same.

"It looks like they'll work, as long as we stay close," Ava said.

"No worries there," Justin said. "Because I'm not going anywhere without you."

They shared a smile.

"Okay, we have to keep moving," Ava said as she put on her helmet.

When Justin tried to put his on, he struggled with the strap.

Ava stepped closer so she could help him. As she was getting everything adjusted, their eyes met.

"It's going to be okay," he said.

"Is it?" Ava asked. She wasn't just talking about their current predicament.

For an answer, Justin took her hand, and they started walking together, moving in sync, as they fought the howling wind and swirling snow, just as they had when they'd climbed up the cliff.

Ava was fighting hard not to spiral, but she knew their reality was brutal. They were alone in the middle of Skydovia's forest during a snowstorm, with no cell service, miles from civilization. To make things worse, the trail was rapidly disappearing under the snow, and powerful gusts of wind were snapping off tree branches, turning them into dangerous projectiles flying through the air.

"Watch out," Ava yelled after one branch almost hit Justin.

He jumped out of the way just in time. "Whoa. Thanks."

Ava was quickly losing the battle of trying to scrape the ice off her face shield. "It's starting to get impossible to see. We need to try and move faster."

"Roger that. Let's go."

When Ava slipped on some ice, Justin caught her before she fell.

"Thank you," she said, giving him a grateful look.

They started walking again in silence.

She glanced over at him. "Justin?"

"Yeah."

"I'm really sorry," she said, fighting back tears.

He linked his arm with hers so they could steady each other as they walked. "Hey, we're going to be fine. We just need to keep going, okay?"

She nodded. "Okay." She was thankful for his ability to stay calm and focused.

# Chapter 23

The Palais de la Lumière in Paris was one of the most sought-after hotels for royalty and celebrities and was one of the queen's favorites. It was especially stunning during the holidays when it was lit up with thousands of gold Christmas lights.

Even the outside entrance was spectacular. The luxurious red carpet, leading up to a palatial front door, was lined with exquisite Christmas trees that all stood exactly six-feet tall and had decadent matching gold decorations.

And once you set foot inside the lobby, it was even more magical. The soaring, vaulted ceiling dazzled with intricate gold leaf details. There were gleaming Carrara marble floors and a collection of priceless crystal chandeliers that gave the space a soft, romantic glow. In the front window, a spectacular thirty-foot Christmas added to the fabulous festive feeling.

All the exquisite holiday decorations were just one of the reasons Queen Kathleen always chose this hotel during the holidays for her visits to Paris. Only this time, she was disappointed to have to cut her trip short.

And it was all because of Henry.

Just thinking about him gave her an instant headache. When she'd first gotten Henry's call she had been surprised, because he never called her. They didn't have that kind of relationship. They had no relationship at all. So, she'd let the call go to voicemail. She couldn't understand why he was calling in the first place.

She'd already told Ava that Henry couldn't propose at the party. So, either she hadn't told him yet, or a more likely scenario was that Ava had told him, but Henry wasn't taking no for an answer.

She knew that, like her late husband, Henry was tenacious when it came to getting what he wanted. And right now, he wanted her daughter. Or more likely, what he *really* wanted was to be part of the royal family. She had always suspected that Henry was much more in love with the idea of having a royal title than he was with Ava.

And that's why she was trying to put off their engagement announcement for as long as possible, hoping and praying that given more time, Ava would come to her senses.

After Henry left his two-minute voice message, he'd also sent her a text saying it was critical that they talk right away because he was worried about Ava.

Skeptical, she'd listened to the message, and she'd been surprised when he hadn't mentioned the Christmas party. Instead, he was upset about seeing Ava in the village with Justin. He was convinced something suspicious was going on. He stressed in his message that Ava was dressed in casual clothes and acting very unusually. It had made her laugh to hear how appalled he was to see Ava in jeans. He also wasn't thrilled that she was with Justin.

Normally, she could have instantly alleviated Henry's fears by calling him back and explaining that Justin was just the dog trainer who was training her new dog, Stormy. But since she didn't want Henry or anyone else to know anything about

Stormy until she made her official announcement at the Christmas party, she simply texted Henry back, keeping their exchange short and to the point.

In her text, she assured him he had nothing to worry about because Justin was just an *old family friend.* When Henry had instantly replied, asking about the clothes and what Ava was doing in the village when she always stayed out of public places, the queen had said she couldn't tell him because it was a surprise about something Ava was getting him for Christmas.

She had no problem telling him a little white lie if it got him off her back. However, while she'd downplayed Ava's unusual behavior to Henry, she, too, wanted to know what was going on.

Henry was right about one thing.

Ava valued her privacy above everything else, and that was why she never went into the village or anywhere in public so that she could avoid the press and paparazzi. When she thought about it, she couldn't remember the last time or any time when her daughter had worn jeans.

The fact that Ava was with Justin only added to her curiosity. Justin was supposed to be training Stormy, and Ava was supposed to be planning the Christmas party. She'd also noticed Edgar had been acting a little strange. Something was definitely going on, and she needed to get home and find out exactly what.

As she walked through the opulent hotel lobby, the general manager—and her longtime acquaintance, Felix—escorted her to the door.

"Felix, thank you again for arranging everything so I could leave early," she said with a grateful smile.

"Or course, Your Majesty. You know we'd do anything for you," Felix said. "But we have been advised that a snowstorm is coming. It would be much safer for you to wait and not fly right now."

She shook her head. "Thank you, but that's not an option. I can't wait. I need to get home right away."

# Chapter 24

The snow was falling so fast that Ava could barely see her hand in front of her face as she hiked down the trail with Justin.

It seemed like each step was getting harder and that it was taking them forever to make any progress. She refused to let herself panic, but the worse the weather got, the more worried she became.

"Test, one, two, three," Ava said, testing the voice-activated mic in her helmet. "Justin, can you still hear me?"

Justin nodded. "Yeah, can you hear me?"

She gave him a thumb up. "Yes."

"Are you sure we're going the right way?" Justin asked. "I feel like we've walked more than two miles."

"I know. It feels like we've been walking forever and hardly moving at the same time, but this is the right way." Ava said. "This is the only trail to the restaurant. We should be close."

"Okay, I'll take your word for it," Justin said. "What kind of restaurant is this to be out here in the middle of nowhere?"

"That's the charm," Ava said. "It originally was a private home, this big, beautiful log cabin on fifty acres that was turned into a special occasion restaurant."

"What's a special occasion restaurant?" Justin asked.

"You know, a restaurant for birthdays, anniversaries, proposals, and things like that," Ava answered. "Special occasions."

"Got it."

"The owner and chef, Samuel, said he wanted to create an experiential dining experience, someplace you could go to get away from it all," Ava continued. "He wanted something small and intimate, a place where you could leave all your worries behind and just enjoy a culinary journey."

"Wow, he should pay you to do his PR," Justin said. "You make it sound great."

"It is, and so is he," Ava said. "I've known him my whole life."

"So, you've been here before?"

"Yes, when I was growing up, but it has been a long time."

"This is good," Justin said.

"The restaurant?"

"No, talking. It's taking my mind off the fact that we're—"

"We're stranded on a mountain in the middle of a snowstorm," Ava finished for him.

"Exactly. What other stories do you have?"

"No, I've said enough. It's your turn to entertain me," Ava said.

Justin brushed some snow off of himself. "My life is pretty boring."

"You said you've traveled all over the world. That sounds pretty amazing to me."

"It is. I'm very lucky. I've been to sixty countries so far, but I have a lot more to go on my bucket list," Justin said.

"What was your favorite you've been to?" Ava asked.

"You know, everyone always asks me that, but it's a hard question to answer. If I just want to relax and disconnect, I love sailing in the Caribbean, island hopping on a small catamaran where the biggest decision I have to make is which beach I want to explore next. But if I'm looking to be inspired and to be reminded of all the things I have to be grateful for, then Africa, for sure."

"Where in Africa?" Ava asked, intrigued.

"I've been to a lot of places. South Africa. Malawi. Have you been?"

"No, but my mother has, many times," Ava said. "We have a lot of royal charities there. I'd love to go some day."

"You should absolutely go," Justin said. "Take a trip with your mom."

Ava laughed. "I don't see that happening."

"Why not?"

"Because…we don't have that kind of relationship," Ava said.

"The kind of relationship where you travel together?" Justin asked, sounding confused.

"The kind of relationship where we do anything together."

They walked a few moments in silence.

"It's complicated," Ava finally added.

"Then uncomplicate it," Justin said. "It shouldn't be that hard for a mother and daughter to travel together—"

"Except when your mother is the queen," Ava said.

"Well, I admit, that's something I know nothing about," Justin said. "Your turn."

"For what?"

"To tell a story," Justin replied.

"I'm afraid I'm not much of a storyteller," Ava said as she tried to get the ice off her face shield again.

"Really? So, I guess it doesn't run in the family."

"What do you mean?" Ava asked.

"Your mother is a great storyteller," Justin said.

Ava tried to look at him, but she could barely see him through the snow. "How do you know that?"

"Because at all the charity events where I've seen her speak, she always tells a personal story and draws people in. I think that's why she's so relatable and people love her so much. She doesn't act like some royal figurehead who's different from everyone else. She tells stories that help get her point across. You're in a lot of them."

Ava, shocked, abruptly stopped walking. "Me? What does she say about me?"

"You know, just family stories, things like that," Justin said as he kept walking.

Ava didn't move. "No, I don't know. I can't imagine what kind of stories she would tell that had me in them. She shouldn't be talking about our family. That's private."

"It's not bad stuff—it's good stuff, funny stories," Justin said as he stopped, too. "I'm sorry, I didn't mean to upset you."

"I'm not upset," Ava shot back at him, though it was clear she was. Her head jerked up when she heard a loud *POP*, like a gunshot going off. Her eyes widened as she saw a massive, ten-foot, snow-covered tree branch snap off above them and come hurtling toward Justin.

"Watch out!" she screamed, rushing toward him. She shoved him aside just as the branch crashed down, hitting her instead. It landed on top of her, burying her as she collapsed to the ground.

## Chapter 25

"Ava!" Justin screamed, but the only thing he heard back was static.

Still in shock, he desperately started digging through the snowy branch that had completely buried her. "Hold on. I'm getting you out of here! Can you hear me? Ava?!"

Nothing.

"Just hold on!" he hollered, as he tore branches off her like a madman. When he could finally see her, he knelt beside her. "Ava?! Are you okay?"

She didn't move.

Her legs were still pinned underneath a branch. He hesitated a moment, torn about what to do. He knew it was dangerous to move her, but he figured it would be even more dangerous to stay where they were with more branches snapping off all around them.

He cringed as he carefully took her hands, praying he was doing the right thing. "You're okay. Just hold on. I'm just going to slide you out from under the tree. If you can hear me, just stay real still, okay? I got you…"

Still nothing.

He slowly, carefully, pulled Ava out from underneath the tree. When she was finally free, she still didn't move. She was unconscious.

Justin carefully lifted the visor on her helmet. "Ava? Can you hear me?"

She didn't respond, but he was relieved to see she was still breathing. He had no idea how hurt she was, but the one thing he did know was he had to get her to the restaurant as fast as he could and get her some help.

"I'm going to pick you up now," he said. "You're going to be okay. I promise I won't let anything happen to you…"

He carefully picked her up and cradled her in his arms. He could barely see the path anymore. The only thing he could do was to keep moving forward and hope the restaurant wasn't too far away.

As he started walking, a gust of wind snapped another branch above them that fell, barely missing them.

"Okay," he said, taking a deep breath. "Let's get out of here."

❄ ❄ ❄

Justin had never been so happy to see anything in his life as when he finally spotted the dim outline of the log cabin that was the Skylight Restaurant.

"We made it," he said to Ava, who was still unconscious.

Even though he was emotionally and physically exhausted, adrenaline kept him moving forward toward the restaurant. It was only a few hundred feet away, but each step was excruciating, with every muscle in his body burning. He was also being extra careful knowing it would be a disaster if he slipped on the icy snow and took them both down.

When he finally got to the restaurant, he could see through the window that there were customers enjoying dinner, so he headed for the back door. He knew Ava wouldn't want anyone seeing her, especially like this.

The snow was coming down fast and furious. Since his arms were full carrying Ava, when he got to the door, he had to kick it several times as his knock.

An annoyed man flung the door open. "What is going on?!" he demanded, but as soon as he saw Ava, he froze. "What happened?!"

"Please, can you help us?" Justin asked. He swore to himself when he realized his helmet was still on, and his face shield was down, so the man couldn't hear him.

But it didn't matter. The man immediately opened the door wide and rushed him inside. "Get her in here, fast! What happened to the princess?! Here, let me take her…"

When the man reached for her, Justin finally was able to flip up the shield on his helmet so he could talk. "No, I've got her. I'm not letting her go," he said in a raspy, hoarse voice.

The man looked as concerned as Justin felt. "I only want to help. You look like you're about to collapse. I'm Samuel. I'm the owner and chef here. Lydia called and told me you were coming to pick up the dog. We've been expecting you."

Justin studied Samuel. He guessed him to be in his sixties. He was handsome, about six-feet tall, physically fit, with salt and pepper hair that was more silver than gray.

"I've known the princess her whole life," Samuel continued. "Can I please take off her helmet and check on her?"

"Yes," Justin said. He knew he needed help, and he had to trust someone. "But please be careful. She's still breathing, but she's been unconscious—"

Samuel gently started taking Ava's helmet off.

Justin held her close. "It's okay. You're safe now. We made it."

When Ava started to stir in his arms, his heart raced with hope. "Ava? Ava, can you hear me?!"

Ava blinked several times like she was trying to focus.

"Ava?! Can you hear me?"

"Yes," she said hoarsely. "Why are you yelling?"

Justin burst out laughing as a wave of relief washed over him.

Ava looked around, confused when she saw Samuel. "Samuel, is that you?"

"Yes, Princess, it's me," Samuel said as he took her hand. "You gave us quite a scare. How do you feel? Does anything hurt?"

Ava touched her head and winced. "I feel like I was run over by a truck."

"Actually, it was a giant tree branch that took you out," Justin said.

Ava nodded. "That's right. It almost hit you—"

"But you shoved me out of the way, and it hit you instead."

"What?!" Samuel exclaimed, giving Justin a furious look. "You let her do that?"

"Do you know her? I didn't let her do anything. She just… did it."

Both men looked at Ava.

"Can you please put me down?" Ava asked.

"Yes, of course," Justin said and carefully sat her down on a chair.

Ava squeezed her eyes shut. "It's all starting to come back to me. The deer. The snowmobile. The cliff and the branch that was going to hit you…" She cringed.

"But you're fine now," Justin said. "You're safe."

Ava frowned. "How did we get here?"

"Justin carried you here," Samuel answered.

Ava's eyes flew to Justin's. "How? We could barely walk on our own. There's no way you could have carried me that far with that snowstorm—"

"Well, somehow he did," Samuel said. "Even though he showed up looking almost worse than you."

"Are you okay?" Ava asked, concerned.

Justin smiled at her. "I'm fine now that I know you're okay."

Ava shook her head like she was still trying to process it all. "I don't know how you were able to get me here."

"I just kept putting one foot in front of the other, like we talked about."

"Thank you," Ava said, looking deeply into his eyes. "Thank you for not giving up."

"Never," Justin said—and he meant it. He knew when it came to Ava, he'd do anything he could to help her.

The last thing he'd planned to do was fall for a princess, but he knew by the way he felt when he saw her helpless, buried under the tree branch, that he'd not only fallen for her, he had fallen hard. Now he just needed to make sure she never found out, so he didn't make a fool of himself.

She was a princess and marrying a duke, end of story.

Ava started unzipping her snowmobile suit. "I need to take this off. I feel like I'm suffocating."

"Okay," Justin said. "Can I help?"

Ava's eyes widened. "Yes, you both can leave and give me a little privacy."

"Of course," Justin said, feeling foolish.

He and Samuel left the room.

Once they were outside the office and had shut the door, Justin leaned against the wall, shut his eyes, and let out a huge sigh of relief.

"You really care about her, don't you?" Samuel asked.

Justin eyes flew open. "What? No! Not like that."

Samuel gave him a knowing look.

Justin rushed on. "Do you know how impossible she is? She's opinionated and stubborn and has so many royal rules it's crazy."

"She's also smart, passionate, dedicated, and loyal," Samuel added.

Justin raked a hand through his hair and sighed. "I know…"

Silence.

"She's like no one I've ever met before, and not because she's a princess," Justin continued. "From the moment I met her she has infuriated me…and fascinated me. The last thing I wanted to do was fall for her."

"But you have," Samuel said.

Justin sighed and nodded. "But it doesn't matter how I feel because she's a princess, and I'm no prince. And she's marrying a duke."

"She hasn't married him yet," Samuel reminded him. "I think our princess is worth fighting for, don't you?"

Justin just shook his head, because at this point he wasn't sure what he thought anymore.

# Chapter 26

In Samuel's office at the restaurant, Ava fidgeted impatiently as Dr. Diane Kelton completed her examination. She always hated when people made a fuss over her, and right now, that was exactly what was happening.

Even though she'd been able to stand up on her own and felt fine, beyond being a little tired and sore, Samuel and Justin had both insisted that she get checked out by a doctor Samuel knew who was having dinner in the restaurant.

"I'm so sorry we had to take you away from your meal," Ava told the doctor. "I feel fine, but these two don't believe me."

"It's not that we don't believe you, but you were hit by giant tree branch, you were knocked unconscious, and you were out in a freezing snowstorm, so I don't think it's being too unreasonable to have you checked out," Justin said.

"I agree," Samuel said. "We have to make sure you're okay."

"Well, then what about him?" Ava asked, jumping up from the couch and pointing at Justin. "You said he was a mess when he brought me in here. He was also in the snowstorm, and he had to *carry* me all the way here. Shouldn't you be checking him out, too?"

"Yes," Dr. Kelton said.

"No," Justin said at the same time.

When Ava looked to Samuel for support, he shook his head. "I'm not getting in the middle of this one."

"I'm fine. I wasn't the one knocked unconscious," Justin insisted. "How is she, Dr. Kelton?"

"Please tell them I'm okay," Ava said. "So they'll stop worrying."

You could tell Dr. Kelton was picking her words carefully. "I was only able to do a basic exam. From what I can tell, you don't appear to have a concussion. You're not nauseous or lightheaded, and no bones appear to be broken, but that doesn't mean you're free and clear. You still need to have your family doctor give you a full and complete exam as soon as possible."

"Agreed," Samuel and Justin said together.

Ava sighed. "And I will, but right now, I need to get what I came for."

"A wonderful meal?" Dr. Kelton asked. "Because you've come to the right place."

"No, there's no time for that. We need to get the dog," Ava said.

"Dog?" Dr. Kelton asked.

Ava rushed to explain, stumbling over her words. "Yes, a friend's dog. Not our dog. We don't have a dog. I mean I don't. Justin does. He has a lot of dogs. He's a vet."

"Actually, a dog trainer right now," Justin said.

Ava gave him a pleading look to help her out.

"But, yes, we're here picking up one of the dogs I'm supposed to be working with," Justin said.

*At least that's not a lie*, Ava thought.

"I wish you could train my dog, Lexie, she really needs it," Dr. Kelton said. "They do have a personality of their own, don't they?"

"They sure do," Ava said. "Thank you for taking time away from your dinner to help me. I really do appreciate it."

"You're very welcome," Dr. Kelton said. "I'm happy I could help."

"And I'm sure you understand, but we'll have to ask for your complete discretion in not telling anyone you saw the princess here and not saying anything about what happened tonight," Samuel said.

Dr. Kelton nodded. "Of course, I value all my patients' privacy. I will not be speaking about this to anyone, I can assure you."

She shared a smile with Ava. "But please make sure your family doctor does a thorough checkup. You are a treasure to our country, and we all want what's best for you. Merry Christmas."

"Merry Christmas," Ava and Justin replied in perfect unison as the doctor left the room. As soon as she was gone, Ava, worried, turned to Samuel.

"You really think she won't tell anyone?" Ava asked.

"We can trust her," Samuel said. "I've known her a long time. She's a good person. You need to relax. You've been through quite the ordeal. When was the last time either of you ate or drank anything?"

Ava and Justin looked at each other.

Silence.

"That's exactly what I thought," Samuel said. "I'm going to go make you something to eat—"

Ava dropped Samuel's hand. "Samuel, thank you. That's very kind, but we really need to go. We're on a tight timeline.

We just need to get the dog and get him home before anything else can happen."

"What I want to know is how did he even get up here in all this snow?" Justin asked.

"He probably jumped on one of the sleighs that brings customers here."

Justin nodded. "That makes sense." He turned to Samuel. "Did anyone say anything? How did you find him?"

"He was playing in the snow outside," Samuel said.

Ava rolled her eyes. "He was probably tearing down your Christmas lights. He loves destroying decorations. Where is he? Hopefully not by a Christmas tree."

Justin laughed.

Samuel didn't.

Ava frowned when she saw that Samuel suddenly looked uncomfortable. "Samuel, what's wrong? Don't tell me he escaped again. Lydia said he was safe, locked up in a room—"

"Yes," Samuel said. "We took good care of him. He didn't escape."

Ava let out a sigh of relief. "Great—"

"But—" Samuel started. He gave Justin a worried look.

"But what?" Justin asked. He was no longer smiling. "What happened? Did he get hurt? Is he sick?"

Samuel shook his head. "No, he is very healthy."

"So, what's the problem?" Ava asked, because Samuel was still looking stressed.

Samuel took a deep breath. "The problem is, the dog we found…wasn't your dog."

"What?!" Ava and Justin exclaimed at the same time.

"What are you talking about?" Ava demanded, her voice rising. "Lydia said you found *our* dog."

Samuel cringed. "I know, and we did find a dog. A black-and-white border collie. I immediately went to the village's website to see if anyone had reported him missing and saw Lydia's post. I called her right away—"

"And she told us, and here we are," Ava said.

"So, what do you mean the dog you found isn't ours?" Justin asked.

"After we found who we thought was Stormy, we fed him, put him in our storage room, and made sure he was comfortable. While we were waiting for you to come, a family showed up asking if we'd seen their missing border collie."

Ava eyes grew huge. "I can't believe this."

"It turns out they're here renting a nearby cabin for Christmas and their dog, Shadow, got loose," Samuel finished.

Justin dropped his head into his hands and groaned.

"I'm really sorry," Samuel said. "I called Lydia right away and told her what happened. She said you guys had already taken off to come here. Since there's no cell service, there was no way to get you a message."

"So, we came up here for nothing," Ava said, pressing her palms against her eyes. "And almost killed ourselves in the process."

"What can I do to help?" Samuel asked.

"Unless you can find our dog, nothing," Ava said, feeling defeated. "So, if Lydia knows, that means she told Edgar—"

"Or not," Justin said. "We don't know for sure."

Ava shook her head and sighed. "No, she would have told him. She had to. We've run out of time. The only question is, did Edgar tell my mother, or is he waiting for me to get back to do it? I need to get home right away."

"How are we going to get out of here?" Justin asked.

Ava turned to Samuel. "Do you have a service vehicle that we can take?"

"Not at the moment," Samuel said. "All of our SUVs are out picking up supplies."

"What about the sleigh?" Ava asked. "I know it's not the fastest way, but it's better than nothing."

"Unfortunately, the sleigh isn't going anywhere right now," Samuel said.

Ava gave him a blank stare.

"That storm you guys were in has gotten worse. A lot worse. There's almost zero visibility right now."

Ava's eyes widened. "So, are you saying we're stuck here?"

"Only temporarily," Samuel said. "The good news is the storm is supposed to let up within the hour. We had four couples ready to leave, but we've let them know what's happening and are offering complimentary desserts and drinks. They're happy to stay a little longer and relax. It's all part of the adventure of dining at the Skylight Restaurant, right?"

Ava couldn't find the words to express how disappointed and stressed she was. When she looked to Justin, he had the same bewildered look on his face that she knew she had.

"So now what?" Justin asked.

"How about that dinner?" Samuel offered with a hopeful smile.

Ava anxiously shifted from one foot to another. "I need to call Lydia before I do anything else."

"How?" Justin asked.

Ava pointed to a landline phone on Samuel's desk.

"Are you going to tell her about our crash?" Justin asked, looking worried.

"Crash?" Samuel asked. "I thought you said the snowmobile just broke down."

"Yes, it did. After it flew over a cliff and smashed into a tree," Ava said matter-of-factly.

Samuel looked horrified. "No—"

Justin shook his head. "Unfortunately, yes."

"But I'm not going to tell Lydia anything about that right now," Ava said. "I need to find out if Edgar has told my mother yet, and if not, to buy us some more time."

"How?" Justin asked.

"By telling her we're following a new lead."

"What lead?" Justin asked.

Ava gave him an impatient look.

"Got it. We don't have any leads," Justin said.

"But she doesn't need to know that," Ava added.

Samuel looked uncomfortable. "I don't know about this—"

"Me, either," Justin jumped in.

"Then why don't you both leave the room and let me do what I need to do?" Ava said.

Justin shook his head. "I think at this point, we just need to come clean."

Ava locked eyes with him. She didn't blink.

Samuel patted Justin on the back. "Come on, let's go. I'll get you a drink."

"But—" Justin started to resist.

"Go," Ava said. "I'll take care of this." She started to pick up the phone.

"Our landline usually works, but sometimes storms take down the phone lines," Samuel warned her.

Ava smiled with relief when she heard a dial tone. "It's working."

"And we're leaving," Samuel said. "Right, Justin?"

Justin didn't look happy about it, but he nodded and left the room with Samuel.

As soon as they were gone, Ava put the phone down and sat back down on the couch, feeling a little shaky. She needed to gather her thoughts together and figure out exactly what she wanted to say. She couldn't be emotional. She had to stay strong and stay focused.

She let out a deep breath and then with determination stood up and picked up the phone...

# Chapter 27

Ava still couldn't believe Samuel and Justin had talked her into having dinner while they waited for the storm to pass. She was so stressed about the dog still being missing that she couldn't even think about eating. The only thing keeping her going was knowing that when she'd talked to Lydia and told her they had a new lead, Edgar had agreed to give her a few more hours to get home so she could tell her mother herself.

She knew Edgar wasn't happy about it, but she figured at this point, he knew he was going to be in hot water no matter what he did for not telling her mother earlier.

Like Justin and Samuel, she was never a fan of lying either, but she told herself it wasn't a complete lie. She did have a lead, sort of. She figured if the other family who lost their border collie was also looking, they might have stumbled upon someone who saw Stormy.

She figured it was worth a try to contact them. She was grateful when Samuel volunteered to call them and find out what he could.

As she followed Samuel into the restaurant's special private dining room, she stopped short when she saw the room was filled with red roses and lit up with dozens of candles, illuminating a single table for two. It was one of the most romantic settings she'd ever seen.

"Samuel, we don't need all…this," Ava said.

"Right," Justin agreed. "We can eat anywhere."

"Actually, you can't," Samuel corrected him. "I don't think Ava wants to be in the main dining room with everyone else who will recognize her."

Ava took a deep breath. "You're right. I can't do that."

"The safest place for you is our private dining room," Samuel said. "Do you remember this room? You used to always use it with your mother when you came here as a child."

"Yes, I remember, but it never looked like *this,*" Ava said.

Samuel smiled. "We transform this room for many occasions. Right now, it's been set up like this for a marriage proposal, but the couple can't make it tonight because of the storm, so someone should enjoy it. It's all yours." Samuel said as he pulled out a chair at the table for her.

Ava hesitated. "I don't know—"

"We can't go anywhere else," Justin said. "This is our only option."

Ava reluctantly sat down.

"And Samuel, I think the room looks amazing," Justin said.

Samuel beamed back at him. "Thank you very much. We pride ourselves on creating magical moments."

Ava picked up her white cloth napkin and put it on her lap, then folded it back up and put it on the table. She stood up. "This doesn't feel right, being here."

"Because of the decorations?" Samuel asked.

"No, because I feel like we should be looking for the dog—Lydia's dog. I know she's very worried about him, especially knowing he's out in this storm. Right, Justin?"

"Yes, we're all very worried about him," Justin agreed. "But you heard Samuel. We can't go anywhere right now."

Samuel gave Ava a sympathetic look. "I promise. As soon as it's safe, you'll be on the first sleigh."

Ava sighed with resignation as she walked over and studied a wall that displayed a collection of black-and-white photographs. It included pictures of her as a child with her mother.

As she looked closer, it surprised her how carefree and joyful they looked.

"I can't believe you still have these pictures of us," Ava said. Her gaze lingered on a photo of her sitting on Santa's lap. Her mother stood next to her, beaming.

Samuel joined her. "Of course. You were some of my favorite customers. It was always my greatest honor to be part of your mother's birthday tradition. We originally built this private dining room for her and your mother-daughter dates."

Ava nodded wistfully…remembering. "I feel like that was a lifetime ago."

Justin joined her and checked out the Santa photo. He blinked several times. "Wait, is that you with Santa? I don't believe it."

"Oh, she loved seeing Santa," Samuel chimed in. "It was a tradition for them to come here to get their Santa Christmas pictures together."

"That was one of our special mother-daughter dates," Ava added. "She also loved coming here, just the two of us, for her birthday. She always had to have Samuel's famous Chocolate Fountain Cake. Another tradition."

"You remember," Samuel said, looking touched.

"Of course," Ava said. "It was my favorite cake, too."

"What exactly is a *Chocolate Fountain Cake*?" Justin asked.

"It's a multi-tiered Belgian dark chocolate fudge cake with a built-in dark chocolate fountain, surrounded by fruit skewers for dipping into the chocolate," Samuel said proudly.

Justin looked impressed. "Wow. That sounds amazing!"

Ava smiled, remembering, "It *is* spectacular."

"Thank you," Samuel said proudly. "We loved making it for you every year, until you stopped coming." A flicker of sadness crossed Samuel's face.

"Why would anyone pass that up?" Justin asked.

Samuel looked at Ava.

"My father started having a big, formal birthday ball for my mother," Ava explained. "So that became our new tradition."

"I couldn't compete with a ball and all the royal trappings," Samuel said. "But you're here now. We can celebrate that. What can I get you? Anything you like?"

"I'd love a glass of Bordeaux, please," Ava said.

Justin shook his head. "I don't think the doctor would recommend *wine*."

Ava gave him a look. "She said I needed to take it easy. So, wine will be perfect."

Samuel chuckled as he left the room.

When Justin walked back to the table and held out the chair for her, she sat down and immediately started brushing off all the red rose petals that were sprinkled across the table. She also blew out the candles in front of her.

Justin's eyebrow arched as he sat down. "You're not a fan of candles or roses?"

"Not right now, I'm not," she said. The last thing she needed was to be in a romantic setting with the one guy who had ever made her feel sparks. She felt like fate was laughing at her, trapping them in a scene straight out of a romantic movie.

Justin surveyed the room. "I bet the girl that was getting proposed to loves roses and candles and that's why her boyfriend had the room set up like this."

"Do you really think he went to all that trouble?" Ava asked, skeptical.

Justin looked surprised. "Yes. Getting engaged is one of the most important days of your life. You want it to be perfect, something romantic and personal that means something to your love story, something you'll remember forever and tell your kids about, right?"

Their eyes met.

Ava had never thought about a proposal in that way before. When she thought about her and Henry's engagement, she saw it as more of a means to an end. Romance wasn't factored into the equation. "Maybe for some people," Ava finally said.

Justin looked surprised. "You're not a romantic?"

"You are?"

"Yes," Justin said proudly. "I'd like to think so, but it surprises me you're not."

"Why?" Ava asked as she flicked another rose petal off the table.

"Because I thought as a princess you would be all about the romance. I mean, isn't that a princess thing?"

"A princess thing? Why would you say that?" Ava asked.

"Because there are literally hundreds of royal-themed romance love stories about a princess meeting their prince charming," Justin said. "I thought every little girl grew up wishing they could live in a castle, get all dressed up, go to beautiful balls, meet their prince, and live happily ever after."

Ava shook her head. "That's not real life for a real-life princess, at least not for me."

"Really?" Justin asked, intrigued. "Okay, then tell me about your proposal. What did your duke do to declare his love for you and win you over?"

"Nothing," Ava said.

Justin stared at her. "Nothing? What do you mean, *nothing*?"

"Just what I said," Ava continued. "Henry didn't do any-thing, because he didn't have to."

Justin waited for her to continue.

"He didn't have to propose or do any grand gesture because our parents matched us up when we were children. We always knew we were going to get married," Ava said.

Justin looked surprised as he leaned closer to her. "So, you're telling me he *never* proposed."

Their eyes met.

"No." Ava said. "Henry has never proposed."

"Interesting," Justin said as he leaned back in his chair.

"What?" Ava asked.

"Nothing," Justin replied.

She gave him a look. "You clearly want to say something, so go ahead and say it."

"There's just no way I wouldn't propose to a person I loved, to make sure they knew how much they meant to me and how much I wanted to spend the rest of my life with them,"

Justin said. "Even if it's a given, like you and Henry, I think words matter, and I don't think a proposal should be taken for granted."

"That's because you're American," Ava said. "You don't understand."

"No, I understand perfectly well. Love is love, no matter where you are in the world. A proposal is a chance to tell someone how much you love them. Why wouldn't you want to say that and celebrate that?"

Ava shifted uncomfortably in her seat.

"I think if you're going to marry someone, there needs to be a proposal," Justin said. "It doesn't have to be as fancy as all this, with candles and roses, but it should still happen and not just be assumed."

"Maybe in your world that's how it works, but that's not how it works in mine," Ava said.

"That's really too bad," Justin said.

"Don't feel bad for me," Ava insisted. "I'm perfectly happy with the way things are."

"Okay," Justin said. "If you say so."

Ava nodded, but as she stared down at the table, she couldn't help but wonder. Was she happy? Or did she want the kind of romance Justin was talking about? She had never thought about a proposal that way before, but now she knew she would never see it the same way again.

# Chapter 28

A fresh coat of snow from the storm covered everything in sight, glistening in the moonlight all around the Skylight Restaurant. Now that it had finally stopped snowing, you could see all the lit-up Christmas trees and the twinkling white lights that outlined the restaurant.

Inside, in their private dining room, Ava and Justin were laughing and drinking wine as they finished their dessert.

"How are you feeling?" Justin asked.

Ava picked up her wine and smiled. "Much better now. This was a wonderful Bordeaux."

"And, of course, you had great company," Justin added with a grin.

Ava rolled her eyes, but she was smiling.

Justin leaned forward. "Can I ask you a question?"

Ava nodded and drank her wine.

"Why did you kiss me back?" Justin asked.

Ava choked, almost spitting up her drink. "What?" she asked as she felt her face turning as red as the Bordeaux she was drinking.

"When the photographers were coming and I kissed you so they wouldn't see you, *you* kissed me back," Justin answered, never taking his eyes off her face.

Ava didn't blink, even though her heart was racing. *Stay cool,* she told herself. *Breathe.* "Did I kiss you back?" she asked as she swirled her wine. "Hmm…I don't remember."

Justin locked eyes with her. "Are you sure? It was quite a kiss."

Ava shrugged and gave Justin her best innocent look. "No. I don't recall. But then I was just hit on the head by a giant branch, remember?"

Justin sat back. "Yes, I remember. You saved me. How could I forget that?"

"I didn't want you to get hurt," Ava said.

Justin picked up his wine. "I think it's too late for that…"

Ava's pulse quickened. She had a feeling he wasn't talking about the accident anymore.

Samuel entered the room, interrupting the moment.

"Your sleigh is ready!" he said with a bright smile.

"Wonderful," Ava said as she stood up eagerly, grateful for the distraction.

❄ ❄ ❄

As Ava sat in the back of a shiny red sleigh that was decorated for Christmas, she glanced over at Justin sitting next to her.

"Are you ready for this?" she asked.

Justin eyed the two strong draft horses that were ready to pull the sleigh. You could see their breath rise in the cold air as their harness bells jingled.

"I'm fine," he assured her. "As long as the horses stay up there and I stay back here and I never have to ride one of them, I'm good."

Samuel chuckled as he gave the reins to Bert, the man who was driving the sleigh. "We've never had that happen yet, have we, Bert?"

"No," Bert said. "But there's always a first time—"

"Bert, don't even joke about that," Justin said in mock horror.

Ava laughed.

"Don't worry, Justin, you're in good hands," Samuel assured him.

"Uh, yeah, that's what Lydia said about snowmobiling," Justin said.

Ava gave Justin a look.

"What?" he asked in a teasing tone. "You almost killed us."

"*Almost* only counts in horseshoes and hand grenades," Ava countered.

Samuel's eyes brightened as he walked up to Ava's side of the sleigh. "Your mother used to always say that. Please tell her I said hello and that I…I mean, *we* all miss having her here."

"I will," Ava said as she smiled back at him. "Thank you again for everything. The meal was wonderful, as always. I'm sorry we disrupted your evening."

"I'm just glad you're both okay," Samuel said. "Please, take care of yourselves, and good luck finding Lydia's dog."

"Thank you, we'll need it," Justin said.

"Justin, there's a blanket under your seat. You'll want to use it." Samuel winked at Justin.

Ava saw the wink but pretended she didn't. She couldn't help but wonder what that was all about.

Justin laughed a little as he got out the blanket. "Merry Christmas, Samuel."

"Merry Christmas!" Samuel replied with a wide smile.

When the sleigh suddenly lurched forward, Justin grabbed Ava's hand.

"Are you okay?" she asked.

"Yes, of course," Justin said. "I was just making sure you were okay."

Ava smiled. She could see how nervous he was, but this time, she wasn't going to give him a hard time about it. Instead, she turned around and waved at Samuel as the sleigh picked up speed. "Thank you again!"

When she turned back to Justin, she was still holding his hand and smiling.

"You look…happy," Justin said.

Ava laughed. "Why do you sound so surprised?"

"Because usually, you're more—"

"Intense?" Ava asked, staring straight ahead.

"Yes," Justin agreed. "That would be a good word for it. Don't get me wrong, I'm not complaining. It's great to see you looking more relaxed. You seemed to really enjoy the time at the restaurant, despite the fact that we were basically trapped here."

Ava nodded. "I did. It brought back a lot of good memories."

"With your mother."

"Yes," Ava said and smiled. "I remember how excited she used to be to come here, and we always took a sleigh, just like this one."

"And you said it was something you two did together. Your father didn't come along?"

Ava shook her head. "No, this kind of place was never really his thing. He was much more…formal."

"That's why he started planning the birthday balls for her," Justin said.

"Yes," Ava said. "And they were always very extravagant. 'The bigger the better,' he'd always say."

"Why was bigger better?"

Ava thought about it for a moment before answering. "I think it's because, as a royal family, we're expected to do things on a grander scale—things most people wouldn't be able to do. The balls and parties aren't just about dancing and elaborate fashion. They're about creating something aspirational, a glimpse into a world of elegance and tradition that sets us apart."

"The fairy tale," Justin said, nodding.

"I guess in way you could say that, yes."

Justin held up the blanket. "I think Samuel's right. We do need this—it's still windy out here." He carefully placed the blanket around Ava's shoulders.

"There's enough for you, too," Ava said as she inched closer to him and offered him some of the blanket.

He looked surprised but pleased. "Thank you."

"You're welcome," Ava said.

They shared a smile.

Justin tilted his head and studied her. "This duke you're marrying, who never proposed to you…do you love him?"

Ava blinked several times, startled by his question. To give herself a moment to compose herself, she wrapped the blanket closer around her.

When it fell off her shoulder, Justin leaned across her and put it back where it belonged.

Ava's heart raced when she felt his body brush hers. While she tried to catch her breath, she stared down the trail in front of them, but all she saw was a blur of white as she thought about Justin's question.

Did she love Henry?

"You must be excited to marry him," Justin continued. "Since it has been planned for so long."

"I don't know if *excited* is the right word," Ava answered truthfully.

"What would be the right word?" Justin asked.

Ava continued staring straight ahead. "Relieved."

"Relieved?" Justin asked, surprised.

"Yes, because like you said, this has been planned for a very long time. I will know I've fulfilled my duty once this is over with."

Justin winced. "I'm sorry, but that's the most unromantic thing I've ever heard."

Ava met his gaze and shrugged. "I told you, I'm not a romantic. I'm a princess. Being part of a royal family brings a lot of responsibilities. Things I must do."

"Like marry a duke," Justin said.

"Yes." Ava nodded. "Henry will make a good partner. He understands this life and what it means to be a royal and all the responsibilities that come with it."

"But do you love him?"

"It's complicated," Ava said, answering as honestly as she could.

"So, you don't love him," Justin replied. "Because saying *yes* isn't complicated at all."

Ava shook her head. "No. You don't understand. You're not—"

"Royal? Yes, I know. You keep reminding me, but that didn't seem to matter when you kissed me."

Ava looked away. She felt overwhelmed by all the things Justin was saying. She was dismayed and embarrassed when a tear trickled down her cheek. She impatiently wiped it away.

"I'm sorry. I didn't mean to upset you," Justin said, sounding sincere. He took her hand in his. "I could be way off base here, but I feel like there's something happening between us."

Ava slowly pulled her hand away and faced him. "There is no *us*."

"But you feel it, too, don't you?"

"No," Ava said, and looked down so he wouldn't see she was lying.

Justin shifted in his seat. "So, you're saying you don't feel anything, and that kiss—"

"That kiss was exactly what you said it was—a distraction. A mistake." Ava took a deep breath before continuing. "For a moment...I forgot who I was."

"Does that happen often?"

Ava looked deeply into his eyes. "No. Never. Only with you."

Justin exhaled sharply, as if her words had knocked the wind out of him. His voice was quieter now. "But you're still going to marry the duke."

"Yes," Ava said, wishing her voice didn't crack when she said it. "I'm marring Henry." Saying the words out loud to Justin sent a chill of dread down her spine.

Justin took a deep breath and stared straight ahead. "Then I guess I know what I needed to know. You're doing what you want to do. Thank you for clearing that up for me."

"You're welcome," Ava said with a formal nod of her head. As she turned away, another tear fell. She told herself of course she was doing the right thing marrying Henry.

But for the first time ever, she wondered if that was what she *really* wanted, and this question scared her to death.

# Chapter 29

Ava and Justin rode the rest of the way in silence. When they arrived at the trailhead, they found Justin's SUV covered in snow.

"Wow, it really did snow a lot," Justin said as he helped Ava out of the sleigh.

"If you two are okay here, I'm going to head back," Bert said. "Some other customers are waiting for a ride."

"Of course," Ava said. "Thank you so much for bringing us back first and please thank Samuel and the rest of the staff for…everything."

Bert smiled. "I will. Be careful on the roads."

"You, too," Justin replied.

As the sleigh headed back down the trail, Justin opened his SUV, turned the engine on, and then tossed his keys to Ava.

"What's this?" she asked as she caught them.

"Get in and get warmed up," Justin said as he grabbed an ice scraper out of the SUV and started scraping the ice off the front windshield.

Ava walked up to the SUV and looked in the back. "Do you have another one of those?"

"One of what?"

"The thing you're using to clear off the window," she said.

"You mean an ice scraper?"

She nodded. "Yes, one of those."

"For what?" Justin asked.

Ava gave him a look. "So I can help you."

Justin laughed. "That's okay. I got it. Just get in and get warm."

Ava crossed her arms in front of her chest and stared him down. "You think I can't do it?"

Justin kept scraping. "Have you ever scraped ice off a car before?"

Silence.

"That's what I thought," Justin said.

Ava's eyes narrowed. "It doesn't mean I can't do it. We need to find the dog and the sooner we get out of here, the faster we can do that. I want to help."

Justin stopped scraping and found another ice scraper and gave it to her. "Okay," he said. "Go for it."

Ava smiled. "Thank you." But when she first tried to scrape the ice off the driver's side window, the scraper slid across the window doing nothing.

"You have to push down harder, at an angle, like this," Justin said as he took her hand and showed her.

Her pulse quickened when he touched her, and they scraped the icy window together.

"It's working!" she said, triumphantly.

Justin laughed at her excitement. "Something to add to your royal resume—princess, tiara wearer, and ice scraper."

"Who says I wear tiaras?"

That stopped Justin's laugh. "Don't you? Don't all princesses?"

"So, you're an expert now on princesses?" Ava asked with a straight face.

"I…uh…" Justin stumbled then gave up. "I have no idea what I'm talking about."

Ava hid a smile. "Then maybe less talking and more scraping would be a good idea."

Justin laughed. "Yes, ma'am."

Ava raised an eyebrow.

Justin cringed. "Sorry, I mean, Your Highness, Princess… Wow, I have no idea what to call you. I'm just going to shut up now—"

"Good idea," Ava said, but she was smiling when she started scraping the window again.

"How about this?" Justin asked as he walked over to her and bowed in front of her. "I'm sorry, Your Royal Highness. I'm pretty sure that's the right thing to say, right? I researched it before I met your mom."

"You're close," Ava said. "The first time you address me should be with my full title, Your Royal Highness, the Princess Ava."

"Really?" Justin asked. "Why do you use *the*, saying *the* Princess Ava?"

"It's a matter of royal protocol and tradition. It distinguishes a specific titleholder from others who might hold similar ranks."

"Wow, okay, that's pretty cool," Justin said. "Let me try again." He smiled his sexy smile as he did another bow with an even bigger flourish this time. "I'm sorry, Your Royal Highness, *the* Princess Ava."

Ava smiled back at him. "Very good." She playfully tapped her ice scraper on his right shoulder and then his left. "You may stand."

Justin stood up, grinning. "Does this make me royal?"

"Do you want to be?" The question flew out of Ava's mouth before she could stop it.

Their eyes met.

Even with the frigid winter weather, the sparks between them sizzled.

Justin eased the tension with a smile. "I don't think I could get all the names right," Justin said. "I'm sure I'm going to forget the right thing to call you and mess up again."

"You can call me Ava, but only when we're alone."

Justin's eyes widened with surprise.

"Just to make it easier to communicate," Ava quickly added.

Justin grinned back at her. "Of course. Thank you…Ava."

Ava's pulse quickened hearing him say her name. She scraped the window harder.

"I wonder, if I were *royal*, would I be able to do this?" Justin gathered up a pile of snow from the SUV's hood and packed it into a giant snowball.

Ava backed away swiftly, but not before Justin threw the snowball, hitting her in the leg.

Ava gasped in shock. "What are you doing?!"

Justin flashed her his sexy smile. "It's called a *snowball fight*. Ever heard of it?"

Before Ava could answer, Justin threw another snowball that hit her arm.

"I could have you thrown in a dungeon for this!" Ava shouted at him.

He laughed. "Look at you. Another joke. You're on a roll."

"No, this time, I'm being serious. It's an ancient rule, but a rule nonetheless. Look it up."

When Justin laughed louder, Ava made her own snowball that was twice as big as any he'd made.

"You need to be punished," she said, dead serious.

As she walked toward him, he kept laughing as he took several steps back. "You wouldn't dare. That wouldn't be very princess-like of you."

Ava never took her eyes off his face. "Remember, you know nothing about being a princess." Ava fired off her snowball. It smacked Justin in the chest.

The stunned look on his face made Ava laugh loudly as she made another snowball and marched up to him until she stood toe-to-toe with him. She looked into his eyes.

"If you really knew me, you'd know I love a good snowball fight," Ava said as she lifted her giant snowball high into the air, dangling it over his head.

"No, no, no, no, no!" Justin hollered.

"And I always win," Ava said before happily dropping the snowball on Justin's head.

It exploded, covering him with snow.

Ava burst into laughter, doubling over as she clutched her stomach.

"Oh, you think this is funny?" Justin asked as he brushed snow off him. "Take me to the dungeon, because you're going down!" Justin was scooping up another snowball when his phone rang, giving Ava a chance to run to the SUV, jump inside, and lock the doors. She was still laughing and feeling pretty proud of herself for outsmarting him until she saw Justin's expression suddenly change as he listened to his call.

He wasn't laughing anymore.

When he turned away from her, she got out of the SUV and walked over to him.

"Justin, is everything okay?"

Justin turned around as he hung up his phone.

She immediately could see by the pain in his eyes that something was horribly wrong.

Her heart stopped. "Is it…Stormy?"

Justin nodded.

# Chapter 30

Justin's SUV was parked outside the Skydovia Animal Hospital. Inside, Ava frantically paced back and forth in the waiting room, while Justin looked numb, staring out the window.

Ava froze when the head veterinarian, Rick, entered the room looking sympathetic.

Justin joined her, taking her hand in his. She could feel him shaking.

"What can you tell us?" Justin asked, his voice was thick with emotion.

"He's in critical condition," Rick answered.

"No…" A small gasp escaped Ava's lips.

Rick continued. "We're prepping him for surgery right now. The driver said he tried to stop, but didn't see him until it was too late, and the roads were icy…"

Ava's eyes filled with tears.

Justin put his arm around her and pulled her close.

"He didn't have any identification when he was brought in," Rick continued. "But, Justin, I called you because I knew you were here and work with dogs and the shelter, and I thought maybe you might know who he belongs to."

Justin nodded.

"We'll do everything we can, but I need to prepare you," Rick said. "He's been through a lot. He's experienced significant trauma."

Ava's knees buckled as she buried her face against Justin's chest. As she heard his heart beating, her own heart was breaking.

She knew this was all her fault. She had driven Stormy away. She was the reason he was hurt. She could feel her body shake as Justin's arm tightened around her.

"Do you want to wait outside?" Justin asked her in a soft voice.

She shook her head. She was shaky but determined. "No. Stormy's my dog. I need to be here. I need to see him before you take him into surgery."

"Okay," Rick said. "If you're sure—"

Ava nodded. "I'm sure."

"Then please, come with me," Rick said as he started walking down the hallway.

With each step she took, Ava felt a growing sense of dread. The last thing she wanted to do was to see Stormy in any kind of pain, but she wanted to make sure he knew he wasn't alone.

She owned him at least that.

❄ ❄ ❄

Ava sat in Justin's SUV staring blindly out the window.

She was still in shock.

When she glanced over at Justin, he looked as numb as she felt.

She anxiously twisted her watch around on her wrist, searching for the right words to say. She didn't know how long they'd been sitting there in silence, but it felt like forever. When another tear slid down her cheek, she didn't move. It was not the first tear she'd cried, and she knew it wouldn't be her last.

She jumped, startled, when Justin gently wiped her tear away. "Are you okay?"

"No. You?"

Justin shook his head.

They both went back to staring out the front window.

"I feel so guilty," Ava finally whispered.

"Because you're relieved it wasn't Stormy?" Justin asked.

Miserable, she nodded her head. "It looked just like him."

"But it wasn't him," Justin assured her. "I told Rick to do whatever it took to save this other dog's life. I'll take care of all the bills. Rick is a great vet. If anyone can save him, he can, and we'll find out who he belongs to—"

"That's the worst part," Ava said, interrupting. "He belongs to someone who is probably worried sick like we've been. Someone is looking for him, just like we're looking for Stormy. Maybe he's a Christmas present like Stormy is and now he could be—"

Justin stopped her. "Don't even go there."

Ava turned her tear-streaked face to him. "I can't stop thinking that could have been Stormy."

Justin took her hand and gave it a reassuring squeeze. "But it wasn't."

"When I thought that was Stormy, I felt like I couldn't breathe. My heart literally hurt, and I'm not supposed to even like him…" Ava said. "I keep thinking about how this would have impacted my mother. She's already been through so much, losing my father."

"So have you," Justin added.

Ava stared at the floor as she twisted her father's watch on her wrist. "I'm fine."

"From what you've told me, you loved your father very much," Justin said. "You said you were a team. I can't imagine this loss for you. You know it's okay, not to be okay—"

"Not as a royal," Ava corrected him. "We're expected to soldier on no matter what happens. It's our duty. It's who we are."

"You're also human."

"People forget that," Ava said in a hollow voice.

"Because you only show them this perfect persona," Justin added. "When you let people see who you really are, with all your flaws and vulnerabilities, that's when people will really start connecting with you."

Ava shook her head, doubtful.

"I think you'd be surprised by how many people would want to help you if you just asked them," Justin said.

"But that's just it," Ava said. "We don't ask for help. We're the ones who help people."

Justin inhaled a deep breath. "Will you let me help you?"

Ava glanced up at him.

"Stormy is still out there somewhere. The longer he's out there, especially in this weather, the more he's at risk. I know this is upsetting. I'm upset, too, but we have to pull ourselves together and focus on finding your dog, okay? Are you with me?"

When Ava looked into his eyes, she felt a renewed sense of strength and determination. "I'm with you," she said softly. She sat up straighter and impatiently brushed the tears off her cheeks. "You're right. We have to find Stormy before something like this happens to him."

"Okay," Justin said. "I agree. First, I need to take you home so your doctor can check you out. I can keep looking, and when you're given the all clear, we'll continue looking together—"

"No," Ava said, stopping him. "I don't want to go home yet. Not without Stormy. I don't need to see a doctor. You said we'd do this together."

"We are," Justin said. "But your health comes first."

"How many times have I told you I'm fine?" Ava insisted. "If I've survived all this stress so far, I can last a few more hours before another doctor checks me out."

When Justin didn't look so sure, she rushed to continue.

"I promise I'll have my doctor do a full checkup, whatever you want, but right now, please, I need to find Stormy. I have to. I was thinking we need to go back to the Christmas market, because that's the last place anyone saw him."

"It's getting dark. We're not going to be able to see much," Justin started, but he stopped when he saw the disappointment on Ava's face. "Okay, I'll make you a deal. We'll go to the Christmas market, but if we don't find him there after an hour, you'll let me take you home so you can see your doctor."

"Do I have a choice?" Ava asked.

Justin shook his head. "No."

"Fine," Ava said, finally giving in.

"You promise?" Justin asked.

"I promise. Now, can we please go and find Stormy?"

"Since you called him Stormy, yes," Justin said.

Ava looked confused.

"This is the first time you've called him Stormy all day. You usually just call him *the dog*. That's a good sign. There may be hope for you yet," Justin said with a teasing smile.

"You're saying that as an expert dog trainer?" Ava asked.

"No, I'm saying that as a dog lover," Justin answered. "Let's go find Stormy."

❄ ❄ ❄

Even though all the holiday vendors were closed up for the night, Skydovia's Christmas market was still sparkling under all the Christmas lights that were strung overhead.

Ava and Justin entered the market looking around for Stormy.

"I think we should split up. We can cover more ground, faster," Ava said.

"Uh, no, I'm not losing you, too," Justin said. "We stick together. We're a team, remember?"

In the distance, a flash of light caught their attention.

Ava turned toward it. "Did you see that?"

"It looked like a camera flash," Justin said.

"Over by the Christmas wreath display. If someone's still here, maybe they've seen Stormy," Ava added, excited. "Let's go—" Ava started to take off toward the wreaths.

"Wait," Justin grabbed her arm. "Someone could recognize you."

Ava kept walking. "I don't care anymore. We need to find Stormy before something happens to him. That's all that matters right now."

When they saw another flash of light, they both picked up their pace.

As they got closer to the wreath display, Ava gasped.

Sitting in the middle of all the wreaths was…Stormy!

Ava ran toward him. "Stormy! Oh my God! It is you! You're okay!"

Stormy barked, excited, as Ava knelt down, wrapped her arms around him, and gave him a heartfelt hug, like she never wanted to let go.

He snuggled closer to her and licked her face.

"I can't believe it's you," Ava said as her eyes filled with tears of joy and relief. She buried her face in his fur. "I'm so sorry I said I didn't want you. I was wrong. We all want you. We love you. I'm so glad you're okay…"

Stormy barked at something behind Ava, making her turn around.

That's when she saw Lydia.

"Lydia, what are you doing here?" Ava asked, confused.

Justin joined them, laughing, ecstatic. "She found Stormy!"

Lydia fumbled around with her phone, trying to cram it in her pocket, but she ended up accidentally dropping it instead.

When it landed near Ava, she picked it up for Lydia and saw a picture of Stormy with the wreaths. She looked closer and she saw Lydia's camera roll was filled with pictures of Stormy—and not just from that night.

There were dozens of pictures of Stormy on different days. There were pictures of him at the candy cane booth and the bakery, different versions of the pictures Lydia had sent her saying Stormy had been found. Ava froze when she also saw there were selfies with Lydia and Stormy.

When Ava's eyes flew to her, Lydia winced.

"What is this?" Ava demanded as she walked toward Lydia, holding out her phone.

Lydia shrunk, her shoulders slumped as she stared down at the ground, looking guilty.

Justin looked up from petting Stormy. "What's wrong?"

Ava gave Justin an incredulous look. "Lydia's phone is filled with pictures of Stormy! The pictures she sent us saying people saw Stormy at the bakery and candy cane booth—Lydia took those pictures. She even has selfies with him."

"What? How?" Justin asked as he looked at Lydia.

When Lydia didn't answer, Ava answered for her.

"Because Stormy was never really missing at all, was he, Lydia?" Ava asked, fuming. "Lydia took Stormy. These pictures show she's had him all along!"

"No…" Justin said.

Ava marched over to him and showed him Lydia's phone. "Yes. Look!" As Ava rapidly scrolled through all the Stormy photos, Justin's eyes grew huge.

He turned to Lydia. "Lydia, what is this? What's going on?"

"I…uh…" Lydia started, but couldn't finish. She looked scared to death.

"Lydia, how could you do this?!" Ava demanded.

A figure emerged from the shadows.

It was the queen!

"Don't blame Lydia," her mother said. "She didn't do this…I did."

Ava stared at her mother in disbelief.

# Chapter 31

The Christmas lights on the castle twinkled like diamonds under the moonlight, creating a peaceful, serene setting. But there was nothing *peaceful* about what was going on inside the castle.

Ava paced around the Drawing Room, rubbing her throbbing temples. She was bubbling over with anger and felt sick to her stomach. She was beyond furious with her mother as she battled to control her spiraling emotions.

Her mother sat in a chair, petting Stormy, as they both watched Ava.

Justin stood by the fire, looking uncomfortable as his gaze shifted from Ava to the queen and then back to Ava again.

When Ava finally spoke, Stormy's head perked up.

"Mother, I don't understand any of this," Ava said, exasperated. "Why did you have Lydia take Stormy and hide him at her house, pretending he was missing?"

"I told you. I did it for you," her mother said, sounding proud.

Ava gave her mother an incredulous look. "That's what I don't understand. How can you sit there and say you did this for me? Why would you want to waste my time and send me on a wild goose chase to find a dog that wasn't really missing, worrying me, and Justin, and everyone else?"

The queen smiled and glanced at Justin.

Ava's eyes widened. "Justin, were you in on this, too?!"

"What? No!" Justin exclaimed. "I have no idea what's going on. This sounds like a private family matter, between the two of you. I should go—"

The queen stood up. "Justin, please don't go. Stay."

Ava marched up to her mother. "Why would he want to stay after what you've done? You have no idea what you've put us through, and for what, I still don't know! What else aren't you telling us? Were you even really in Paris?"

"Yes," her mother said, offering her most dazzling smile. "I went to get you a gift." Like an excited child, her mother hurried over to the Christmas tree, picked up a beautifully wrapped small present, and handed it to Ava. "Open it."

Ava tried to hand it back to her mother. "I don't want this. I want answers."

"Ava, please," her mother pleaded. Her eyes were filled with hope.

Frustrated, Ava ripped the bow and wrapping paper off and found a jewelry box. She impatiently opened the box and saw the stunning diamond-and-sapphire watch inside. "What is this?" she asked, angry. "Why would you give me a *watch*?"

Her mother smiled brightly. "Because I know how you like to stay on schedule, and I wanted something special for you. It was designed just for you. Read the inscription on the back—"

"No," Ava said impatiently as she gave the watch back to her mother. "I don't want this. I have a watch, Father's watch, and that's the only one I need. I don't know why you'd get me this."

All the hope disappeared from her mother's eyes as she took the watch back.

The tense moment was interrupted when Justin's phone rang.

He checked his phone and cringed. "I'm sorry, but I really need to get this." He headed for the door.

"Hurry back," the queen called out as he disappeared.

"If he was smart, he'd run and never come back again," Ava said to her mother. "Do you know how worried he's been about Stormy and about letting you down? He hasn't slept. He's been looking for Stormy around the clock—"

"I knew you'd like him," her mother said with a smug smile.

Ava blinked several times. "What are you talking about?"

"Justin," her mother said, grinning back at her. "He's a good, smart, caring man. Someone you could build a life with. I've seen the way you two look at each other. I knew you'd hit it off if you just had some time together."

Ava's eyes grew huge as her mother's words hit her like a freight train. She backed away from her, stunned.

"Oh. My. God! That's what this is all about!" Ava exclaimed. "You did this whole Stormy charade to try and set me up with Justin!"

Her mother's victorious smile said it all. "And it worked, right?"

Ava was so furious that for a second, she couldn't even find her words. She locked eyes with her mother. "I need you to listen to me *and* hear me. Your crazy little scheme did *not* work. I couldn't care less about Justin."

Her mother's smile faded.

"I'm with Henry, remember him?" Ava said, seething. "The duke *you* matched me up with years ago. The person I'm supposed to marry!"

Her mother didn't blink. "Your father planned your marriage to Henry, not me."

"But you obviously never stopped him, because me marrying Henry has always been the plan. It's the only plan I've ever known, and you know this! So, I don't understand how you could do something like this to me."

"I did it because I love you," her mother said passionately as she stood up and faced her daughter. "And I don't want you making the same mistakes I did, being in a marriage where there is no love—" Her mother stopped talking abruptly, looking like she regretted what she'd just said.

Ava felt like the room was spinning. "Are you saying you *didn't* love my father?"

Her mother hesitated for a moment, then she looked into her daughter's eyes. "I didn't love him in a romantic way. I've only had that kind of love once, and it wasn't with your father."

"What?" Ava gasped, backing away from her mother. She couldn't believe everything she was hearing.

"It was before we met," her mother quickly added.

Ava shook her head, stunned. "But I thought you had a great marriage."

Her mother took a deep breath. "What we had was a… partnership, more of a business relationship. We both knew the roles we were expected to play. I was only twenty when I took over the monarchy and got married. I worked very hard to uphold my father's legacy. My parents knew I needed someone like your father to help me rule. They believed his levelheadedness and sense of duty balanced out my more passionate, untraditional personality. Over the years, I honestly hoped we would grow to love each other. I tried, Ava. I really did, and I'm not saying it was his fault. He never promised to love me. He promised me security and that he would always stand by my side and support me. He did that. He kept his promise."

Ava's hand shook as she twisted her watch around and around on her wrist. She felt betrayed by both her parents. She felt like everything she had believed was wrong. "Why are you telling me all this now?"

"Because I don't believe you love Henry or that he loves you," her mother said. "Do you know he called me when I was in Paris—"

"What?" Ava asked, shocked. As far as she knew Henry had never called her mother.

"After he saw you in the village."

"Oh, that," Ava said. "I know he was worried about me—"

"No," her mother interrupted. "That's my point. He wasn't worried about *you*. He was worried about how it would look if anyone saw you in the village with another man. You were with Justin, right?"

Ava nodded.

"And that's all he cared about," her mother said firmly. "I wished he had called because he was worried about your well-being, but the only thing he talked about was how your"—she held up her hands and made air quotes—"'reckless actions' would reflect poorly on the monarchy if anyone saw you or if there was gossip. Not once did he mention being worried about you or your safety."

Ava refused to let her mother know how much hearing this upset her. "You know Henry—he's just like father. He's worried about appearances—"

"Exactly!" her mother jumped in, adamant. "All Henry cares about is your title and image. He doesn't love you. He loves that you're a princess and the heir to the throne. That doesn't make a good life partner."

Ava got out her phone. "I'm going to call him right now and clear this up."

"What are you going to ask him?" the queen asked. "Do you really love me or just my title?"

"No, of course not," Ava said as she called Henry.

"Actually, you *should* ask Henry that question," her mother said. "Because I'd love to know how he'd answer it. Give me the phone. I'll ask him."

When her mother reached for the phone, Ava backed away. "Are you crazy?"

"No crazier than you marrying someone you don't love," her mother shot back.

Ava was speechless and grateful that Henry never answered the call. She didn't want her mother shouting out something inappropriate. She sent him a text instead.

*Please call me ASAP it's important.*

She knew Henry would get right back to her. She'd never asked for him to contact her ASAP, so she figured this would get him responding right away.

She waited for a text back.

Nothing.

She frowned.

"Problems?" her mother asked.

"With Henry? No," Ava said. "But with you, Mother? Yes. I have a lot of problems with what you've done."

"I'm not going to apologize for trying to help you," her mother said. "I know you're an adult and you make your own decisions. I know when you take over as queen, you'll want to be and do the best for our people—"

"Of course," Ava interrupted.

"But to do that, you have to be the best version of yourself. I haven't been, and I've struggled. I've done all this because we need to stop this destructive cycle of marrying people we don't love because we think it's our duty and—"

But before her mother could finish, a loud crashing sound echoed from the hallway.

"What was that?!" her mother asked.

Ava looked around. "Where's Stormy?"

❄ ❄ ❄

Ava, the queen, and Justin were speechless as they stood in the Grand Hall, staring at Stormy as he sat next to the once stunning twenty-foot Christmas tree that was now toppled over, laying on the ground. Tangled lights and broken ornaments were scattered everywhere.

"Whoa!" Justin was the first to speak.

"Oh my God!" the queen exclaimed.

Ava rushed up to Stormy. "Stormy, are you okay?!"

Stormy was trying to pull one of the angel ornaments off a broken branch. He was covered with Douglas fir needles.

As Ava struggled to pick him up, Stormy wouldn't let go of the angel ornament.

"Stormy, let go of the angel," Justin ordered.

Stormy let go of the ornament and barked, wagging his tail. He wiggled around in Ava's arms and tried to lick her face.

"I think he's okay," Ava said, breathing a sigh of relief.

"But this room isn't," her mother said, looking stunned as she glanced around, taking it all in.

When the giant Christmas tree had fallen, it had also taken out all the life-size vintage nutcrackers, Ava's special twirling wreath display, and dozens of smaller Christmas trees and poinsettias.

The more Stormy squirmed around, the harder it was for Ava to hold him.

Justin rushed over to help, taking Stormy from her. "I got him."

"Thanks," Ava said. "Can you check him out and make sure he's okay?"

"Yes, of course," Justin answered.

Her mother gave her a surprised look. "Have you looked around? I can't believe you're not more upset about this room. It's a complete disaster. I know how hard you've worked to make everything perfect for the party."

"Uh-huh," Ava said as she checked Stormy's paws, not really paying attention to her mother. "I can deal with that later. Right now, we need to make sure Stormy is okay."

# Chapter 32

Back in the Drawing Room, Ava sat on the couch with Stormy on her lap while Justin picked Douglas fir tree needles out of his fur.

Now it was her mother's turn to pace back and forth in front of the fireplace.

"Stormy, what have you done?" her mother in a tone that was unusually stern. "You've destroyed all of Ava's hard work and everything we'd set up for the Christmas party. Ava's right. You have to go."

Ava's head jerked up to give her mother an incredulous look. "Wait, what?! Mother, no. We can't send Stormy back to the shelter. It was an accident. He didn't mean to do it—"

"Not to the shelter—to Justin's Puppy Bootcamp," her mother clarified.

Ava let out a sigh of relief as her mother walked over to her desk, opened a drawer, and took out a sparkling new red dog collar and matching leash. She handed them to Justin.

"Justin, please take Stormy and work your magic. Only bring him back when he's ready. However long that takes," her mother said.

Stormy tilted his head as if he was listening to her.

"You got it," Justin replied as he picked Stormy up off Ava's lap, put him on the floor, and started putting his new collar on.

"Wait, Mother, I thought you wanted to introduce Stormy at the Christmas party tomorrow night."

She gave her daughter a surprised look. "I did, but obviously, that can't happen now since we're canceling the party."

Ava jumped up from the couch. "What are you talking about? We're not canceling this party. It's been a royal tradition for decades. The charities are counting on us—"

"Have you seen the Grand Hall?" her mother asked. "Everything is ruined. We can make a donation to the charities—"

"No," Ava interrupted her. "It's not the same. People count on this. They look forward to it all year. It's a Christmas tradition, and this year, we're honoring Father. We're having the party. I'll handle it," Ava said with more confidence than she felt.

Her mother gave her a skeptical look. "In less than twenty-four hours?"

"I can do it," Ava said. At the moment, she had no idea how, but she knew she couldn't give up. She had no intention of breaking tradition and letting the charities or her father down.

"And I'll help," Justin jumped in. "I'm not much of a party planner, but I'll do whatever you need me to do."

Her mother gave him a grateful look. "Thank you, Justin. Right now, I think the best thing for everyone would be for you to take Stormy with you and bring him back for the party tomorrow. This way, we know he's being well taken care of while we figure all this out."

"That I can do," Justin said happily.

"And of course, you're invited to the party as well," her mother said with her most charming smile.

Ava's eyes narrowed. She couldn't believe her mother was still trying to play matchmaker. She was grateful that at least Justin didn't know anything about it.

"Mother, I'm sure Justin is very busy and has other plans. It's Christmas Eve."

"Do you have plans, Justin?" the queen asked.

Ava saw Justin squirm a little. *Just say yes*, she thought. *Say you're busy…*

When her mother walked up to Justin, took his hand, and looked into his eyes, Ava groaned. Her mother was pulling out all the stops.

"Justin, I know you're away from home this Christmas, away from your family, and I feel responsible for that," her mother said. "Because you so graciously agreed to come here and train Stormy I would hate for you to be alone—unless, of course, you have other plans?"

Ava sighed. Now she was starting to feel bad thinking of Justin being all alone at Christmas. When he caught her eye, she nodded. "My mother's right. You should come."

Her mother grinned. "Can you say that again, please? The part about me being *right*? I don't believe I've ever heard you say that before. It's a Christmas miracle—"

"Okay, enough," Ava interrupted. "Justin, please, just agree to come so we can all get back to work. I have a party to replan."

"With that lovely invitation from you, how could I say no?" Justin said with a twinkle in his eyes as he smiled at Ava.

Before Ava could say another word, Edgar rushed in, looking frantic.

"Princess, you need to come right away," he said. "It's Midnight. Something's wrong. Justin, you should come, too."

Ava laughed and gave her mother a look.

"Seriously, Mother, now you're even trying to include Midnight in your plan, thinking this is another way to try and throw Justin and me together?"

Justin looked confused.

So did her mother.

Ava continued, looking smug. "Well, obviously, you didn't know Justin's afraid of horses. So whatever plan you were cooking up won't work this time."

Edgar and the queen shared a concerned look.

"Ava, I know nothing about Midnight. I didn't do this," her mother said.

Ava looked from her mother to Edgar and then to Justin. When they all looked equally confused, her heart stopped. "Wait, is Midnight really in trouble?"

"Yes!" Edgar said.

Ava didn't wait to hear more. She was already running out of the room.

❄ ❄ ❄

Inside the royal stables, Midnight was lying down in his stall with a Christmas blanket draped across his back. His breathing was labored.

Ava sat next to him, petting him, trying to reassure him and not let him sense her panic.

"It's going to be okay, Midnight. Everything's going to be okay," she said in almost a whisper. She only wished she believed it. She had never seen Midnight in pain like this before.

Justin tentatively approached, holding a black leather veterinarian's bag. He looked at Midnight like the horse was a loaded gun.

"Justin, are you sure you can do this?" Ava asked. She could see how uncomfortable and scared he was. "We can wait until our vet gets here—"

"No, we can't," Justin said. "You said your vet is stuck up north because of the storm. Who knows how long she will be? We can't afford to wait."

Midnight snorted and tossed his head.

Ava watched Justin freeze. She could sense his dread, and she knew if she could sense it, so could Midnight.

She was terrified for both of them.

Justin shut his eyes, took a deep breath, and then continued walking toward Midnight. "Easy, there, Midnight. We're going to take this nice and slow."

Ava gave Justin a grateful look as she hugged Midnight. "Justin is going to help you. He's our friend. He's a good guy. I trust him. It's going to be okay…"

❄ ❄ ❄

A half-hour later, Ava and Justin stood outside Midnight's stall watching the stallion sleep peacefully.

"We're very lucky we caught this when we did so I could drain the abscess on his foot before the infection spread any further," Justin said. "It could have caused blood poisoning and that would have been—"

Ava shuddered, hugging herself. "Don't even say it. I know. Just tell me he's going to be okay."

Justin looked into her eyes. "Midnight is going to be okay."

Ava nodded. "Thank you." She shivered.

"You're shaking," Justin said. "You should go back inside—"

"I'm not going anywhere. I'm staying here with Midnight," Ava said.

"He's stable right now, and that's a good sign. I can stay with him until your vet gets here," Justin offered.

Ava saw how exhausted Justin looked, and she felt a rush of gratitude. "Thank you so much for taking care of him. You were wonderful with him. I know it wasn't easy for you. No one would know you're afraid of horses."

"Except the horses," Justin said. "And you."

"Your secret is safe with me," Ava said and crossed her fingers across her heart. "Cross my heart. Did I do that right?"

"Very nice," Justin said. "You were perfect."

They shared a smile.

"I couldn't have done this without you," Justin said. "I think that pep talk you gave Midnight about me being a good guy really helped."

"I had to say something—you looked terrified."

"Honestly, I was," Justin said. "A healthy horse is bad enough, but with a sick animal, any animal, you never know what they're going to do."

"Then how were you able to do this?" Ava asked.

"I just kept telling myself he was a giant grass-eating puppy."

Ava laughed. It was amazing to her that even during the most stressful times, Justin always found a way to lighten the mood and make her laugh.

She checked her phone to see if Henry had answered any of her texts yet. She'd sent him several and had tried calling twice. Still no response.

Justin glanced at her. "You keep looking at your phone. Are you waiting to hear from someone? Your mom?"

"Henry," Ava answered.

Justin arched an eyebrow. "The fiancé. What's the problem? Is he ghosting you?"

Ava put her phone away. "No, he's just busy."

"You are never too busy to make a quick call," Justin said.

"Maybe you're not, but he is, obviously," Ava said, trying to pretend she didn't care when she was actually very frustrated. She stifled a yawn as a wave of exhaustion suddenly hit her. She'd been running on adrenaline. Now that she knew Midnight was going to be okay, everything that had happened over the last twenty-four hours was catching up to her.

"You need to go inside and get some rest," Justin told her.

Ava shook her head. "No, I'm not going anywhere. I'm going to wait with you for the vet. We'll do this together."

She took two blankets from the stall and handed one to him.

"Thank you," Justin said, looking touched. "And for the record, I'd always call you right back I'm just saying..."

"Say less," Ava urged, but when she turned away from him, she couldn't help thinking about how he probably would call her back. She couldn't imagine Justin ever ignoring her like Henry was doing.

❄ ❄ ❄

It was past one in the morning by the time everything with Midnight was finally settled. Standing next to Justin's SUV, where Justin and Stormy were already inside, Ava felt a rush of gratitude that everything had all turned out okay.

She wasn't surprised when her vet confirmed Justin's diagnosis and credited him for probably saving Midnight's life.

Even though she'd thanked Justin, multiple times, she doubted he understood the true depths of her gratitude. She blamed herself for not doing more when she'd first noticed Midnight was limping. Even though her same vet had told her Midnight just had a bruised hoof, she knew she should have kept a closer watch over him. Midnight was her best friend. He'd deserved better, no matter how busy she'd been trying to chase down Stormy. She felt terrible, like she'd let Midnight down.

"Hey, what's wrong?" Justin asked her, seeing her frowning. "You look like you just lost your best friend."

"I almost did," Ava said.

"But Midnight is going to be fine, and we found Stormy. You should be celebrating!"

Ava sighed, unable to shake her doom and gloomy mood. "That was the plan at the Christmas party tomorrow, but oh, that's right, all those plans have been ruined."

Justin gave her a look. "You're obviously exhausted."

"Why do you say that?"

"Because the princess I know doesn't give up. She doesn't take no for an answer, and she'd fight with everything she had to make sure this Christmas party was going to happen—"

"I know, but that was before everything with Midnight—"

"But now everything's fine. Stop beating yourself up, get over it, and go find a new Christmas tree. You're the Princess of Skydovia—make it happen!"

Ava's mouth dropped open.

"Too much?" Justin asked. "Am I heading to the dungeon?"

Ava laughed. "No, this time, you're safe. You're right. I think I'm just tired. I can do this. Thanks for…"

Justin winced. "Being rude?"

"Being honest," Ava said.

They shared a smile.

Ava leaned in the window so she could pet Stormy. "You be good for Justin."

"What fun would that be?" Justin asked with a boyish grin.

Stormy barked and wagged his tail, as if in agreement.

"You two are impossible," Ava said, but she was smiling.

"Thank you very much," Justin said. "We'll take that as a compliment, won't we, Stormy?"

Stormy barked twice.

When Justin flashed her his sexy smile, she melted a little.

"I'll bring him back tomorrow for the party," Justin said as he petted Stormy. "So go be…the Princess of Party Planning, because if I'm coming, it better be a good one."

Ava laughed. "That's not one of the names they call me."

"Well, it should be, and it *will* be after you pull off this party tomorrow night," Justin said.

"You really believe I can do it?" Ava asked.

"Yes, because I've seen you in action. I believe you can do anything you set your mind to."

Ava blushed. "Thank you."

"For what?"

"For the pep talk. I needed it," Ava said.

Justin smiled. "Anytime. I got your back. And now, I better get Stormy some rest because he has a big day of training tomorrow if he's going to dazzle everyone at the party."

"You really think he can learn anything in one day?" Ava asked, sounding skeptical.

"Look at all we've learned in one day," Justin said with a wink.

Ava laughed. "Touché."

"Call me if you need help with anything."

"Thank you, Justin…for everything. Goodnight…"

Stormy barked.

Ava laughed. "And goodnight to you, too, Stormy. See you tomorrow."

As Ava watched Justin's SUV disappear down the road, she stood up straighter and lifted her chin high.

*Justin was right*, she thought.

She was the Princess of Party Planning, and she needed to get to work.

# Chapter 33

When Ava entered her mother's bedroom, she found the queen sitting at her vanity trying on a dazzling emerald necklace.

Their eyes met in the mirror.

"We need to talk," Ava said in a serious tone.

Her mother sighed and nodded. "I know." She put down her necklace.

As Ava worked on choosing her words carefully, she walked over to the fireplace where the flames flickered and popped. That was when she saw a framed photograph of her with her mother and Samuel at the Skylight Restaurant. She'd never noticed this picture before, but then she was rarely in her mother's bedroom. She picked up the picture and studied it closer. In the photo, they were eating Samuel's famous Chocolate Fountain Cake.

Still holding the picture, she turned to face her mother. "Was Samuel also in on this Stormy charade?"

Her mother nodded. "Yes."

Ava shook her head with disbelief.

"He knew you'd be coming to the restaurant with Justin, and he planned a romantic meal for you."

"He said the private dining room was set up for a proposal, but all along, it was for us," Ava said. "Unbelievable…"

"It was supposed to be a wonderful night, until you showed up hurt. You scared us to death. If anything had happened to you…" Her mother's voice trembled with emotion.

Ava was surprised by her mother's level of concern. She walked over to her and took her hand. "Our doctors say I'm fine," Ava reassured her. "There's nothing to worry about."

"Except you marrying someone you don't love," her mother said.

Ava pulled her hand away. "I don't understand. If you're so against this marriage, why haven't you ever said anything all these years?"

"I should have. I regret that I didn't," her mother said, clasping her shaky hands. "You and your father had such a strong bond. I didn't want to interfere with that. I didn't want you to have to choose between us, because I knew who you'd choose…" She stopped to wipe away a tear.

Ava opened her mouth to disagree but stopped. She realized her mother was right. She would've chosen her father. She felt a rush of guilt. She struggled to find the right words to say when nothing seemed like enough. Finally, she settled on simply saying, "I'm sorry."

"You have absolutely nothing to be sorry about," her mother said. "You and your father made a great team. There just wasn't any room on that team…for me."

Now it was Ava's turn to fight back tears.

All this time, she'd grown up feeling like a failure in her mother's eyes, believing her mother had no time for her, because she didn't approve of her. She thought that was why they weren't close, and why they never did things together.

But now the real truth was sinking in.

While her father had meant well, he had definitely monopolized her time. He always said they needed to stay out of her mother's way because she was the queen and had a country to rule. He'd always reminded her that that was mother's focus and most important job.

She had grown up believing she wasn't important to her mother, and that belief had cut deep, leaving her feeling like no matter what she did, she would never be good enough.

And since her father had always been there, always showering her with attention, her loyalty had naturally belonged to him.

She turned and faced her mother. "I always thought you never wanted to spend time with me because we are so... different."

"No," her mother said passionately. "Ava, you have always been the most important thing in my life. I know I've made a lot of mistakes. There are a lot of things I should have done differently. I should have spoken up sooner, but I'm here now, promising you I'll always put you first. I'm hoping we can start over..."

"And what happens if I decide to marry Henry?" Ava asked.

Her mother took a deep breath. "I will support whatever you decide to do, as long as you know you don't have to marry Henry or anyone else you don't love. It's your choice, your life. I trust you."

"Really?" Ava asked, surprised.

"Really," her mother said. "I realize I may have gone a little overboard with having Lydia take Stormy—"

"A little?" Ava laughed.

"Okay, maybe a lot, but time was running out. You wanted to announce your engagement at the Christmas party. I had to do something drastic—"

"So, that's why you adopted Stormy?"

"No," her mother said smiling. "I love Stormy, and I meant it when I said I thought he would be good for both of us. I also was already planning to hire Justin, because he really is the best of the best. I've been following his career and admire him and what he does so much. This all started out very innocently…"

Ava gave her mother a look.

"I'm serious," she said. "Cross my heart." She crossed her heart with her hand.

"Wait, Justin does that," Ava said.

Her mother smiled a bright smile. "I knew I liked him."

"So, how did we go from you hiring him for Stormy to you playing matchmaker?"

Her mother shrugged. "Honestly, it all just snowballed really fast. When you started pushing your engagement, I panicked. I didn't know what to do, but I knew I needed to buy some time to figure it out. I thought maybe if you could be around someone like Justin, you'd see there are some great guys out there, and that Henry didn't have to be your only choice. So, I asked Lydia to take Stormy, so you and Justin would spend some time together. Lydia feels terrible for deceiving everyone, so please don't blame her, blame me. I didn't mean for all this to blow up like it did, or for anyone to get hurt. I have a lot of people I need to apologize to, starting with you and Justin. Do you think Justin will forgive me?"

"I have no idea," Ava said. "Especially after he learns *why* you did this."

"He should be honored that I was trying to match him up with my daughter," her mother said. "You're a princess."

"Justin doesn't care about any of that," Ava said.

"And that's why I like him for you," her mother jumped in. "But I'm done matchmaking. I've learned my lesson."

"I hope so," Ava said.

Their eyes met.

"Can you forgive me?" her mother asked, sounding truly sorry and looking scared.

For an answer, Ava wrapped her arms around her mother in a heartfelt hug. It was the first real hug they'd had in years. "I forgive you," Ava said with tears in her eyes. "I hope you can forgive me for only spending time with Father. I wish I had known then what I do now—"

"There's nothing to forgive."

As they continued to hug, like they both never wanted to let go, Ava felt an overwhelming sense of love. In that moment, she knew it was the beginning of healing old wounds.

They both wiped away tears when they pulled back from the hug.

"I do have another question, if that's okay?" Ava asked tentatively.

"Anything. What would you like to know?"

Ava took a deep breath. "You said you loved someone once, before Father. How did you know…it was real love?"

Her mother smiled softly, a faraway look in her eyes, as if she were remembering. "Because when I was with him, I could just be me. I felt free. I didn't feel like a future queen with the weight of the world on my shoulders. We had so much fun together. We laughed all the time, and we challenged each other. He was always making sure I was okay, putting me first, no matter what. Together, we made each other better, and that's what I want for you, too."

Ava reached for her hand. "I'm sorry things weren't different with Father."

Her mother brushed a strand of hair from Ava's face, her voice soft but sure. "I wouldn't change a moment, because he gave me you—the most precious thing in my life."

Tears welled up in Ava's eyes as she wrapped her arms around her mother. "I love you."

"I love you, too."

Ava drew back gently and smiled. "And I know the perfect way we can start over. I have a plan…"

Her mother laughed and hugged her again. "Of course you do."

❆ ❆ ❆

Ava cringed as she stood in the Great Hall with her mother, surveying all the damage that Stormy had done when he taken down the Christmas tree.

It was worse than she'd remembered.

When she had first run into the hall after hearing the loud crash, her focus had been on Stormy and making sure he was okay. Now that she had a chance to really look around, it was beginning to sink in what an abysmal disaster the entire room really was.

The showstopper Douglas fir Christmas tree was a complete loss. There were broken branches everywhere and the top of the tree had snapped off when it hit the wall. The marble floor was covered with broken ornaments. Her wreath display invention was totaled, and the vintage nutcracker collection looked like it had just gone to war—and lost.

She was going to have to start completely over to decorate the room, and the clock was ticking if she was going to transform this space in time for the Christmas party.

"Ava, are you sure you can do this?" her mother asked, worried.

"No," Ava said. "I can't do it…"

Her mother's shoulders slumped with disappointment.

"But *we* can," Ava continued.

"We?" her mother asked, surprised.

"Yes, *we*," Ava said emphatically. "If I'm going to pull off a Christmas miracle, I'm going to need your help."

"You really want *me*…to help *you* save this Christmas party?"

Ava laughed. "Yes, Mother. Why do you sound so surprised?"

"Maybe because you've never asked me for help…ever."

"But we're starting over, remember?" Ava asked with a warm smile. "And who knows a party better than you?"

"This is true," her mother said, her smile lighting up the room. "But I'll only do this if Santa can come."

Ava laughed. "Yes, Santa can come."

"Ho! Ho! Ho! Then let's go!" the queen exclaimed, excited.

Ava put her arm around her mother. "I know we're going to make a great team."

"The best team ever," her mother agreed as they shared a smile.

# Chapter 34

As the sunrise spilled over Vailgate Castle, it illuminated a flurry of activity.

Vendor vans from Icescape Catering, Skydovia Christmas Tree Farm, Gary's Lighting, and Finn's Floral filled the driveway as a steady stream of workers hurried in and out of the castle, preparing for the day ahead.

Inside the Grand Hall, Ava felt surprisingly at ease in jeans and a red flannel shirt as she supervised one crew hauling out the remains of the demolished Christmas tree while another brought in a new one, an even taller and more magnificent thirty-foot Douglas fir. Delivery workers followed, carrying in new boxes of ornaments and lights, life-size nutcrackers, wreaths, and every other festive touch imaginable.

One of the nutcracker designers nervously approached Ava.

Ava smiled. "Yes, can I help you?"

The designer nodded. "Yes, Your Royal Highness. Thank you. Where would you like the new nutcrackers to go? I know they're a little larger than the original ones, so would you like them here, or closer to the tree?"

Ava studied the new, stunning vintage nutcrackers. "What do you think?"

The designer blinked, surprised. "Me?"

"Yes," Ava said. "You're the expert. Where do you think they would look best?"

The designer relaxed and smiled. "I think they would look wonderful closer to the tree."

"Great, then let's do that," Ava said.

They shared a smile, and then the designer got back to work.

Next, Ava turned her attention to her rotating wreath display, which she had managed to put back together. The crashing tree had taken out all the hanging wires and wreaths, but the mechanism she had invented remained intact. It hadn't taken her long to string up new wires, add fresh wreaths, and restore everything to look as good as new. She was smiling, adjusting one of the wreaths' bows, when Edgar walked up. He looked around, impressed.

"I can't believe you've been able to do all this so fast," he said. "Dare I say everything looks even better than before?"

Ava gave him a grateful look. "Thank you, Edgar. That means a lot, coming from you. I know you've seen a lot of parties in here."

"Dozens," Edgar agreed. "But what you've done for this party will make it the most magnificent one we've ever seen. I know your father would be very proud of you."

"I didn't do this alone. It has been a team effort. Mother and I were up all night calling people, asking for help. Justin was right."

"About?"

"He said if we ever needed help, we should ask for it, and that we'd be surprised by how many people would show up for us. You know that's not how we usually operate."

Edgar nodded.

"We're not takers, we're givers," Ava continued. "But this time, in order to *give* this Christmas party to everyone, we needed help, and everyone came through. It's really unbelievable. I'm so grateful."

Edgar smiled. "So, you and Justin…"

For a moment, the question hung in the air.

Finally, Ava answered. "There is no Justin and me."

"But you'd like there to be," Edgar said. "And before you try and deny it, remember I've known you since you were born." He gave her a pointed look.

Ava blushed. She picked up an angel ornament out of the box of decorations and walked over to the new Christmas tree.

Edgar followed her. "Justin seems like a very upstanding young man. I know your mother has worked with him over the years with her animal shelter charities. She thinks very highly of him."

Instead of facing Edgar, she concentrated on finding the perfect place to put the angel ornament on the tree.

"Yes, Mother has told me," Ava said.

"And you don't agree?" Edgar asked.

"I've never met anyone like him." Ava chose her words carefully. "He's driven, dedicated, smart, and kind. He's passionate about what he does. He always seems to find a way to make things better, and he always finds a way to make me laugh…" She smiled as she hung the angel. "But what I like best is that he doesn't care that I'm a princess. He sees the real me, not just the tiara."

Edgar smiled and nodded. "Those are all very admirable traits, wouldn't you agree?"

"Yes," Ava said. "They are." She turned to face Edgar. "I know what you're doing."

"But do you know what *you're* doing?" Edgar asked. "I think you two would make a great team."

Ava took a deep breath and gave in. "Edgar, how I feel doesn't matter. Justin lives in a different world, a different country. Once he's done training Stormy, he's going back to New York, to work with his father."

Saying the words out loud made it real. The weight of it hit Ava hard, making her heart ache.

"And you know very few people can handle our royal life," Ava continued. "And Justin, he's more of a rule breaker than a royal rule follower. I don't see how it could work, even if I wanted it to. I'm afraid there's no fairy-tale ending in our story.

"You're an inventor," Edgar said. "Use the brilliant imagination of yours and I'm sure you can figure out something. We all write our own stories, how yours ends is up to you…"

Ava twisted her watch around her wrist, thinking about how her whole life had felt like a story already written. Duty had dictated her path, and following it had always given her a sense of security. But stepping off that path into the unknown, where nothing was guaranteed? That scared her more than she wanted to admit.

"I'm sorry if I overstepped," Edgar said. "We just all want you to be happy."

"It's okay, Edgar. I appreciate your concern," Ava said. "I've just never put my happiness first or really thought about what would make me happy."

She gave him a quick hug. "Thank you for always being here for me." When she stepped back she looked around the room. "Now, I need to focus on making sure our Christmas Eve party is a success because a lot of charities are counting on us That's what my father wanted, and I'm going to do everything I can to make that happen."

❄ ❄ ❄

As Ava worked side by side with her mother party planning, dealing with the different chefs, caterers, florists, and musicians, they were both surprised at how effectively and efficiently they were able to work together.

While Ava prided herself on making sure every last detail was taken care of, she had to admit she was impressed by her mother's fresh, creative ideas—especially the way she kept their cherished royal traditions with also having some modern, magical moments.

One idea from her mother in particular felt especially brilliant. It didn't require extra time or money, yet it added a touch of fairy-tale elegance. She had arranged for a beautiful photo area to be set up, featuring one of the sparkling tiaras from their royal collection, where guests could try it on and get photographed.

Ava could already imagine the joy on their faces. For a brief moment, they wouldn't just be guests at a royal party—they'd be part of something truly special, stepping into a storybook memory they could cherish for years to come.

Ava was especially touched when her mother let her pick the tiara that would be used. She had chosen the one that had been her favorite as a child. It was covered with dazzling diamonds and emeralds. It was one of the more extravagant and ornate tiaras her mother had that had belonged to her grandmother. She also loved the story behind how it had been given to her mother at Christmas as a present from her parents.

They were just finalizing the details with the caterers when her mother brought her a glass of champagne.

"Where did you get this?" Ava asked, surprised.

"I have my connections," her mother said with a bright smile as she clinked her glass to Ava's. "To a job well done."

"I'll drink to that, and to you. You've been amazing to work with."

Her mother smiled. "See what you've been missing all these years?"

They shared a laugh.

"But seriously, thank you for allowing me to help. I can't remember the last time I enjoyed myself so much."

"We couldn't have done it without you," Ava said and meant it.

"Since we're done here, I think we should go upstairs and start getting ready. I have a few surprises for you."

"Really" Ava asked with a laugh. "I don't know if I can handle any more surprises from you."

Her mother smiled back at her. "This is a good surprise, I promise. I've brought you several dresses from Paris. Celine designed them just for you, for the party!"

"I had a dress I was going to wear," Ava started, but stopped when she saw the disappointment on her mother's face. "But who could resist a Celine original, right?"

Her mother's face lit up with joy. "Right!"

"You go ahead, and I'll be there in a moment," Ava said. "I just need to get ahold of Henry."

Her mother's smile faded. "You still haven't heard back from him?"

"I did," Ava said. "He sent one quick text saying he'd talk to me tonight, but I told him I needed to talk to him *before* the party. It's critical."

When her mother arched an eyebrow but didn't say anything, Ava knew it would be best to drop the topic. She didn't need to give her mother even more reason to not like Henry.

She gave her mother a quick hug. "I'll see you soon."

❋ ❋ ❋

Ava entered her bedroom and exhaled slowly. This had always been her sanctuary, her peaceful escape. For the decor, she'd chosen soothing shades of ivory for a clean, classic look that contrasted beautifully with her traditional mahogany furniture, including some priceless royal family heirlooms.

But right now, all she felt was anxious as she left Henry another voice message.

"Hi Henry, it's Ava again. I really wanted to talk to you *before* the party to tell you this. I hate leaving it on a message, but you need to know…"

She took a deep breath before she continued.

"I know I told you earlier my mother approved for you to propose tonight, but something has come up…there has been a change of plans I need to update you on. I'm sorry, but you can't propose tonight. Please call me back right away."

Ava hung up, hating that she'd had to leave a voice message about him not being able to propose. She knew they'd been planning it for months and he wasn't going to take the news well. That was why she'd wanted to tell him in person, or at least during a phone conversation, not in a voice message.

"Well, maybe this will get you to call me back," she said to herself.

She walked over to her fireplace and added the Santa photo with her mother to her collection of photos with her father.

Smiling, she then turned to her attention to her antique dresser. At first glance, it looked like a regular piece of bedroom furniture until Ava tapped the side of the dresser twice. Suddenly, the top of the dresser slid open, revealing a secret compartment of stunning tiaras that slowly rose up about twelve inches high.

"I know you were one of my first inventions, but you're still a favorite," Ava said to the dresser as she picked up a stunning diamond-and-pearl tiara.

When her phone buzzed with a text, she eagerly put the tiara down. "Henry, finally!"

But when she checked her phone, the text wasn't from Henry…it was from Justin.

*Black or red bow tie for Stormy?*

Ava laughed when she saw Justin had sent different adorable photos of Stormy modeling bow ties in both colors.

She texted back.

*Red. We'll match.*

Justin responded.

*Done! Everything going okay?*

Ava smiled as she texted Justin back.

*It's great. Thanks for asking.*

She couldn't help but wish Henry had been as considerate about checking in with her, knowing how important this party was to her, especially when she'd been trying to reach him.

She went back to studying her tiaras, which sparkled from the light of the crystal chandelier hanging above them.

"Okay, which one of you beauties wants to go to a party?"

❄ ❄ ❄

As the sun set over the castle, Ava stood in her mother's bedroom in front of a gold-gilded mirror, studying her reflection. She was wearing a dazzling red cocktail dress with a stunning ruby-and-diamond tiara and matching jewelry.

"That's my favorite," her mother said, clapping her hands, delighted. She was wearing an ivory silk robe.

Ava self-consciously adjusted the neckline. "Are you sure it's not too much?"

"You look perfect!" her mom said.

Ava turned and faced her mother. "I have something to tell you."

"Oh my, you suddenly look very serious," her mother said. "Is everything all right?"

"It will be," Ava said, still looking worried. "I hope…You know I've been trying to get ahold of Henry."

"Yes."

"And you know, before you left for Paris, we wanted to make sure we had your permission for him to propose at the party," Ava continued.

A flicker of concern crossed her mother's face. "Yes, you were very insistent about it."

"And you told me we couldn't get engaged yet, and that we had to wait until Valentine's Day…"

Her mother took her hand. "Yes. I'm sorry, but I was trying to do anything I could to stall you—"

"I know," Ava said. "But I told Henry you gave your permission for him to propose at the Christmas party tonight."

"What?!" her mother exclaimed as she dropped Ava's hand. "But I was very clear—"

"I know," Ava said, cringing. "He was pressuring me, and I didn't want to let him down."

The queen took a deep breath. "Are you saying you want to me to give my permission now, so he can propose tonight? I will if this is what you really want."

"No," Ava said. "It's okay. You don't need you to do that. I just told Henry he can't propose tonight."

Her mother's eyes grew huge with hope. "You did? How did he take it?"

Ava shrugged. "I don't know. I wanted to tell him in person, but I never got a chance, so I had to leave it on a voice message."

Her mother winced.

"I know," Ava said. "I hated doing that but there was nothing else I could do."

"No, you did the right thing," her mother said. "He had to know before the party."

"Exactly."

Her mother suddenly looked nervous. "So," she started. "Does this mean you want to get engaged on Valentine's Day?"

"No," Ava said. "This means I don't want to get engaged to Henry at all. I'm not going to marry him, Mother. You were right—I don't love him. He doesn't love me. I want more than just a business arrangement. If I'm going to be the best person I can be to rule our country I need someone by my side to support me and love me, just like I love them."

Ecstatic, her mother's face lit up with joy as she threw her arms around her. "This is the best news ever! I'm so happy for you!"

Ava couldn't help but laugh. "You have to be the only mother in the world who would celebrate her daughter breaking up with a duke."

"So, does this mean you and Justin—"

Ava held up both hands to stop her mother. "Mother, stop. I can't even think about that until I handle this."

# Chapter 35

Vailgate Castle was lit up like a Christmas fairy tale as limousines and luxury cars lined up to drop off elegant party guests who were dressed to impress.

As people walked down a luxurious red carpet, they were greeted by the jolly old-world Santa who was at the Christmas tree farm. He was wishing everyone Merry Christmas as they entered the castle.

As soon as you stepped into the castle's Grand Hall, you could hear a chamber orchestra playing "Carol of the Bells," creating a mesmerizing and regal atmosphere that was perfect for the spectacular, festive setting.

The first thing guests saw when they entered the Grand Hall was the jaw-dropping new thirty-foot Christmas tree that was glittering with even more sparkling lights, placed exactly five inches apart, and dazzling ornaments. All the Christmas decorations in the room sparkled brilliantly beneath the hundreds of white twinkling lights that were strung overhead.

A master of ceremonies and a royal trumpeter appeared at the entrance.

With a triumphant flourish, the trumpet burst into a regal fanfare, signaling that the night's festivities were about to begin, capturing everyone's attention.

The master of ceremonies spoke in a deep, rich, booming voice.

"Ladies and gentlemen, may I have your attention, please? It is my honor to present Her Majesty, Queen Kathleen of Skydovia, and Her Royal Highness, Princess Ava of Skydovia."

A hush fell over the crowd as the doors opened, revealing the queen and Princess Ava arm in arm.

The queen's emerald-green gown, along with her matching royal jewels and tiara, shimmered under the lights, exuding regal grace. Beside her, Ava looked equally stunning in a sparkling red dress, paired with a ruby-and-diamond tiara and jewelry.

Together, they created a striking contrast—the perfect pairing of holiday elegance and royal sophistication.

Ava's eyes darted anxiously around the crowd.

"Are you looking for Justin?" her mother whispered.

"No, Henry," Ava said. "He still hasn't responded."

"Well, there's Justin," her mother said with a radiant smile as she nodded toward where Justin was standing on the sidelines with Stormy.

Ava's eyes flew to him, and her heart raced when he winked and adjusted his red bowtie before pointing to Stormy, who was also wearing a red bowtie.

She laughed, unable to resist either of them.

"Are you ready?" her mother asked.

"Born ready," Ava said, smiling back at her mother.

As the orchestra began to play, they stepped forward in perfect unison, their presence commanding the room as the guests bowed in respect. They stopped next to the Christmas tree.

The orchestra fell silent.

Her mother looked around the room, smiling at everyone. "My daughter, Princess Ava, and I want to thank you all for being part of our family's Christmas tradition and helping to support so many charities that change lives." She turned to her daughter.

Ava smiled. "We promised you a big announcement tonight…" When she glanced over at Justin and Stormy, Justin smiled, giving her a thumbs up. "And we have one."

Her mother, excited, continued, "We'd like to introduce a new, very special member to our royal family." Her mother motioned for Justin to bring Stormy up.

But as Justin moved forward, his path was suddenly blocked by Henry, who stormed up to Ava.

Ava froze, shocked. "Henry, what are you doing?"

Justin and the queen looked equally stunned.

Everyone gasped when Henry got down on one knee in front of Ava and took her hand.

"Henry, no!" Ava said, horrified. She tried to pull her hand away, but Henry held on tight.

When the crowd applauded, Stormy started growling and barking at Henry.

Suddenly a group of paparazzi surrounded them, taking pictures and blinding Ava with the flash. She wanted to run, but Henry squeezed her hand tight and started speaking in a voice that was loud enough so everyone could hear.

"Your Royal Highness, Princess of Skydovia, it would be my greatest honor to be part of this royal family you've invited me into as we follow another Skydovia royal tradition with this Christmas Eve proposal," Henry said proudly.

Ava felt like she was going to pass out as Henry crammed a ring with a gumball-sized diamond onto her finger. When she tried to pull her hand away, Henry shot her a look.

It wasn't loving.

It held a threat.

Ava's blood ran cold. She knew she was trapped as more photographers swarmed around them.

She frantically looked around for Justin. When their eyes met, she saw his pain. It broke her heart when she saw him hand Stormy's leash to her mother and walked away.

"Justin," she tried to call out to him but was silenced when Henry kissed her.

As more paparazzi surrounded them, Ava could no longer see her mother or anyone else. All she could see were camera lenses in her face and Henry's menacing smile.

❄ ❄ ❄

As a light snow started to fall over Vailgate Castle, there were no limousines or cars left at the front entrance.

Everyone was gone.

The party was over.

Inside the Library, Ava furiously yanked off the engagement ring Henry had forced on her finger. "Here. Take this. I don't want it—"

Henry refused to take it. "We can get you another ring."

Ava gave him an incredulous look. "Didn't you get my message? I told you we couldn't get engaged tonight. I've been trying to call and text you, and you just disappeared."

"Oh, I got your messages," Henry said calmly.

"Then how could you do this and bring the paparazzi with you?!" Ava demanded. "My security told me you brought all the photographers to the party and told them I authorized it. Why would you do this knowing how the paparazzi has repeatedly tried to destroy this family?"

When Henry smiled, it sent a chill down her spine.

"I thought you'd rather have our engagement photos going viral than these pictures," he said as he held out his phone.

When Ava saw a photo on his phone of her and Justin kissing in the park, she recoiled.

"How did you…?! This isn't what it looks like," Ava insisted. "This kiss was Justin protecting me from the press, something you should be doing—"

Henry held up his hand to silence her. "Stop!"

She flinched.

"None of this matters," he continued, smugly. "I don't care what happened between you two. We just got officially engaged in front of everyone. We're getting married, just like we've always planned. Your father trusted me to make sure the monarchy was protected, and that's what I'm doing."

Stunned, Ava shook her head. She couldn't believe she hadn't seen this side of Henry before, but now it was all so crystal clear.

She locked eyes with him. "Henry, this isn't your decision, or my father's. It's *mine*. This is *my* choice. *My* life. You only see us as a…business deal…a job—"

"Yes, one I take very seriously," Henry fired back.

Ava stepped toward him. "But you've forgotten, I'm the boss."

She slapped the engagement ring against his chest.

"And you're fired. We're done!"

Henry's eyes flashed with anger. "You can't just…*fire* me. I have pictures of you kissing…an American! Do you know what the press would do with this?"

Ava's eyes narrowed. "Are you trying to threaten me—blackmail me? You really think that's going to convince me to marry you? This just makes me even more sure that I'm doing the right thing."

"You won't do this. You won't risk a scandal," Henry said smugly.

Ava glared back at him. "Get out of my castle. Now!"

❅ ❅ ❅

The next morning, Ava woke up exhausted. She'd hardly slept at all. Her mind kept replaying everything that had happened the night before.

After Henry's proposal, she'd been in such shock that she just stood there, numb, until her mother had stepped forward and told the press and all the guests they'd be answering questions tomorrow, but for tonight, it was a celebration, and everyone was invited to enjoy the party.

When the orchestra had started again, Ava had tried to leave the room, but Henry, in front of all the press, had insisted on a dance first.

Before she knew what was happening, they had been dancing, and the paparazzi had been photographing their every move.

She clutched her stomach, feeling sick just thinking about it.

Henry had proven himself to be a master manipulator.

She looked out her window and saw all the news vans and cars parked in front of the castle. "They're all here," she muttered to herself as she walked over to her desk and picked up the newspapers and tabloids Edgar had brought earlier.

Her engagement was front-page news. In every picture she looked shocked, like a deer caught in the headlights.

She cringed reading the tabloid headlines. They were big, bold, and brutal.

ICE PRINCESS MELTS! PRINCESS AVA IS ENGAGED
PRINCESS AVA FINALLY PUTS A RING ON IT
PICKY PRINCESS SAYS YES

Her disastrous engagement to Henry was the last thing she wanted to deal with on Christmas Day, but she knew the longer she waited to face the media, the worse it would get.

To face her press firing squad, she'd chosen another classic red pantsuit, the one that always made her feel powerful.

This morning, she needed all the help she could get.

As she left her room, she checked her phone. Her heart sank when she saw that Justin hadn't responded to the text she'd sent last night, asking if they could talk.

"I don't blame you for not getting back to me," she whispered to herself. "I wouldn't want to get caught up in this mess, either."

❄ ❄ ❄

In the entrance of the Grand Hall, Ava, the queen, and Stormy all watched as TV news crews and photographers gathered around the Christmas tree, waiting for them to make a statement.

When Ava touched the watch on her wrist, her mother's face lit up when she noticed.

"You're wearing the new watch I got you from Paris," her mother said, surprised.

Ava nodded. "Yes. I will always cherish Father's watch as part of my past, but this watch is the one I want for my future."

Her mother touched her heart. "You read the inscription."

Ava nodded and gave her mother a hug. "I love you."

"I love you, too," her mother replied, fighting back tears.

Ava took a deep, shaky breath. "Okay, let's do this." When she started walking toward the press, her mother reached out and grabbed her arm.

"Wait. Ava, are you sure you're okay to do this today? It's Christmas. We could always set this up for another time—"

"No, the longer we wait, the harder it will be," Ava said. "I want to get this over with. This is something I have to do. I'm done hiding and letting the paparazzi or anyone else rule my life. Henry thought he could use the press to blackmail me into marrying him. He thought I'd never risk a scandal. He was wrong."

"Okay, it's your call," her mother said, but she sounded worried. "I'll support whatever you want to do."

When her mother offered Ava her hand, she gratefully took it, and they approached the Christmas tree together.

Everyone in the press stopped talking.

*The calm before the storm,* Ava thought wearily.

She jumped when a flash from a cameraman testing the lighting blinded her. She let go of her mother's hand and gripped her hands together tightly to try and stop them from shaking.

As she glanced around at the media, she didn't see any faces. Everything was a blur. But she saw all the cameras pointing at her. She started to panic as her entire body began to shake.

She cleared her throat, hoping her voice wouldn't sound as terrified as she felt.

"Thank you all for coming on Christmas morning for this press conference," Ava started, but before she could continue, she was cut off by reporters firing questions at her.

"When are you marrying the duke?!" one reporter asked.

"Where will the wedding and honeymoon be?!"

"Why aren't you wearing your ring?!" another reporter jumped in.

In a frenzy, everyone gathered closer to take pictures of her hand.

Feeling claustrophobic, Ava swayed, feeling like she would faint. She was grateful when her mother stepped forward.

"Please, everyone, take a step back," the queen requested.

The press immediately stopped taking pictures and moved back.

The queen smiled. "Thank you. We invited you here this morning to answer your questions, and that's what we're going to do, but we'll only be taking questions one at a time. You will all have your chance, I assure you."

Ava gulped and nodded.

The queen pointed to an older gentleman in a tweed suit. "Charlie, do you have a question?"

Charlie looked surprised and pleased to be singled out to go first. "Yes, Your Majesty, thank you very much. My question is actually for you. How do you feel about having Duke Henry as your new son-in-law?"

When Ava saw her mother's eyes flash with anger, she quickly stepped forward. She knew how furious she was with Henry, and that anything she said would make headlines.

"I will be the one answering questions today," Ava said. "And let me start with the question about when I'll be marrying Henry."

The press eagerly leaned in…

# Chapter 36

In New York City, as Justin hurried down the street toward his parents' brownstone, his mind was thousands of miles away, back in Skydovia.

What had happened at the Christmas party still stung.

Ava had said the big announcement was going to be about Stormy becoming their first royal pet. She'd never once mentioned Henry proposing. Now, not only did he feel deceived and blindsided, but he was embarrassed to have even let himself hope, for a moment, that Ava could be feeling what he was feeling, and they could have a chance together.

If he had known about the proposal, he could have at least mentally prepared himself. Then again, if he was honest, had he known about the proposal, he wouldn't have gone to the party in the first place.

It was especially crushing because he had secretly hoped she was starting to feel the same sparks he was. Now, he wondered if he'd just made up their connection in his head. He would never know, because he'd left Skydovia before talking to her.

As soon as he'd left the party, he'd booked the next flight back to New York. He felt bad leaving before finishing his job with Stormy. He had never run out on a job before, but then he'd never fallen in love with a princess before, either.

He was grateful that when he'd called the queen from the airport, she'd been very understanding when he rambled on about a family emergency he needed to get home for. She'd also been very gracious when he'd promised to send her recommendations for people he trusted to finish training Stormy. She'd told him to take his time and to focus on his family because being there for loved ones was what mattered the most.

He glanced at his phone and saw Ava had sent him another text asking to talk. He deleted it instantly. He didn't see the point. She'd already made a fool of him once. He wasn't going to let it happen again.

When he got to his parents' place, he took a deep breath and told himself he was done thinking about Ava. He knew he needed to put her and Skydovia behind him. Because no matter what he'd wanted or hoped for, the reality was she was a princess marrying a duke.

When he knocked on his parents' door, it only took a few seconds for his mom to answer. When she saw him, her expression went from looking surprised to confused to ecstatic.

"Justin! What are you doing here?!"

Justin held out his arms. "Surprise! Merry Christmas!"

"I can't believe it," Justin's mom exclaimed as they hugged. "It's my Christmas wish come true! I'm so happy the queen gave you time off—"

"She didn't," Justin said as he walked in. "I quit."

❄ ❄ ❄

A beautiful Douglas fir Christmas tree sparkled in the bay window as Justin opened presents with his parents in their stylish but still cozy living room.

When Justin inhaled the tree's fresh evergreen scent, it reminded him of Ava's Christmas tree in the Grand Hall.

*Stop it*, he told himself. But it seemed no matter how hard he tried, his thoughts kept drifting back to her.

To try and distract himself, he grabbed another dark chocolate peppermint donut and took a big bite to try. His mother always made these donuts for him every Christmas as one of their holiday traditions. His favorite part was the peppermint icing covered with crushed candy canes. But right now the candy canes were only reminding him of the picture of Stormy at the candy cane hut at the Christmas market.

"Here, open this one next," his mother said, jarring him back to the present. She was smiling brightly. "It's really more from your dad than me, but I know you're going to love it."

"I hope so," Justin's dad said as he gave his wife a loving look.

Justin took off the large silver satin bow and ripped open the shiny silver foil paper, revealing a box underneath. When he opened the box, his eyes grew huge as he took out a black leather bag. It was a deluxe veterinarian tool kit, filled with all the essential tools and supplies needed to diagnose, treat, and care for animals.

"Wow, this is really amazing," Justin said. "I don't have anything like this." He didn't mention the reason was that he only carried carry-on luggage when he traveled, so everything he had was small and compact.

His dad proudly beamed back at him. "Only the best for my son and my new business partner!"

"That's right," his mom agreed. "Your dad is so excited to start working with you."

Justin forced a smile. "Thank you both. It's…top-of-the-line, for sure."

The song "God Save the Queen" suddenly started blaring from Justin's pocket.

"What on earth is that?" Justin's mom asked, laughing.

Justin grabbed his cell phone. "Sorry, it's my phone. I have an alert set for when the queen is trying to reach me, so I don't miss anything."

His parents gathered around him while he checked his phone.

"Did the queen of Skydovia just call you?" his dad asked, sounding amazed.

Justin laughed. "No, she sent me a text."

"What does it say?" his mom asked, trying to see it.

Justin looked perplexed. "I don't know. She sent me a video."

"Does she always send videos?" Justin's dad asked.

Justin shook his head. "No, never."

"Play it," his mom insisted. "She's probably wishing you Merry Christmas."

But when Justin played the video, it wasn't the queen. He saw it was a video clip from the news conference Ava just held.

Justin's eyes grew huge. "I can't believe this…"

"What?" his parents asked at the same time.

"It's Ava. The princess. She's talking to the press, and she hates the press."

"Shhhh," his mom playfully scolded him. "I can't hear what she's saying. Can you please turn it up?"

Justin turned up the volume, and they all watched Ava address the press.

"I'm here to set the record straight," Ava said. She took a deep breath and held her head high. "I am not marrying the duke. Not now or ever."

Justin jumped up, excited, pumping his fists into the air. "Yes! She did it! Way to go, Princess!"

"Did what?" Justin's dad asked, confused.

"She just got her life back," Justin answered with a huge smile.

# Chapter 37

In Manhattan, outside Justin's dad's business, the Erikson Animal Clinic, there was a charming Christmas tree with animal-themed ornaments that matched the clinic's colorful mural showcasing joyful pets.

The sign on the door said *Closed for a Private Party – December 27th.*

Inside, the clinic's lobby was buzzing with a lively celebration. Clients had been invited to bring their pets. There were dogs, cats, birds, and even an adorable potbellied pig wearing a giant red velvet bow.

As Justin took it all in, his mom came over and put her arm around him.

"Thank you for doing this for your dad. He's so excited to announce this new partnership."

Justin nodded. "I know. He's planned for this for as long as I can remember. He's worked hard to expand the clinic. He deserves this."

"You're a very good son."

"That's because I was raised by wonderful parents," Justin said as he hugged his mom.

Then they both laughed as they watched his dad take a selfie with the potbellied pig while several dogs raced by them, barking.

"Watch out!" his mom warned as a bird flew by, almost hitting him.

Justin jumped out of the way just in time. "Is it always this crazy around here?"

His mom smiled brightly. "Yes, isn't it wonderful?"

Justin laughed.

His dad caught his eye and waved him over.

"I gotta go. The boss is calling," Justin said to his mom.

She smiled proudly. "I bet your dad wants more pictures with you."

"Do you think we'll have to include the pig?" Justin asked, laughing.

"Would you rather we have a horse?"

"No!" Justin exclaimed in mock horror. "No horses, please."

They shared a laugh.

"You know what, I take that back. Today, I'll do whatever Dad wants," Justin said. "This is his day."

His mom kissed him on the cheek. "And it's your day, too. I'm happy for you. I love you."

"Thanks, Mom. I love you, too."

# Chapter 38

On New Year's Eve at Vailgate Castle, a long line of limousines and luxury cars dropped off dazzling party guests dressed in spectacular costumes paying tribute to *The Great Gatsby* theme.

Inside the Grand Hall, couples were dancing to a live band playing jazzy, upbeat classics. The men impressed in vintage tuxedos, while the women sparkled in gorgeous beaded gowns that shimmered with fringe, perfectly capturing the decadence and spirit of the Roaring Twenties.

The thirty-foot Christmas tree had been reimagined with all gold-and-black Art Deco decorations, adding to the timeless theme.

Suddenly, trumpets rang out. The band stopped playing. Everyone stopped dancing.

A wave of anticipation swept through the crowd as the lights dimmed and a single spotlight illuminated the top of the Christmas tree.

Ava's heart raced. *So far, so good,* she thought.

She stood poised in a shimmering gold gown, the perfect mixture of vintage glamour and royal elegance.

Her fingers trembled slightly as she pressed the silver button on a sleek black remote control.

This was the moment of truth…

As the drummer began his dramatic drumroll, a golden, gilded, throne-like chair started slowly descending from the ceiling.

Perched regally on the throne was the queen with Stormy by her side.

The crowd gasped in awe.

The queen waved at everyone, excited. "Happy New Year's Eve!"

Thunderous applause erupted.

As friendly photographers captured the moment, Stormy barked happily, his tail wagging.

The queen laughed, pulling him closer. "You're a good boy, Stormy."

Ava breathed a sigh of relief as she watched her mother's throne descend smoothly. Even though she had tested it dozens of times herself to make sure it was safe, there was always a chance something could go wrong.

She smiled, thinking how this wild, grand entrance had, of course, been her mother's idea.

Originally, her mother had wanted to fly down from the ceiling using the harness the tree decorators had used. But when Ava had firmly vetoed that idea, together they'd come up with the plan for Ava to create a special throne her mother could safely sit on and slowly be lowered to the ground. While her mother at first grumbled that sitting in a chair wouldn't be as fun, she'd ultimately agreed after Ava had told her that this way, she could include Stormy, too.

Now, watching her mother pose effortlessly for pictures in her breathtaking gold-beaded gown, Ava marveled at how comfortable she was in front of the cameras. It amazed her how her mother seemed to blossom under the spotlight, and because she embraced the media, they adored her just as much as she enjoyed them.

When her mother had first suggested hosting a New Year's Eve party, Ava had been surprised. They'd never done one before. While her mother insisted it was something she had always wanted, Ava knew her mother was worried about her and wanted to give her another project to keep her mind off of what had happened with Henry and Justin.

With Henry, she was mad at herself for wasting so much time on him.

But Justin? That was different.

That still hurt.

She couldn't believe he'd just disappeared without saying goodbye and that now, he wasn't answering any of her texts.

As she watched her mother's throne almost touch the ground, she saw Edgar standing by to help her. Lydia was on the other side, waiting to take Stormy from her.

As soon as the throne hit the marble floor, Ava pressed the remote again—flooding the room with light.

The crowd cheered, clapped, and took more pictures.

When Lydia took Stormy from the queen and put him down on the ground, he raced straight for Ava, barking.

Ava stepped forward and held up her hand. "Stormy, no barking. Sit."

Stormy immediately obeyed. He stopped barking and sat down in front of her.

"Are you trying to take my job?"

Ava spun around.

Her breath caught.

It was Justin.

He looked more handsome than ever in his tuxedo.

Her heart pounded. "You came…"

Justin smiled, nodding. "Your invite said it was going to be an amazing party. How could I pass that up?"

"You couldn't," the queen chimed in, joining them. "This is going to be our new tradition, having a New Year's Eve party that's all about new beginnings and starting the new year with the people you love. You both deserve one, and so do I."

Ava followed her mother's gaze and nearly gasped when she saw Samuel, from Skyline Restaurant, enter the room. He was pushing a silver cart with a gigantic Chocolate Fountain Cake.

Ava's eyes widened as she watched her mother and Samuel light up the moment they saw each other.

"You two have fun," her mother said with a twinkle in her eyes, "because I know I'm going to."

And with that, her mother walked toward Samuel, beaming.

"Oh my God…" Ava whispered, shaking her head in disbelief. "It's Samuel. That's who my mother dated before my father. That's who she truly loved."

"Is this a good thing?" Justin asked, confused.

Ava studied her mother talking and laughing with Samuel. She couldn't remember the last time she'd seen her looking so happy.

"Yes," Ava said, thinking about it. "I think it's a very good thing. She deserves to finally be happy."

Justin turned back to her. "And what about you? Are you happy?"

Ava touched the new watch on her wrist as she met his gaze. "I'm working on it."

"You're wearing the watch your mother gave you," Justin said, surprised. "I hope you didn't lose your father's."

"No, it's safely put away," Ava said. "But I won't be wearing it anymore. My father's message of *Time for duty* is important, but I think my mother's message is even more important."

She carefully took off her watch and turned it over, showing him the inscription.

He read it out loud.

*"Time for love…"*

Their eyes met.

Justin smiled slowly and looked into her eyes. "I like this one."

She smiled back at him. "Me, too."

"I saw your press conference."

Ava cringed. "I was terrified."

"I couldn't tell," Justin said. "You were amazing. You looked strong. Smart. Beautiful."

Ava blushed. Her pulse quickened.

When she'd sent him the invite, she'd never expected him to actually come. She told herself inviting him would be her closure. A way for her to tell herself she tried, and then go on pretending everything was fine when her heart ached for something she couldn't have. The fact that he was actually here, standing in front of her, was still something she was trying to process.

"If I looked strong, I have you to thank for that," she said. "You were right. Hiding from the press gave them all the power. I needed to take my power back."

"Well, you sure did that," Justin said, looking impressed. "And I also saw your interview talking to kids about the importance of science and math and showing them some of the things you invented. It was very cool."

"Thank you," Ava said. "They really seemed to enjoy it and so did I. I'm looking at creating some programs to help inspire students to go after their dreams. I want them to know they can be anything and do anything they set their minds to."

"I think that's amazing," Justin said. "As a princess and future queen, children will look up to you. You could be a great role model for them. We need more positive and empowering people like you in the world."

Ava smiled, touched. "Thank you. I will do the best I can."

"I know you will," Justin said with a warm smile.

"I invented something for you," Ava said.

"Really?" Justin asked, surprised. "What?"

"You said you needed to be cloned to help more animals, right?"

Justin laughed. "Yes…should I be worried?"

Ava smiled back at him. "No, hopefully you will like it. It's a work in progress. A pet matchmaker app I'm calling 'VidPet.' Shelters can have QR codes for each animal that people can scan for videos showing their unique personalities and get special training tips."

"This is genius," Justin said, impressed. "It will help so much. I can't believe you did this. Wait until I tell my dad and everyone else."

"How is working with your father?"

"I took your advice and told him I don't want to be a full-time vet," Justin said.

"Really? How did he take it?" Ava asked.

Justin grinned. "It went really well, especially after I hooked him up with a friend from college who is a perfect fit to work with him in his clinic."

"So, what does that mean for you?"

"It means that I can get back to what I love," Justin said. "That's why I came here…"

Ava's heart skipped a beat.

He looked into her eyes. "Because Stormy, clearly, still needs some work."

Ava smiled, playing along. "He does. He needs *a lot* of work."

When they glanced at Stormy, he tilted his head, listening to them. He was sitting calmly, perfectly behaved, acting like a *little angel.*

"But it might take some time," Justin said. "A lot of time…"

Ava stepped closer and looked into his eyes. Nothing in her life had ever felt so right. "That's okay," she said. "Because someone once told me things that really matter are worth the wait…and worth running toward once you find them."

When Ava kissed him, she found something she hadn't even known she was searching for, something she never wanted to live without again.

As Justin deepened the kiss, Stormy raced around them, barking with joy.

Ava pulled back when she saw flashes from photographers taking pictures of them. She looked at Justin, smiled, and kissed him again.

She wasn't letting anyone get in the way of her happily ever after.

As they kept kissing, Ava knew this was the beginning of everything…

Thank You For Reading
***A Ruff Royal Christmas***

It would mean so much if you could take a moment
and leave a review on Amazon, BookBub, Goodreads, B&N,
on social media, or your favorite place. Reviews
make such a difference and help other readers
find the stories they'll love the most.
Thank you so much!

**My Free Gift for You!**

I've created a special FREE downloadable DIY *Christmas
Camp Guide* that I update every year with new festive and fun
content for you! This includes exclusive recipes and holiday
activities from all my Christmas movies and novels.
As a special bonus, you'll also receive some of my beautiful
coloring book pages from my bestselling coloring book
*Color Your Christmas Dreams* for adults!

**Download Here**

# Acknowledgments

Everyone loves a comeback story—I know I do. But I never expected to be the main character in one. When I broke my hand on Christmas Eve hanging stockings, writing became impossible for months. Sure, I could dictate emails and small notes, but that clunky process didn't mesh with how my brain works. There was no way I was finishing a novel for 2024. That's why finally completing this one means so much—I've never been more grateful for the ability to write, something I once took for granted.

None of this would have been possible without my amazing team, who make my books better in every way. To my brilliant editor, Elizabeth Mazer, and my wonderful copy editor, Mira S. Park—your dedication, patience, and keen eye elevate my stories beyond what I ever imagined. To my interior designer, Ramesh Kumar Pitchai, your work brings my books to life in ways I never could have dreamed. And to the incredibly talented cover artist, Kristen Ingebretson—thank you for always pushing creative boundaries with me to capture the Christmas magic on every cover.

To my legal eagles, Neville Johnson and Phillip L. Rosen—your unwavering support lets me soar. Thank you for always having my back and guiding me forward.

To my first and favorite "editing elves," my moms, Lao Schaler and Kathy Bezold—your honest feedback, insight, and belief in me mean everything. You read every word and always tell me exactly what works and what needs more love. I couldn't do this without you.

To my fellow writers in the Morning Howl—where I host 5 A.M. to 7 A.M. writing sessions three times a week—Birgit, Todd, Celina, Gary, Kawan,

Ambra, Vicki, and anyone else who pops in—thank you for showing up, cheering me on, and reminding me that the writing journey doesn't have to be so solitary. This novel exists because of those early mornings, shared struggles, and victories, big and small.

To my "stars in the sky"—John, Heather, Tim, Lee, Elise, and my beloved grandparents, Pat and Walter Crane, and Irene and Harry P. Schaler—I miss you every day, but you are always in my heart, guiding me forward.

And finally, to the incredible animal rescue community, your work changes lives, both human and animal. *A Ruff Royal Christmas* is my heartfelt thank-you to you. I hope this story reminds you just how important you are.

Wishing you a heathy, happy, and hopeful holiday season!

# Meet Karen Schaler

**KAREN SCHALER** is a three-time Emmy Award-winning storyteller, screenwriter, bestselling author, journalist, and national TV host. Known for her uplifting, feel-good, and empowering romantic comedies and dramas, Karen has written eight beloved Christmas novels and holiday movies for Netflix, Lifetime, and Hallmark, including the Netflix sensation *A Christmas Prince* and Hallmark's beloved *Christmas Camp*. She also wrote the Audible Original *Once Upon a Christmas Carol*, which became an instant Top 10 Audible Bestseller.

Sharing her love for Christmas, Karen is bringing her *Christmas Camp* Hallmark movie and books to life by creating magical *Christmas Camp* experiences for grown-ups that she personally hosts at resorts, hotels, conferences, and destinations around the world—where you'll feel like you're starring in your own holiday movie!

These unforgettable immersive experiences are an extension of Karen's *Travel Therapy*® brand, where she has traveled to more than sixty-eight countries, reporting on the most inspiring and empowering trips to take based on what you're going through in life. As the creator and host of *Travel Therapy TV*, airing globally, Karen showcases transformative travel experiences. No matter what she's writing, Karen's stories are always uplifting, empowering, and filled with heart and hope. Be sure to visit www.karenschaler.com for your exclusive, free *Karen Schaler's Christmas Camp Guide*.

**Free Zoom Chats with Karen, VIP Newsletter, and Special Deals!**

You can also sign up for my VIP newsletter at www.karenschaler.com.
I only send it out a few times a year when I have special deals,
the dates for my free Zoom chats, sneak peeks of my latest projects,
and giveaways of free books to share.

**Let's Stay Connected!**

I love staying connected with all of you! Please post pictures with your books
with #ARuffRoyalChristmas and tag me, and I'll repost as many as I can!

FACEBOOK: @KarenSchalerOfficial

TIKTOK: @KarenSchaler

INSTAGRAM: @TravelTherapy

THREADS: @KarenSchaler

BLUESKY: @karenschaler.bsky.social

WEBSITE: www.karenschaler.com

STANSTORE: https://stan.store/karenschaler

ETSY STORE: etsy.com/shop/WritingTips4Success

# More Novels by Karen Schaler

*Every Day is Christmas, 2023*

*Love Always, Christmas, 2022*

*A Royal Christmas Fairy Tale, 2021*

*Christmas Ever After, 2020*

*Finding Christmas, 2019*

*Christmas Camp, 2018*

# Karen Schaler's Magical Adult Coloring Books

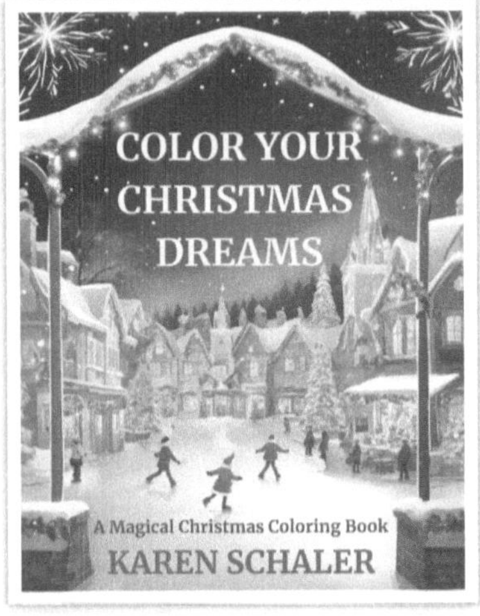

*Color Your Christmas Dreams*

*Color Your Travel Dreams*

120-pages of relaxing, calming coloring pages
paired with inspiring famous quotes

**Find Karen's Books Here**

# Karen Schaler's Full Cast Audible Original

## Top 10 Audible Bestseller

### *Once Upon a Christmas Carol*

Celebrate the magic and music of the season with this scripted holiday romance featuring award-winning actors and musicians by Emmy Award-winning writer Karen Schaler!

# Karen's New Etsy Store for Readers & Writers!

I'm so excited to share with you my new Etsy store, WritingTips4Success, where I've personally created and curated unique gift ideas to inspire and empower readers and writers. It also *includes* my bestselling writing guides and checklists. I can't wait to hear what you think!

## RECIPES & FESTIVE ACTIVITIES!

A holiday tradition I love sharing with you started when I wrote my debut novel, *Christmas Camp*, inspired by my *Christmas Camp* Hallmark movie. I included recipes and activities from the movie and book in the novel. You all told me you liked it so much that now I do this for all my books as a fun and festive way for us to connect with the story and each other! I hope you try some of these out, and I can't wait to see when you share your creations on social media using the hashtags: #ARuffRoyalChristmas and #ChristmasCamp.

For more original Christmas recipes and holiday activities, be sure to download my FREE *Karen Schaler's DIY Christmas Camp Guide* at www.karenschaler.com, which I update every year with new content! Enjoy!

*A Ruff Royal Christmas*
# Skydovia Christmas Butter Balls

This is fast and simple recipe, inspired by Skydovia's Christmas market in my story. I hope it becomes one of your new family favorites. The best part, besides being delicious, is that it's super easy to make during the hectic holiday season.

**Makes:** 24 cookies

## Ingredients:
- 2 ¼ cups all-purpose flour (spooned & leveled)
- ¼ teaspoon sea salt
- 1 cup unsalted butter softened but still cool
- ½ cup powdered sugar for dough & ½ cup for rolling after baked
- 1 teaspoon vanilla extract
- 1 cup finely chopped walnut

## Instructions:
- Preheat to 375°F (190°C).
- Line a cookie sheet with parchment paper (not greased).
- Spoon flour into a measuring cup so it doesn't get too packed down and level off the top with a knife.
- In medium bowl, add flour and salt and whisk together.
- In large bowl, use hand mixer to beat butter and powdered sugar until smooth. Add vanilla extract.
- Gradually add flour mixture to large bowl. Mix only until combined. Do not overmix.
- Stir in walnuts.
- Roll dough into 1-inch balls and place on the cookie sheet 2 inches apart.
- Bake for 8-10 minutes until bottoms are lightly golden (tops will stay pale).
- Let cool 5 minutes before removing from cookie sheet.
- Roll in a bowl of ½ cup powdered sugar.

**OPTIONAL:**

- I let them sit for 5 minutes and then roll again for a snowy effect.
- You can add red and green sprinkles to the powdered sugar for an extra festive look.
- You can add finely crushed candy canes to the powdered sugar.

**KAREN'S TIP:**

- If your cookies spread, avoid overmixing the dough and refrigerate dough for at least one hour before baking.

## *A Ruff Royal Christmas*
## Dark Chocolate Peppermint Bliss Donuts

In our story Justin's mom makes these blissful donuts every Christmas as one of their holiday traditions. If you've never made donuts before, don't worry. I made this an easy recipe so everyone can enjoy making these delicious donuts that you'll want to make part of your Christmas traditions, too!

Makes: 16 regular-size donuts

### Ingredients for the Batter:
- 1½ cups all-purpose flour
- ⅓ cup unsweetened dark cocoa powder (preferably Dutch processed)
- 1 teaspoon baking powder
- ½ teaspoon baking soda
- ¼ teaspoon sea salt
- ¾ cup dark brown sugar (pack firmly into measuring cup)
- 2 large eggs—room temperature
- ¾ cup unsweetened almond or whole milk room temperature. Add a splash more if batter is too thick.
- ⅓ cup melted butter (should be liquid)
- 1 teaspoon almond extract
- ⅓ cup hot water (to bloom the cocoa powder and intensify chocolate flavor)

### Ingredients for Frosting:
- 1 cup powdered sugar
- ¼ cup heavy cream (you can add a little extra if you want a thinner frosting)
- ½ teaspoon peppermint extract (or adjust to taste depending on how minty you like it)
- ¼ teaspoon vanilla extract (to balance the mint flavor)
- 1 tablespoon almond or whole milk
- ¼ cup finely crushed candy canes

**Donut Instructions:**

1. Preheat oven to 350°F (175°C) and grease donut pans with real butter.
2. Mix dry ingredients in a medium bowl, whisk together the flour, cocoa powder, baking powder, baking soda, and salt. Set aside.
3. Mix wet ingredients in a large bowl, whisk together the eggs, almond milk, melted butter, and brown sugar until smooth. Stir in almond extract.
4. Add the hot water. Slowly mix in the hot water to wet mixture. This will bloom the cocoa powder when it's added for a deeper chocolate flavor.
5. Combine wet & dry ingredients. Gradually fold the dry mixture into the wet ingredients, stirring until just combined. Do not overmix.
6. If the batter feels too thick, add a little more almond milk (1 tablespoon at a time). You want it thick, but able to pipe or scoop it into your donut pans.
7. Fill the donut pan. Pipe, pour, or spoon batter into the 12 donut molds, filling each about ¾ full.
8. Bake for 10-14 minutes, or until a toothpick inserted in the center comes out clean. Watch closely, as ovens vary.
9. Let the donuts cool for 5 minutes in the pan before transferring them to a wire rack to cool completely before frosting.

**Frosting Instructions:**

1. Mix the frosting. In a medium bowl, whisk together the powdered sugar, heavy cream, peppermint extract, and vanilla extract. Add almond milk as needed to reach your desired consistency. You want it thick enough to stick to the donuts but still get a nice drip.
2. Dip the donuts. Once your donuts have cooled, dip the tops into the frosting, letting any excess drip off before placing on a cooling rack or parchment paper.
3. Place the frosted donuts on a wire rack to decorate and set.
4. Decorate by sprinkling finely crushed candy canes on top.

**KAREN'S TIPS:**

- I like to break off pieces of candy canes and put in two 1-quart plastic bags, that have been doubled up, and then use a rolling pin or hammer to crush the candy canes into a powder that includes some tiny pieces to sprinkle on top of the donuts.
- You can also double dip the donuts in frosting for added sweetness before decorating.
- I've also added a touch of green food coloring to the frosting for another festive look.
- You can also decorate with red and green sprinkles for some extra sparkle!
- Best if eaten that day but can store in airtight container in the refrigerator for up to 48 hours.

## *A Ruff Royal Christmas*
## Stormy-Approved Christmas Activity:

Here's an activity I know Stormy in our story would approve of! To make sure this treat is both delicious and safe for dogs, I consulted with a veterinarian. Many store-bought dog treats contain reported to be harmful ingredients, like Xylitol—a sugar substitute that is toxic to dogs—or dairy, which can cause digestive issues since many dogs are lactose intolerant. Even chocolate, a favorite human treat, is dangerous for dogs and can lead to serious health issues. Nutmeg is also toxic to dogs. Instead of taking risks, why not make a healthy, homemade treat yourself? I love baking these as gifts for my dog-loving friends, and they've been a hit with every pup who's tried them!

Important note: Before making any treats, please check with your veterinarian to make sure your furry friend isn't allergic to any of the ingredients.

### Stormy's Paw-sitively Delicious Dog Treats

These little dog treats, endorsed by Stormy, are bound to make tails wag! Packed with wholesome ingredients, they're as tasty as they are healthy—perfect for spoiling your pup while keeping them nourished. And the best part? They're super easy to make! For added festive fun, you can use your Christmas cookie or heart cookie cutters to show love for your precious pets! There are also a lot of great dog treat molds online if you want to go that route.

Yield: About 75 small (1.4-inch) heart-shaped treats

### Ingredients:
- 2 cups almond flour
- ¼ cup + 2 tablespoons ground flax seeds
- ¼ cup mashed blueberries (fresh or frozen)
- 1 egg
- 2 tablespoons extra virgin olive oil
- 2 tablespoons unsweetened applesauce

**Directions:**

1. Preheat oven to 350°F and line a baking sheet with parchment paper.
2. Mix dry ingredients: In a large bowl, combine almond flour and ground flax seeds.
3. Mix wet ingredients: In a separate bowl, whisk or use hand blender to mix together the mashed blueberries, egg, extra virgin olive oil, and unsweetened applesauce.
4. Combine: Pour the wet ingredients into the dry ingredients and stir until a dough forms. Dough should be slightly wet but still firm enough to roll out. If the dough feels too dry, add a tiny splash of water (1 teaspoon at a time) until it holds together but is firm enough to roll out. If it feels too wet, add almond flour (1 teaspoon at a time) until it's the right consistency.
5. Roll out the dough: Lightly dust a work surface with almond flour and roll the dough to about ¼-inch thickness. It should roll out easily without sticking.
6. Cut out shapes: Use 1.4-inch heart-shaped cookie cutters to cut out small treats.
7. Put on baking sheet 1 inch apart.
8. Bake for 12-15 minutes: Bake until the treats are firm to touch and lightly golden. Start checking at 10 minutes to avoid overbaking. Bake time depends on size of treats. This is for 1.4 inch treats.
9. Cool completely on metal rack before serving to let them set.
10. TO NOTE: These will be firm but slightly soft, perfect for older dogs. If you want them crunchy, you can roll the dough thinner and/or cook longer at 350°F but watch closely so they don't burn.

**KAREN'S TIPS:**

- Instead of blueberries, you can use a ¼ cup of mashed strawberries or blackberries.
- Check your oven: Oven temperatures can vary, so check the first batch and adjust the bake time if needed.

- When rolling out the dough, you can also use a sheet of parchment paper on top of the dough to prevent sticking.
- Storage: Store completely cooled treats in an airtight container at room temperature for up to a week. For longer freshness, refrigerate the treats for up to 2 weeks and add a paper towel to absorb moisture. If you want them to last even longer, you can freeze them for up to 3 months.
- Because all our dogs are different and we know some are pretty finicky, I always advise starting with a small batch as a test to make sure your pup loves these!
- Texture Tip. If a dog prefers softer treats, bake for less time, or add a tiny bit more applesauce.
- Get ready to be the most popular person with all the pups!

**FUN FACTS:**

1. Almond Flour: It's a dog-friendly alternative to regular flour, providing a healthy, gluten-free base. Most dogs can easily digest almond flour, and it's packed with protein and fiber.
2. Ground Flax Seed: It's a great source of omega-3 fatty acids, which support skin and coat health, as well as fiber for digestive health. Flax also helps keep your dog's energy levels steady.
3. Blueberries: These are full of antioxidants, fiber, and vitamins that support your dog's immune system. Dogs tend to love the slightly sweet, tangy flavor, and they're easy to digest in small amounts.
4. Extra Virgin Olive Oil: It's healthy for your dog's coat and skin and helps keep them feeling full longer. It's also heart-healthy and has anti-inflammatory properties.
5. Unsweetened Applesauce: The natural sweetness of applesauce is appealing to dogs, and it provides a bit of moisture to the dough without being too rich.
6. Eggs: High in protein, eggs support strong muscles and overall health for dogs. Plus, most dogs love the taste!

**WHY DOGS LOVE THEM:**

- Flavor: The combination of fruits (blueberries and applesauce) and a bit of olive oil will make these treats naturally flavorful. The slight sweetness from the applesauce is something dogs find irresistible!
- Texture: These biscuits, once baked, should be crunchy on the outside but not too hard, which dogs love to munch on.
- Potential Health Benefits: Dogs will love that these treats taste good, but they'll also feel good knowing they're getting a healthy snack with lots of nutritional value!

**STORAGE & SHELF LIFE:**

Room Temperature Storage:

- Store in an airtight container at room temperature for up to 5-7 days.
- Make sure they are completely cooled before storing to prevent moisture buildup.

Refrigerator Storage:

- If you need them to stay fresh longer, store in the fridge in an airtight container for up to 2-3 weeks.

Freezer Storage (Best for Long-Term Keeping):

- Store in a zip lock bag or airtight container in the freezer for up to 3 months.
- To serve, just thaw at room temperature for a few minutes or give them straight from the freezer for a crunchy treat!

**PLEASE REMEMBER:**

Before giving your dog any treats, including homemade ones, always check with your vet, especially if your dog has any dietary restrictions or health concerns. Also, remember to give treats in moderation as part of a balanced diet. Enjoy! I'd love to hear your feedback and what your furry friends think!

Merry Christmas to you and your loved ones!